LIFE AFTER

and other stories

LIFE AFTER DEATH
and other stories

Susan Compo

Faber and Faber, Inc.
50 Cross Street
Winchester, MA 01890

First published in the United States by Faber and Faber, Inc., 50 Cross Street, Winchester, MA 01890.

This paperback edition first published in 1991.

Library of Congress Cataloging-in-Publication Data

Compo, Susan.
Life after death and other stories / by Susan Compo.
p. cm.
ISBN 0-571-12914-5 (pbk.)
1. Los Angeles (Calif.) — Fiction. I. Title.
PS3553.04839L5 1990 90-3207
813'.54—dc20 CIP

This is a work of fiction. All characters and events are products of the author's imagination. The author's use of names of actual persons, living or dead, is incidental to the purposes of the plot and is not intended to change the fictional nature of the work.

Cover painting by Heather McAdams
Cover and interior design by Lois Stanfield

Printed in the United States of America

Contents

LIFE AFTER DEATH

1

Nobody knows Zelda Zonk's real name and in truth she's had so many that, if strung together like party lights, they'd make her sound like some extreme form of English royalty. Her present one, Zelda, was an alias often favored by Marilyn Monroe when she was in her self-portrait phase. Norma Jean would draw pictures of her body, oddly, all sharp lines, and then obliterate her face.

Zelda worships Marilyn Monroe of late and thinks herself the only one who really understands her. Zelda can talk to Marilyn, help her, as she summons her reluctant ghost to slummy, flat, poverty-row Hollywood from which Marilyn tried so hard to escape. Zelda believes that one day she'll find Monroe's mysterious ruby red diary and sees it in a vision, in a shoe box all tied up with shoelaces.

Zelda is going out tonight, a warm, lifeless night, to a trendy rock club which is sort of a mock English pub. The Fan and Flames has a painted sign out in front so the illiterate won't miss the symbolism, but because it's dark no one can see it anyway. Zelda wants everyone there to know that she's Marilyn's only true fan, that she has suffered absolutely for her painstakingly platinum hair and her *Seven Year Itch*-y dress.

Orange, a local celebrity, deejay, and record store owner, is holding court in a corner of the club, telling his admirers why he won't honor Elvis Presley with a window display on the King's birthday—which happens to be the same day as David Bowie's. Orange's equally flamboyant wife, Cruella, is known for her red fingernails and hair plus her sharp wit that strikes as expediently as a letter opener. She's sitting next to Orange and waiting for the right moment when she can breathe in deeply and make her announcement. She finds it and says, "What I always hated the most about Elvis," she pauses to look over at Zelda, "and Marilyn Monroe for that matter, is that they were basically low-life white trash hicks masquerading as something else but never really succeeding. That's why they came to such bad ends."

"Great," says Orange. "Hey, what do you say to that, Zelda? Cruella's calling Norma Jean white trash."

Zelda shrugs and dismisses the whole thing as pretend-salon banter. She figures they rehearse this stuff while they're doing their hair. She walks into the next room which has a lower ceiling and sees the stage is being set up for a band. A roadie with magenta hair (no trace of nature) and ermine-colored skin asks her if she's looking for someone.

"No, no. Who's playing tonight?"

"Orphan Charm. They're kind of glam." He wrinkles his nose.

"Oh." Zelda turns and starts to walk away.

"Hey, don't leave," calls the roadie, whose name is Vex. His real name is Asunción but he gave it up long ago since it really didn't suit the scene. Vex was a punk-rock name which is not where he is now. It doesn't match his present David Bowie/Ziggy Stardust incarnation but he is still known by it. He thinks Zelda would make a very good Angie Bowie for him, considering her platinum hair.

"I've just got to go to the bathroom," Zelda says. "Maybe I'll see you later." She goes to the ladies' room and has to fight several boys for a position at the damaged, broken mirror, portions of which appear to have been whitewashed. She feels the terminal boredom of the club and decides to go home.

Vex is guarding the back door in case anyone tries to steal the band's equipment. He sees Zelda attempting to make her escape. "Hey, blondie, blondie, wait!" he shouts, like a truck driver. "At least let me give you my phone number."

Something about his eyes makes him look like a fifties film star (they look like they could cut glass), Zelda decides, so she says okay. She fixes on his flaming hair as he writes his number on a matchbook.

"Are you parked very far away? Because I can walk you to your car if it's not that far."

They go to her Valiant and he stands by the passenger door, twisting the toe of his silver boxing boot into a stream of ants.

Zelda looks down until his action registers. "Stop that!" she screams. "You're killing them! You're killing them and they're helpless and innocent!"

"Okay, okay, sorry," he says. "I'm sorry to upset you."

"I just can't stand animals being hurt," she explains.

"I said I was sorry."

"Well, please be." She is rubbing her eyes. "Say, are you a big Bowie fan or something?"

"Yeah, but . . . "

"I mean it's funny because, well, usually with Bowie fans they try to keep up with the latest image and you're, you know, at least ten years behind."

"I know, I know. But you see, I think the thing about being a fan is like knowing when to freeze, like cryonics. You have to know when to thaw, too. It's like playing statue in the schoolyard."

More rhetoric, Zelda thinks, annoyed, as Vex leans her against the car door. "I dropped out of school," she tells him, "and anyway I have to get going." She turns away as he tries to kiss her.

At six A.M. the next morning Zelda's phone rings. It is a woman from the Living Dolls Casting Agency, for which she works as an extra. Will she, the voice wants to know, report to this fifties-style diner and dress in the period?

I could have starring parts, Zelda thinks, if I didn't live so much at night and my complexion were better. She turns on her curling iron and takes coffee and Vivarin. Walking across the floor of her tiny apartment, she goes to open a crusty Venetian blind and let in a line of light. She doesn't bathe, because, like Marilyn, she's not all that clean, but when she looks at the clock she jumps, since unlike Marilyn she can't afford the luxury of being late.

"You look like you just got up," says her contact at the diner as he gives her some forms to sign, which she does with a flourished script.

"Zelda! Zelda!" calls Cruella, whose trademark red hair is tied back in a taut ponytail. She is hard to recognize in ordinary makeup. "I'm glad to see you. Listen, I'm sorry about what I said last night. About Marilyn."

"Quiet, girls, please," says a man.

On her way home that night Zelda stops at a bar and has a martini. She thinks of Vex, of how she liked his icy gray eyes, and she decides to call him. She starts to leave a message on his machine but he cuts in. He's screening his calls like a superstar. Vex asks Zelda if she wants to stop by but explains that he has a rehearsal later that night.

"Are you in a play?" Zelda asks.

"No, no. I'm in a band called 5-Years. I'm the singer."

She drives her Valiant up his steep street and goes up the steps to the ornate Queen Anne house. The pale green shutters look as if they were crocheted. At the casement glass front door a dark-eyed child tells Zelda to go downstairs by pointing to the ground.

Vex opens his door and as Zelda enters his basement apartment she feels uneasy, like she's stepped into the belly of a piñata. Turquoise and pink *papier mâche* skeletons and devils, black-and-white coffins and skulls dance suspended on strings from the ceiling. The walls are covered with religious icons, sacramentals, novena cards, and crucifixes. A glass case displays a collection of faded *santos*. Posters break the religious zeal: Zelda recognizes David Bowie (as Ziggy Stardust), Sid Vicious, and Elvis Presley, but has to read the border to get Rudolph Valentino.

"Where'd you get all this stuff?"

"You like it? Let my show you my favorites." Vex leaves the room. He returns with two intricately painted staffs, one of which he hands to Zelda. It is weighty and has a sharp gold tip.

"Now take this one," he commands.

She takes the other and gasps. "It's light as air!"

"They're props," he says. "From the original *Ten Commandments*. The light one is called the 'hero' 'cause it's for the star to use, to make him look tougher. The heavy ones are for everybody else."

"How'd you get these?"

"I stole them from the Studio Museum when I was working up there with sound equipment. I do that sometimes."

"You're lucky you didn't get caught," says Zelda.

"Yeah, well. Do you want a beer or something?"

"Okay."

He gets her a Corona and motions that she sit on the overstuffed couch. His coffee table is made from a tombstone.

"Tell me about yourself," he says.

"There's not really anything to tell." Zelda rarely speaks about her pre-Marilyn life. "How long have you lived here?"

He thinks for a moment. "About six years. I was measuring it by what job I had when I moved in."

"Oh." She notices a framed photo above the heater. "Is that you?"

"Yeah, me in my Sid Vicious days."

Zelda walks over to get a closer look. "Is that girl really Nancy Spungen?"

"Her? No. That was my girlfriend at the time. It's a pretty good likeness, though, isn't it?"

"I guess so. Are you religious or something?"

"I used to want to be a priest," Vex says. "I come from a hard-core Mexican Catholic family. Like my real name is Asunción." He exagerates the *u*.

"What happened?"

"I woke up."

Zelda draws on her beer and goes back to the couch. The phone rings but Vex doesn't answer it and out of deference to Zelda he doesn't even bother to check who it is.

He reminds her, "You haven't told me anything about yourself."

"Yes, I did. I told you there was nothing to tell."

"For instance, what bands do you like?"

"Oh, none, really. It's not my scene."

Vex laughs. "Oh, come on. I don't buy that for a minute."

"Well, never buy what you can't afford." She gets up abruptly, her stiletto heels scratching the grooves of his hardwood floor like a record needle. "Anyway, I'm going to leave since you're not going to listen to me or take me serious."

"No, wait," he says. "I like your hair."

Zelda glares at him.

"How long have you had it like that?"

"I have no idea. This is the way I have it now. You of all people should understand that. This is where I've *frozen*."

Her sarcasm stuns him. "Look," he says, "why did you come here?"

"You invited me."

"Cut the cute replies, sweetheart," he says, undoing the long fringed scarf he wears around his neck. He loops it around her, pulls her close and into his bathroom. Hairspray, bottles of dye, and glitter are on the counter and spilled over the tile floor so that it looks like Hollywood Boulevard. "Listen," he says, "I don't know who you are or where you came from but stuff like that is just window-dressing anyway. All I know is I wanted to talk to you, to see you in the mirror with me. Look." He pulls her head up.

Zelda looks at her reflection and is relieved to see that the resemblance to Marilyn is there. But Vex is not quite right, she thinks. Unless she can change him, and she knows he's changed before.

Zelda goes home that night and finds Whitey, her cat, waiting for her at the front door. She feeds him and then gets ready for bed. She phones Cruella but the line is busy so she calls Vex and hangs up when the machine answers.

After Zelda gets into bed she lays in her last boyfriend's spot. He was a tall boy who played baseball in college and signed with a major league's farm team (he is a pitcher). Then she hurls as if thrown back into her own space.

She can't sleep. She hears someone doing their laundry and she tries to change the sound of the washer and dryer into the hum of ocean waves.

Zelda thinks, if only I had some Nembutol. She gets out of bed and puts on her white, knee-length terrycloth robe. She's going to call on Marilyn.

The first thing she does is take the phone off the hook so no one will interrupt her concentration. Then she sits on the edge of her bed and starts to think until her forehead hurts.

The water's roar gets as loud as Niagara Falls and then tapers off to a hyped-up hum so Zelda can barely hear Marilyn's soft, faded-photo voice. She sees Marilyn standing on a bluff overlooking Santa Monica beach, her champagne-colored hair blown back by the wind. Marilyn's wearing sand white matador pants and her skin is the color of moonlight. She's both a young model and a tired star. She's very sheer and wears plexiglass, platform-wedged shoes.

"I'm trying to reach my locksmith," Marilyn says. "He's close by." She drops the coin she intended for the pay phone and it falls into the sand, which has shifted directions with the wind.

Zelda gets a paper from her nightstand to write this down.

"Let me go," says Marilyn but not, Zelda thinks, to her. Zelda concentrates. "The diary, Marilyn, the red diary."

"That man," she whispers, "on the corner knows."

Zelda jumps up. "The coroner?" But Marilyn's gone, vanished as if she hadn't signed off but just put the phone receiver down.

Zelda's filled now with a loneliness and confusion as to her next step. How will she get to the coroner—while she's still warm, that is? She walks over to close a window because a Santa Ana wind has started to blow.

The phone rings as she hangs it up and Zelda nearly jumps out of her skin. It's Vex who just wanted to say hi, so Zelda says hi, distantly, with the certainty that from now on each time they speak or get together they'll be more and more uncomfortable, for that's the nature of love.

When she falls asleep Zelda dreams about the diary. That it's been left somewhere in the rain and the ink is running and dripping like the blue blood from a fine-point pen.

II

Vex is sitting in the barber's chair at Appointment with Destiny, a new hair salon on Melrose Avenue. He is sticking to the chair; his red vinyl pants don't coexist too readily with the chair's similar fabric. Each time he moves a horrid sound occurs—like wet plastic being scratched—and it's worse than nails on chalkboard.

He tries to be still while having his hair trimmed in anticipation of a date with Zelda (their first, really) later that evening.

The hairdresser asks Vex if he works so he tells him about his band and that he should come to see them. "But what do you do for money?" the guy asks. Vex answers with a shrug and the guy tells him he has a friend who runs a limousine service and is always looking for drivers.

Vex likes the idea and asks for the friend's name and number. He leaves the hairdresser a nice tip and a flyer advertising 5-Years' next performance.

He drives across the city to the downtown flower market where he buys some discounted carnations. He removes them from the paint bucket they've been withering in. When he arrives at Zelda's apartment, he's swinging this old bouquet.

Zelda, who has spent the whole day in her Murphy bed, quickly throws a cover over it to disguise the twisted and knotted sheets. She's been thinking she would be good at being dead; she spends so much time lying down.

She is nowhere near ready, still in her terrycloth robe. "Vex?" she asks through the door in her best babydoll voice. "Can you come back in about fifteen minutes?"

Vex passes time by walking around her bungalow-style building and checking to see if the laundry room is locked. He's gotten some of his favorite clothing, like his leopard-print socks, from other people's laundry. He decides against breaking into the room and goes instead to the corner where he uses the pay phone to call the limo service. A man answers by saying, "Ernest," and asks Vex if he has ever had his license suspended. "No," says Vex, relieved.

"Any major convictions?"

"No," Vex lies. He makes an appointment to go see Ernest in Venice the next afternoon.

It has been half an hour and Zelda is still in the bath. When she hears the doorbell she gets out, dries off, throws on a dress (no underwear), and applies makeup: a rose of red lipstick, eyeliner, and finally a mole that sits like a period on her left cheek.

Vex hands her the flowers and kisses Zelda, his tongue extending like a stamen. She worries that he has messed up her lipstick so she checks it in the bathroom mirror before they leave to go ice-skating, a passion of Zelda's and one of her few carry-overs from childhood. As Vex drives her out to the San Fernando Valley she thinks about her old skating costume and wishes she still had it. "It had this white rabbit fur trim," she explains. "It was really regal."

Vex is confident he will be able to skate since Zelda has told him it's all in the ankles—his are very strong from the platform shoes he wears, especially when performing.

The two make a remarkable couple at the "S" Capades Skating Chalet, which is populated by teenagers and children who stare at and whisper about the strange duo. Zelda holds onto Vex tightly as he gets used to the skates and even when he's clearly proficient. They skate around and around to music by Prince. The frigid air drifts up Zelda's dress, tingling her thighs like pin-sized icicles. She pulls her sweater's fur collar up around her neck.

Zelda leaves Vex to go to the bathroom where junior high school kids are swapping drugs. She brushes her hair and then finds the snack area where Vex is standing, staring into the fake fireplace. They sit in front of it and, over hot chocolate, begin to feel uneasy with the innocence of their outing.

"Maybe we should go," suggests Zelda, who has a sudden craving for a martini. They exchange their skates for street shoes—Zelda's stilettos and Vex's silver boots.

When they see Hollywood upon emerging from the Cahuenga Pass, it looks like a miniature. Zelda yawns and says, "I'm glad it's overcast tonight. I don't like to see the stars. They're so oppressive." Vex takes her hand, feeling a little queasy. Maybe she's really insane, he thinks.

Back inside her apartment they kiss and she takes him to the bed. He removes her dress and sighs when he sees she isn't wearing underwear. Later he fashions a stole for her out of the sheet.

At two A.M. Zelda is wide awake and shaking Vex's shoulder. "I have to ask you something," she says. Her eyes are wild and dark. "Have you ever broken into anywhere?"

"Yeah, once or twice. Why?"

"Well, do you know the county coroner?"

"Not personally, no."

"You know what I mean, the one who did all the famous people."

"You mean 'Heaven's Hollywood Agent?' I saw him once." Vex sits up. "I had to go to the morgue to identify a friend of mine."

"You *saw* him?"

"Yeah, as he was leaving. Did you used to know a girl named Penny Dreadful?"

"Maybe. I'm not sure. It sounds familiar."

"She was really tough," Vex explains. "She used to always want to get tattoos and I told her, 'Sweetheart, with your arms it'd be like playing connect-the-dots.' She had so many marks."

"She OD'd?"

"Sure. What else? But what do you want with the coroner?"

Zelda sighs and tells him it's a long story.

III

Around lunchtime the next day Vex is sitting at the desk in his study, which is covered with store-bought picture frames that have their original photographs of anonymous people still inside. For Vex the faces are his pretend family—even though they're mostly blond and blue-eyed. He is writing out a resumé, which he assumes Ernest at the limo service will ask for. He won't.

The resumé is a litany of lies except for the part about the seminary.

His work is interrupted by the clanging of a skateboard as it dives down his front steps. When he opens his door he sees one of the children from upstairs. "*Lo siento*," says the little boy.

"Go to school," says Vex, slamming the door shut.

Ernest is a flashy man who doesn't bat a clouded eye as the magenta-haired Vex enters his tiny combination living room/office, resumé in hand.

"You'll wear a cap," he directs. "All my drivers wear caps. And get a tie."

"I have one."

"Good, good. And are you sure you never done time? 'Cause I ain't gonna lie to you. I have—for not paying child support. Shit, my old lady don't need it. She spends every thin dime on herself."

Ernest twirls a big ring that sits accusingly on his right index finger. "So you can keep your nose clean? A lot of situations in this business be demanding that. A lot of temptations. Yes, sir, a lot of temp-tations." He taps his fingers in time on the desk.

Vex doesn't answer because he's looking at the girlie calendar that hangs crookedly on the wall. He thinks he knows Ms. Snowfall and he does—it's Cruella.

"Check it out, check it out," laughs Ernest as he removes the calendar from the wall. "See anything you like?" He slaps the calendar down onto the desk.

When Vex turns the pages and sees Ms. Sandy Dreams he realizes how stupid he's been. Zelda thinks she's Marilyn Monroe.

"I didn't know you punkers was straight," says Ernest. "Glad to see it."

Ordinarily, Vex would be angry at having been mistaken for a punk-rocker—I'm an original, he would defend—but for now his mind is on Zelda. As Ernest writes down the details of his first assignment, Vex decides to stop by Orange and Cruella's record store on the way home.

Cruella and Orange have just changed the name of their record store and they could have done it with mirrors because the new name is Rat/s/tar. As Vex arrives, Cruella's on a ladder in the window hanging up tinsel and David Bowie album sleeves in honor of his birthday on January 8.

"Hi, Cruella," Vex says.

"Oh, hi, uh, I'm sorry, I know I've seen you around but I can't think of your name."

"Vex," he says, holding up his hand that Cruella descends a few steps on the ladder to grasp. Vex sees his face reflected in her black vinyl miniskirt.

"Vex. That explains why I didn't remember—it doesn't suit you." She folds the ladder as she continues, "Aren't you in a band?"

"Yeah, 5-Years. I've got some flyers in the car."

"Oh, please, no more flyers. The store looks like a giant-confetti factory as it is. What are you staring at?"

He keeps seeing her as Ms. Snowfall. "Nothing. I came in to look at the new imports."

"Well, they're over there."

He still stares. "Is there something about my outfit that grabs you?" Cruella asks.

"I like vinyl."

"Do you now?" She smiles. "Well, you've come to the right place."

Silence. Vex doesn't know what to say.

"You're in a record store!" Cruella laughs at her joke.

Vex laughs too and goes over to the magazine rack which is cluttered with local fanzines, glossy English magazines, and the calendar.

"If you're going to buy that calendar," says January's Cruella, "don't wait until next month."

He takes it over to the checkout counter.

"Sold, American," says Cruella, "or are you English?"

"I lived in England when I was little."

"Yeah? My husband Orange and I are going next month."

"On vaca . . . on holiday?" Vex asks.

"More like a working vacation," Cruella responds as she stuffs the calendar into a bag decorated with little skulls inside ice cubes. "Sorry we don't have the bags with our new logo yet. They come next week and they're going to be really cool. They say Rat/s/tar and have rats crawling around on the faces of Elvis and Marilyn Monroe."

"That's okay," says Vex, thinking ahead. "Say, how'd you come to do the calendar?"

"Through my job as an extra, through the agency I work for. I wanted April 'cause that's the month I was born. I wanted the world to be able to say, 'April is Cruella's month.' " She pauses. "You don't read poetry, do you?"

"What? No." He starts to leave.

"That's, sort of like, T. S. Eliot," she explains.

"Oh, Bowie reads him," Vex replies, turning back.

"Right. He's in town, you know. Bowie, that is. A friend of mine saw him buying magazines down the street. Oh, and Vex," Cruella says, "if you want to, go ahead and bring some flyers in."

When Zelda gets out of bed at last, Vex is gone. She notices that Whitey, the cat, is hungry and so is she. She dresses and walks to the corner liquor store to buy whole milk and the *Herald Examiner*. Zelda drinks whole milk because she needs the calories—no one ever heard of a skeletal Marilyn.

Before Zelda goes back to her room she stops to check her mail and finds she's received a postcard from her last boyfriend, the pitcher for a Cactus League team in Arizona. The words he wrote seem devoted but also self-absorbed. Zelda feels a little love for him, runs her finger over his written name as if it were erotic braille. "He fits me better than Vex," she whispers.

Zelda pours milk for Whitey and for herself. She thumbs through the *Herald* and spots an ad for a porno film she had a part in. It's playing downtown and Zelda considers going to the five P.M. show. It could cheer her up. Who knows, someone might even recognize her.

The Mayan Theater is near the bedraggled end of downtown Los Angeles's Broadway, which is a lot like an ever tawdrier Hollywood Boulevard. The theater's facade is very ornate and colorful, featuring replicas of Mayan gods and gilt-flecked masks, and it reminds Zelda of Vex's apartment. She is the only girl at the show and this makes her uncomfortable as she shifts and turns in the balding, velvet seat.

Her movie is called *Blonde Ambition* and she waits through half of it for her scene, which she did with Cruella who wore a blonde wig. In it they play girls named Harlow and Harlot who are auditioning for a part in a Big Money porno flick in the 1930s. Zelda recalls how she'd overheard the director tell Cruella it was meant to be a metaphor for Hollywood, as in layer upon layer, tinsel upon tinsel. Cruella had said it was more like life imitating life.

Zelda thinks she handled her role with considerable aplomb and imagines she's writing this about herself in a review. She decides against sticking around for the second feature and as she walks through the lobby she notices a man staring at her. He's older, smarmy-looking in his outsized chinos, but he has this endearing flat-top haircut that gives him a contradictory aura of cleanliness and familiarity—as if he were an older friend. Zelda finds herself standing next to him on the street corner as they wait for the signal to change.

"Can I buy you a cup of coffee, miss?" the man asks.

"I was just on my way home."

"Where's home?"

"Hollywood," Zelda says proudly.

"Funny, that's where I was thinking of," the man says. "I know a nice little place there called Musso & Frank's. Know it?"

Zelda knows all of Marilyn's haunts and this is one of the most famous. "Sure," she says, agreeing to meet the man, whose name is Fred, in half an hour.

IV

Vex has been calling Zelda for the past three hours but can't leave a message because she doesn't have a machine. She doesn't believe in them. He tries to reach her one final time before he leaves to drive. No luck. He adjusts the skull and crossbones clip on his western bolo tie and straightens his beret.

He picks up the limo near Ernest's house in Venice and heads south for Marina del Rey. The car is deceptively hard to drive—no cars will yield for him and Ernest had lectured him repeatedly not to look in the rearview mirror out of deference to the passengers. "That's what they're paying for," Ernest had said, "so they can be alone. Pri-va-cy."

Vex collects his passengers—a young man and his very blonde wife—and they instruct him to take them to the Magic Castle in the Hollywood Hills. He does so, careful not to look back as he drives. Once they arrive at the private club, Vex is told he can wait in a separate room they provide for drivers. The room is smoky like a bar and has a color t.v. perched up high. Vex looks for a place to sit down when one of the other drivers offers him his seat. "I've got to go now, anyway," the driver explains. "My passenger's got to record."

"Who are you driving?" Vex asks.

"David Bowie."

"Man," he says, "I've got to meet him, just shake his hand or see him. I won't make an ass of myself, I promise."

"Sure, man," the driver says. "Just follow me. But act like it's a coincidence, okay? I could lose my gig."

Vex sees this wafer-thin guy who looks like a pixie with a suntan. It can't be Bowie, but it is. Vex offers his hand which Bowie brushes lightly, an unfiltered cigarette dangling from his fingers. He leaves and Vex stays standing for a few moments. Then he starts to tremble.

He goes back into the drivers' room and sinks into the deep red leatherette booth. He can't fight his sudden sleepiness, a feeling he hasn't had since his narcoleptic days as a seminarian.

He's back in his apartment, which seems to have been turned on its side so that all the contents have fallen into one corner. He sees himself in a Mexican silver mirror only it's not Vex now but rather Vex as he was when he was Sid Vicious. His girlfriend, Julie, is across the room, over at the top corner. He's begging her to nag and torment him but she's refusing and nearly crying. "I just don't know what to say," she keeps repeating. "I love you. Why would I want to hurt you?"

"To help me! So I can have ideas! So I can create," Sid says, but it's no use. He'd like to kill her but he can't even reach her.

A photograph falls off the wall, one of Vex's make-believe relatives, only it's the couple he's driven tonight. They spring to life and don't notice him as they weightlessly fly out the side window.

Vex decides he doesn't want to live and struggles to find a bag of heroin that's tied with pink yarn. As he feels the sharp seduction of the needle, who appears but Penny Dreadful, looking much worse than she ever did in real life.

She asks him what he's doing and he tells her to leave him alone. "Okay," she says, "as you wish." All of a sudden he sees himself as a child in East Los Angeles. He's walking under the Sixth Street bridge looking at all the train tracks and then fighting with the other kids, his hair a tangled mixture of blood and gravel, like barbed wire graffiti.

Then he's wearing his little league uniform while his father belts him for having lost the game. His mother is screaming, "Leave him alone. For heaven's sake, he's an altar boy. What will the Father think?"

It is Vex as a seminarian who cuts his wrists unevenly but systematically with a blunt crucifix and bleeds onto the floor of what becomes the Fan and Flames Club. He is setting up equipment for a punk band. He's performing with 5-Years while people are talking, picking up and putting down their drinks.

"Penny, take me away," he's saying as a man shakes him to. As soon as he's aware, Vex knows he's a better David Bowie than that imposter he met earlier.

This is exactly what he's telling Zelda down the phone lines a few hours later. "Z, honestly, I'm more Bowie than he is."

Zelda is hearing but not really listening, waiting for a break in his story so that she might tell him what happened to her. But he goes on and on. She tries to visualize him, to see him as she'd tried to imagine him in the crown of Fred's balding head when he'd looked down at his coffee. Instead she saw Vex looking all wrong, as he'd appeared that night in the mirror with her—a bad match. In his apartment she'd seen a picture of him performing onstage, sharing the microphone with his guitar player, and side by side they were like a symphony of cheekbones. Maybe he was the kind of guy who looked best with other boys and not with starlets.

No matter what, she'd decided over dinner, although she was drawn like blood to Vex, if he wanted to see her again he'd have to change his look.

"Hang on a minute, can you?" she hears him ask. "I had to get a towel," he explains when he comes back on the line. "My hair dye was dripping in my face and black's such a bitch to get out."

Black? Like technicolor fan-magazine black? Zelda is hopeful. "Why are you dyeing your hair?"

"I don't know. I just needed a change. Maybe it was the Bowie thing. Do you like the idea?"

"I have to see it first. Vex, can I tell you about my evening?"

Slowly he says, "Sure." He's afraid of what she might say and doesn't want to hear about her life apart from him.

"Remember when I asked you about the coroner? Well, I met this man who maybe can help."

"Why don't you come over and tell me in person?"

When Zelda arrives at Vex's the sun is a headachey light through a slat on the city's east side.

Vex is different with black hair slicked back like, Zelda tells him, a post-punk Montgomery Clift. He holds Zelda and kisses her each time she starts trying to tell her story. She uses all her strength to push him away.

"I met this man tonight," she says, although it's already morning. "He might be able to help me find what I've been looking for."

"What's that?"

"It's a long story but if you know anything about Marilyn Monroe and I'm assuming you do or you wouldn't be interested in me . . . anyway, I want to find her red diary. You won't tell anyone, will you?"

"Who would I tell?"

"I don't know, Cruella or someone. But anyway, this man tonight, Fred, he claims he was married to her."

"To whom?"

"Marilyn. And, you know, I *believe* him. I've seen his face. He claims they were married in Tijuana right after she made *Niagara.*"

"Oh, come on, Zelda."

"No, really. He says he has proof and that he's writing a book about her. I think he can help me get the diary."

"Can we talk about this later?"

As Zelda and Vex go to bed, they're like two ice cubes in a tall glass: they can meet but they can't merge, absorbed as they are in their own worlds.

Before long, Zelda wakes up and sees Vex all huddled and far from her, sleeping completely by himself. His pillowcase is smeared with black dye, the life she wants for him stubbornly refusing to stick.

She slips out of bed to go to Fred's house in the Hollywood Hills. Zelda walks barefoot to her car which sits tilted on the steep street.

Upon waking, Vex is shattered to find her gone. He takes a vase full of dirt (from David Bowie's property in Switzerland) and throws it in the trash.

V

Zelda finds herself lying partially on top of Fred and dispassionately giving him head. Once again, she thinks, I'm paralleling Marilyn.

Fred is happy with his new protégée, as he refers to Zelda. Earlier he'd shown her a photograph of himself with Marilyn, which Zelda had held for a long time. It displayed Fred and Marilyn cheek to cheek – Marilyn is fresh and flowerlike against Fred's desert-clay complexion.

Zelda wants to see Fred's marriage certificate plus the book he's writing and also needs to bring up the diary but knows she must wait for the right time. She puts her blue and white polka dot blouse back on and smooths her hair.

Fred sits up and says, "I want to take my protégée out and show her off."

He drives her downtown to the Alexandria Hotel, which was elegant when it opened in 1906 and all through the 1920s, but fell, like the silent era, into disrepair. In the hotel bar Zelda learns that Fred has a weakness for Scotch so she keeps smiling her best Marilyn half-smile and kissing him whenever he finishes one drink and orders another.

"I'll spring for a room here, babydoll," he tells her, as if they were at the Beverly Hills Hotel. He leaves her at the bar and walks over to the front desk, stopping for a moment to shake off a soiled paper bag that has gotten stuck to his shoe.

Zelda props him up in the elevator and as they walk to their room.

"Wait," says Fred. "I think I know what's in here." He points to partially open double doors that are loosely bound with rope. When he pushes them open the rope parts like gossamer. Revealed is a dark ballroom with mirrors for walls and aging chandeliers hanging precariously overhead.

"Zelda," Fred says, his arm once again around her waist, "Valentino used to dance here. They all did."

She remembers that name from Vex's wall. "Not Marilyn."

"Wanna bet?" asks Fred. "I brought her here. She loved old Hollywood, kid, all of it."

Suddenly the room takes on life as Fred slowly twirls Zelda around on the floor and rats watch from the corners like wallflowers.

By the time they get to their room, Fred is really reeling and Zelda convinces him he should lie down. She starts to loosen his shirt but he stops her. "No, please, babydolly, you first."

She gets up from the bed and walks toward the door. Turning to face Fred, she undoes her polka dot blouse and steps out of her skirt. She pats her silk slip and then slips it down over her breasts, her hips, her spike heels.

She massages Fred's back until her hands find a scar (like a fat needle mark).

"Norma Jean gave me that. She threw a high heel at me from across the room and bull's-eye!"

Zelda's hands linger. "You were fighting?"

"Yeah, over something she'd put in her diary. Wish I could get my hands on that diary."

"Have you ever seen it, you know, since?"

"No, but I have a hunch who has it. I think the coroner's office does. They took a lot of her stuff: phone bills, medical receipts, shoot, probably even some of her organs."

"Ooooh," says Zelda, envious.

Vex has broken into Zelda's apartment and left a flyer that contains a song he's written for her. He's placed it on the pillow of her unmade bed. The song is called "Graven Image" and 5-Years will be performing it tonight at their show which Zelda better be at or, the accompanying note assures, Vex doesn't want to go on living.

Zelda finds the note and song beneath Whitey, who loves to sleep on top of paper. His claws have made pin holes in it so she can't make out every word. She plans to go to the concert, if for no other reason than she's impressed with Vex's skill in breaking and entering.

As she starts to draw a bath she decides to check in with Marilyn. She takes the phone receiver off its cradle and then gets in the tub. Marilyn is also in the tub, white bubbles on her white skin and a red rosebud against her shoulder. She holds the rose out to Zelda who replies, "I can't reach it, Marilyn. What's the point?" but Marilyn doesn't answer. Instead Norma Jean knocks a glass of champagne from the edge of the tub onto the cracked tile floor and starts to cry as she evaporates, as surely as the bubbles do. Zelda's left sitting in dirty, lukewarm bathwater, two inches below a ringline.

Zelda, great," greets Orange as he leads her toward the bar at the Fan and Flames. Cruella is there, examining her now-black fingernails. Orange keeps obsessively straightening the sleeves on his knee-length satin tunic.

"Are you okay?" Zelda asks him.

"Sure."

"Orange took a little too much speed," Cruella explains.

"I didn't know you had any vices, Orange," says a friend.

"I do, I do," he laughs. "They hold me prisoner."

"Believe it," says Cruella. "He's a prisoner of his own deep vices."

"Have you seen Vex?" asks Zelda.

"You know him?" replies Cruella.

"Yeah."

"He came into the store the other day and bought a calendar."

"Great," says Orange. "We need the royalties. We're going to England."

"Orange, we don't get any royalties from the calendar," sighs Cruella.

"That's funny. He didn't say anything to me about the calendar," says Zelda as she goes to look for him. She doesn't find him until he's onstage. 5-Years plays a long set—nearly ninety minutes—and by the end only a few people are left standing near the front. The others have migrated to booths, bathrooms, and parking lots.

"Not only is this our last song tonight," Vex tells the audience solemnly, as if there were ten thousand of them, "but it's the last song we'll ever do." They perform "Graven Image" and Vex puts special emphasis on the lines, "You're my graven image / I wish you were dead."

"Great," says Orange. "He's retired. No one even knows the band yet. Great career move."

There's no demand for an encore and when Vex comes back onstage to pick up his p.a. Zelda catches him. Standing as she is on the floor she's about eye level with his spandex-covered knees.

"Vex, what's going on?" she asks in an injured, childlike voice.

"I just want to get out of here," he replies, dramatically. Over Chinese food, he's still moody and it's made worse when the cookie fortunes are irrelevant. "Look afar," one reads, "and see the end from the beginning."

"You know, Vex," Zelda tries, "I think I know who has Marilyn's diary."

"Oh, goddamn it, Zelda, not the fucking diary again." He puts his head in his hands on the tabletop but when he looks up and sees that Zelda is about to cry he's filled with a kind of compassion for her. "I'm sorry," he says, softly. "What do you want to do?"

"I need to go to the coroner's office."

"Well," says Vex, "seeing as my life is over, I guess there's no time like the present."

VI

As Vex and Zelda drive to the county coroner's they pass the hospital where Marilyn was born.

"Oh, really?" says Vex distractedly when Zelda tells him this. "I was born at the Queen of Angels—on Good Friday. What about you?" He feels nervous and curiously compelled to talk about his and Zelda's pasts.

"How should I know?" she replies. "Some boring hospital somewhere."

They turn into the medical examiner's parking lot and Vex (who's been here before, after all) is trying to think of the best way to approach the situation.

"We could say we're looking for a body," Zelda offers.

"No, no, too direct."

"Direct? What are you talking about? It's a lie."

"What I mean is I don't think we should be seen at all. It's not the bodies that we're interested in, but the records."

"How can we avoid being seen, though?"

"I don't think it'll be that hard. It's a really messed-up place."

Vex slips on a pair of menacing-looking leather gloves and gives Zelda black lace ones that belonged to his last girlfriend, Julie. From the glove compartment he gets a flashlight which he places in the inside pocket of his leather jacket.

They go in a side door of the examiner's office building and proceed down a long, dark corridor. Opening another door they enter the morgue, a low-ceilinged room with no windows.

"Come on, let's keep going," Vex tells Zelda who has slowed

dreamily, thinking that the morgue looks like a video room at a local club. They pass silently through the embalming room, which has stainless steel tables equipped with water hoses, sinks, and scales.

A door at the edge of the room is marked "No Admittance," and since it is locked Vex takes out a switchblade and tries to coax the lock. That doesn't work so he grabs a sharp tool from a nearby table and pries the door, which opens into a series of cubicle offices. Zelda closes the door behind her and Vex turns on the flashlight. One room is filled with fireproof file cabinets which are stacked like card catalogs.

"Marilyn was Case Number 81128," Zelda whispers. Vex finds the corresponding cabinet, also locked. He tells Zelda to go back and retrieve the sharp tool from the embalming room.

"You want me to go alone?" she asks, incredulous.

"Go! Don't freeze up now!"

Zelda goes back inside the embalming room and stands still, unable to move. She surveys the cold and lifeless tables and thinks, one of those held Marilyn! She strokes the edge of the nearest one, and it's as slippery as mercury. When she thinks she hears a sound, she quickly grabs the tool, which looks like a letter opener.

"What took you so long?" asks Vex, who's still at work on the cabinet.

"I was just thinking."

"Well, save that for later. While I'm doing this, you should try to find Heaven's Agent's address. Try to find a business office."

Sifting through papers in a metal in-basket, Zelda finds the coroner's address on a tax withholding form. She writes the address on the back of her hand and goes back to Vex who's standing over the opened cabinet. "What's there?" she asks him.

"There's nothing here—nothing. Just a file marked 81128 with nothing in it."

"Just take that, then. It's something, anyway."

He puts the folder under his jacket and as they start to leave they hear movement in the next room. Vex looks at Zelda, who stops, doesn't even breathe. Once the sound is gone Vex walks slowly to the door and looks into the embalming room. Someone has wheeled in a body on a gurney.

"Come on," he tells Zelda, "we have to move fast before they start working." When they are in the embalming room they hear voices in the hall, coming closer. Instinctively, they duck beneath the sheet-covered gurney as two men enter the room.

"Before we begin," says one of the men, "how about some coffee?"
"Sounds good," says the other.
Zelda and Vex hear the men walk toward the office door. "Hey," says one, "this lock's been jimmied." They open the door and throw on the lights as Zelda grabs Vex's arm, urging him to run for it. They move quickly, crouched low, until they reach the corridor and finally the side entrance they had come in by.
They speed away in Vex's car, forgetting to turn on the headlights until another passing car winks at them as if in on their secret.
In nearby Elysian Park, Vex turns off the car motor.
"Why are we stopping here?" asks Zelda.
"I need to relax before we go home." He leads her over to a point where they can see the freeways meet below them. He takes out a joint as neatly rolled as an i.v. tube.
"That was strange being there," says Zelda, taking the cigarette.
"I know," says Vex. "I mean, I was thinking, there can't be an afterlife. I mean, not in the sense that there's no heaven and hell but I mean even if it's just a state of being or something, there's just no way there can be another dimension that can hold like, both Sid Vicious and my fucking father."
"I didn't know your father was dead," says Zelda.
"He isn't," Vex says.
He starts to take her hand but drops it when he sees the vein-like blue smear. "Christ, Zelda, what's on your hand?"
"Relax!" she laughs. "It's just the coroner's address. I couldn't find any place to write it."
"Beautiful child," he says, hugging her. "Why didn't you just take the paper you found it on?"
He drives Zelda back to the Fan and Flames where she'd left her car. He holds her tight and tells her he loves her. "I loved you the first time and first place I saw you. Love at first sight and love at first site."
"That sounds like something Cruella would say," says Zelda, pushing Vex away and picking up Marilyn's file folder from the dashboard.
When Zelda gets back to her apartment Cruella and Whitey are waiting on her doorstep.
"Zelda, I've been trying to call you all morning," she says, eyeing the folder. "What's this, are you working as a temp?"
"What's up?" says Zelda, feeling a sudden headache.

"We have a gig, a film. Zelda, this could be the big one. Prince is doing it and I hear he's easy to get to know."

Zelda unlocks her door and Whitey runs inside. "Oh, Cruella, I can't work today. I'm exhausted."

"Forget that. Do some speed. I'll feed Whitey."

"Maybe I should change clothes," says Zelda, pulling at the neckline of her black lace peasant-style dress.

"Nah, what you're wearing is great. Especially the fishnets."

Zelda's phone rings as she and Cruella are going out the door. "Don't answer it," commands Cruella. "It's probably the agency and they'll scream if they find out we're not at the shoot yet. We'll be ex-extras."

Zelda lets it ring so she doesn't find out it's Vince, the fastball-hurling love of her life, who's in town for three weeks.

Also desperate to reach her, but without any way of doing so, is Fred. He's left alone in his house, exposed like a heart without the shell of a body to hide in.

VII

Vex is back in his basement resting on a pile of pillows, his spikey black hair leaning on a sign that he took from one of his jobs as a valet. The sign says "No Grace Period" and at the moment his hair is forming a smudgy comma between the words grace and period.

He needs to sleep but he can't, so he plays back his phone messages. Several are from band members saying things like, "You fucking poseur, why couldn't you have warned us?" Another is from Ernest and there's one from his brother, plus one he hasn't heard before, from Cruella.

"This is Cruella," it says. "I'm glad you're listed and not, uh, listless. I'm trying to reach Zelda and I know she knows you so I thought she might be there. If she is can she please call me at 555-3500 or," she pauses, "you can call me there too, if you know anything."

Vex dials her number but hangs up when Orange answers. He slumps back onto the pillows, where he sees himself now as sort of a combination of identities, which is in itself something new. He's chic like Rudolph Valentino, cultivatedly tormented like Montgomery Clift (good for Zelda), and he senses also the recurrent, romantic soul of the late (they're all late) Sid Vicious. It's got a lot to do with his hair color, but Vex doesn't consider that as he falls fast asleep.

An hour after they leave, Zelda and Cruella are back at Zelda's and Cruella is holding a carton of take-out Chinese food.

"I hate it when that happens," says Zelda, kicking off her heels and referring to the cancelled shoot.

"I know, I know, but I guess Prince is like that."

"It's such a waste of time."

"Zelda, relax, it'll work out. We'll probably work tomorrow. Anyway, let's eat."

Zelda goes to the sink where she starts to wash some dirty dishes. Suddenly, she screams. "Oh, no! Goddamn it!"

"What?"

"Goddamn it! Goddamn it, I've washed my hand!"

"What's the big deal?"

"God, you don't understand."

"Well, if it's what you had written there you can stop screaming 'cause I memorized it."

"Oh, Cruella, did you?"

"Yeah, it was in the Marina. What's the deal? Another porn film?"

"No, nothing like that."

"Well, tell me what it was and I'll tell you the address."

"It was the address for a party."

"Great. Tonight?"

"Yeah—no. Shit, Cruella, if I tell you, do you promise you won't tell a soul?"

"Sure. I'm your best friend."

Zelda, who considers herself essentially friendless, pauses for a moment. "It's the address of the coroner—the famous one. Heaven's Agent."

Cruella shrugs. "Am I supposed to be starstruck? Is he kinky or something?"

"No, it's nothing like that. It's just that he has Marilyn Monroe's diary."

"The one with the stuff about the Kennedys?"

"Yeah, but I don't care about them. They're cold, like coins and granite. No, I want the diary because she wants me to have it. And I have an idea that maybe you can help me with."

"Sure." Cruella sits down at the formica table. "But can we eat first?"

They eat in silence and then Zelda collapses on the bed while Cruella does the dishes. The phone rings and it's Vex who's just gotten out of the shower.

"Tell Zelda I have to drive tonight," he says.

"Are you a truck driver?"

"No," he laughs, "a chauffeur."

"I'll tell Zelda you called when she wakes up. Should she call you?"

"Yeah."

Cruella hangs up and dials Orange at the record store. "You won't believe what's happening here," she tells him in at most a stage whisper because she knows Zelda is out cold. "It could mean big bucks for us. You didn't throw out that English newspaper, did you? Well, get it. Listen, I'll be there soon."

Cruella taps Zelda's bare shoulder and to her surprise she stirs. "I had the most amazing dream," Zelda says, rubbing her eyes. "And it's like I was dreaming really hard and it's given me a headache."

"Vex called and he said to tell you to call him and that he has to drive tonight."

"Oh, perfect! Except he's not going to drive who he thinks he's going to. What are you doing tonight?"

"I was going to dye Orange's hair purple, but it can wait."

About eight o'clock that evening Zelda and Cruella are standing in front of the Penguin Café in Santa Monica. They are waiting for Vex to arrive with the limousine. Zelda has gone all out as the last Marilyn: she wears a shimmering, tight emerald green dress like the Pucci one Marilyn was buried in, plus all the makeup she can apply. In the coffee shop's neonesque light she most resembles the Marilyn that's stuck in the Hollywood Wax Museum.

Cruella has set her hair in an odd flip like Natalie Wood sometimes wore hers. She has no second thoughts about being involved in Zelda's scheme, for she knows precisely what is at stake. As she told Orange earlier, she'd seen an article in an English newspaper about a man who was offering a reward for Marilyn Monroe's diary. He was promising fifty thousand dollars, but Cruella is certain she could get at least twice that.

When Vex pulls up, the two girls rush over. Zelda starts to get in the front, but quickly thinks better of it and hops in back. They drive south to the Marina, to the coroner's address.

Vex is nervous and keeps looking in the rearview mirror at his calm passengers. Wearing all black and with his hair slicked back he looks like a B-type movie vampire. He pulls up in front of the complex, gets out, and says, "Wish me luck."

"You'll do fine," says Zelda. "It's easy; like acting."

Vex pushes the doorbell of the two-story condominium and it rings with a sound like wind chimes. The door opens to reveal a tiny, elderly man who has a head of hair that looks like it has been rubbed with carbon paper. Vex recognizes him to be the coroner, although he looks much older than the last time he'd seen him.

"Good evening, sir," he says. "Your car is here."

"I'm confused," says the man. "I thought I was cooking dinner here."

"I only know my orders, sir, and they are to come and collect you." Vex dislikes being so formal—it reminds him of how he had to talk to his father, an ex-Air Force sergeant.

The little man wrings his hands together. "Okay. Give me a moment." He turns back to face Vex. "How do I know your information is correct?"

"I assure you it is. But if you'd like me to call . . . "

"I'll call," the man says. "You wait here."

Vex twitches and worries that he might faint. He thinks he can avoid doing so by pretending very hard that he's onstage. He even goes so far as to sing a song called "Lust for Life" that his old band had covered. When he spies a samurai sword on the wall in the entryway, he moves forward to get it, to use as a prop microphone. Just as he's about to touch it, the man returns.

"I didn't tell you to come in."

"I'm sorry, sir. I was admiring the sword."

"Admire it from a distance," the man says. "There was no answer," he continues. "Why is that, can you tell me?"

"Because they're waiting for you," Vex improvises. "Please, come this way."

The man follows Vex to the limousine but stops before getting in when he sees Zelda and Cruella in the backseat, leaning on each other and beckoning him.

"Is this some kind of a joke? Who sent you?"

"No joke, sir," says Vex nervously.

"Hi," says Zelda. "We're a present to you."

The coroner smiles at her and slowly gets in the car. Vex closes the door after him.

"Toby sent you, didn't he?"

"Yes," says Zelda. "We're a present to you," she repeats.

"And a past," says Cruella, under her breath. She puts her hand on his knee.

"Are we meeting him later?"

"No," says Zelda, bending over Cruella to further affect her cleavage. "He says to tell you he'll call you tomorrow." She kisses his slender cheek.

Cruella, noticing that Vex keeps looking at them in the mirror, slides the glass partition closed.

"Here," offers Zelda, "why don't you sit between us?" She crawls over him, careful to brush her gartered thigh against his wrist.

Cruella begins to unbutton his shirt. "Don't worry," she whispers in his ear. "Have some champagne."

The petite, clenched man begins to relax as his clothes are loosened. "Can't we go somewhere?" he asks. "This, being in a car, maybe isn't too smart."

"Can we go back to your place?" asks Zelda, kissing his fingers dizzily. "And, please," she glares at Cruella, "can I have you first?"

"Driver," says Cruella as she opens the partition, "take us back to this gentleman's home."

After they arrive Vex walks behind Cruella and Zelda, who are hand in hand with the coroner. Vex feels for the camera that's in the pocket of his black cashmere jacket before he's told to wait in the car. Then he goes out, careful not to close the door tightly behind him.

Slightly up the coast in Venice, Ernest has just taken a call from an irate man complaining that his driver had failed to show. "I'm sorry," Ernest says. "I'll have another one sent on the double. And it's on us." He is furious to think of the new kid screwing up already, and on one of their best customers. Also, there is the problem of the car, stocked as it was with the client's favorite drugs.

"I'll have to teach the kid a lesson," he mutters before he picks up the phone again and says, "I gotta job for you. Find this punk and rework his pretty mama's boy face a little."

Vex goes back into the condo and follows the sound of giggling and moaning to the bedroom door which, he finds, is locked. He sneaks through the gourmet kitchen to the back door. Once outside, he matches a sliding glass door to what would be the master bedroom. He uses his Swiss army knife to slip the lock and bounds in through the flapping drapes.

He begins taking pictures of the startled nude man as he leaps off Cruella, who is on all fours on the floor. Zelda is asleep on the bed, on her side, partially covered by the silk sheet.

"No!" says the little man to Vex. "No! Who are you? What do you want from me?"

Zelda wakes up and she and Cruella tackle him and pin him to the bed.

"I want," says Zelda, "what's rightfully mine."

"What? Who are you?"

"I want Marilyn Monroe's diary."

"I don't have it! Please, I'm a respectable man. I have my career . . . Who do you work for?"

"I work for myself," says Zelda, "and I want that diary."

"I told you I don't have it!"

"Who does?"

Vex takes off his tie and approaches the pinned man threateningly. He wraps it around the coroner's throat.

"Okay, okay! I saw it. I had it. Please, I'm an honorable man and I did the only honorable thing."

"Such as?" asks Zelda.

"I saw to it that it was buried with her."

Downtown, the medical examiner's office is receiving a new body. It's Fred, who has hanged himself from his bedpost and left behind what is considered to be a laughable suicide note. "To Zelda," it says, "I loved you more than life. Now I've gone to join my other love, my wife, Marilyn Monroe."

In the limousine, Vex, Cruella, and Zelda are solemn.

"What really slayed me," says Cruella, trying to break the mood, "is the way the old guy kept saying to us, 'Haven't I met you somewhere before? You look familiar.' "

"I know one thing," Zelda says after a long silence. "I'll kill myself before I give up on getting that diary. And I'm not ready to die yet."

"Do you think Marilyn killed herself, Zelda?" Cruella asks.

"Sure. In her book she wrote 'I was the kind of girl they found dead in a hall bedroom with an empty bottle of sleeping pills in her hand.' "

"Sounds like a premature suicide note," says Cruella.

"I'd never commit suicide," adds Vex. "I mean, I am a Catholic."

"Call a priest!" laughs Cruella, alone.

Vex leaves the girls at the Penguin Café and goes to drop off the limousine in an alley near Ernest's. If he'd checked the mirror he would have realized he was being followed.

In their storefront apartment above the record store Orange has been trying to get this purple patch to appear just right in his mostly tangerine-colored hair. At present, the spot looks like an Easter egg. It makes him feel edgy so he sits down to smoke a cigarette.

Orange thinks about Cruella, whom he still loves from afar, like a Valentine, even though they've been married for five years. He has his doubts about her diary story and thinks that what she's really doing is having an affair with Zelda. He drinks a glass of whiskey, which gives him the confidence to drive over to Zelda's, singing along all the way with Frank Sinatra.

He's standing on tip-toes peering into Zelda's window when he feels this big hand on his shoulder and then a blunt thud on his skull.

"You better not be after my girl, punk!" says the tanned, athletic Vince, who's holding a small aluminum baseball bat.

"What the fuck?" stammers Orange. "You're crazy! What girl? I'm looking for my wife." As proof Orange waves his hand to display a fast food giveaway wedding ring.

Vince lets go of him and Orange puts his hand to his head. The once-stiff purple is now cracked and blending with maroon blood. "Shit, man," he says, "what's the deal with the baseball bat?"

"I'm sorry," says Vince. "It's just that you never know—a lot of weirdos here in Hollywood. Anyway, I'm not that good with the bat. I'm a pitcher. Name's Vince."

"Great. Orange." He holds out the hand he's been pressing to the top of his head.

"So far this year I've been batting .113 but I could probably do better if I could get in more practice time. Are you a friend of Zelda's?"

"She's a friend of my wife's. I don't think they're home."

"I'll wait," says Vince. "Any idea where they went?"

"I think they went to the movies," says Orange, stumbling as he backs away down the cracked cement walk.

VIII

While Vince was using Orange's head for batting practice, two *West Side Story*-style thugs were seeing to Vex, their punches providing a steady rock 'n' roll backbeat to Vince's swing. Vex's cheeks, once so beatific, are going to need some stitches and the ones he gets in the emergency room at Saint John's Hospital soak with blood until his swollen face looks like a baseball.

Zelda and Cruella, tired of waiting at the café, are standing on Lincoln Boulevard, trying to hitchhike back to Hollywood.

When Vex finally arrives at the Penguin he finds no trace of either girl. He sits down on the brick planter (careful not to fall backwards into the trash-cluttered ivy), covers his eyes with one large hand, and starts to cry.

How could you leave me?" he's screaming at Zelda. "And why are you looking for something when my love for you is enough? Don't you know that I don't even dare look at anyone else's face because it breaks my heart that it's not yours?"

"It's no use," he hears Zelda saying, quite far off. "I can't love you back the same. Never, because you've been unable to make me forget how different you are from the one who came before. And the only reason to be in love is to forget."

"No," he says and he wants to kill her. He looks up into the elaborately painted ceiling of his apartment. It's fluorescent and, with the black light turned on, Day-Glo, like the clotted oil-on-velveteen rendering of Elvis that lies on his floor. The ceiling splits and rolls back like a tarp to reveal a heaven full of bones.

The Santa Monica dawn is heavy as a canvas dropcloth. When Vex looks at a shadow of himself in the café window he reluctantly sees he's like Sid Vicious again and for him, right now, that's as random and imposing as stigmata.

Vince and Zelda are still up, Vince reading her like he would his catcher, alternately nodding and shaking his head as she rattles off irrelevant, innocent chatter, the sorts of things she'd never say to anyone else.

The coroner, habitually early for work, is alerted to a special case. When he goes to view Fred's body he believes he's the victim of another trick, for there's nothing there.

Vex takes the blue Santa Monica bus to Century City and transfers to the Number One, which meanders slowly down Hollywood Boulevard to Sunset, finally past Dodger Stadium and then close to where he lives. When he gets home he doesn't listen to his messages, he just calls Zelda, who doesn't answer.

A few days later when she still hasn't called him he changes his message at least a dozen times, trying to get the right one that will magnetically attract her call.

She still doesn't call so he phones Cruella at the record store and has to explain who he is to Orange. "Whatever you do," says Orange, "I'd stay away from Zelda's place. There's this maniac over there with a baseball bat."

When he's alone inside Zelda's apartment Vex observes the nylon sports bag with athletic gear as well as the huge bowls of food and water left for Whitey and suspects that Zelda's either eloped or been kidnapped. In case his first assumption is true he shoves the heavy Murphy bed back into the wall while Whitey cowers beneath the couch.

"I think she's been kidnapped," Vex explains to Cruella and Orange in their apartment. Cruella is eating a leopard-print banana that matches her shirt.

"Great; great concept," says Orange. "But, like, no way. For one thing, how can you explain all the extra cat food?"

"You don't know Zelda! She couldn't bear to see animals suffer. She probably pleaded with the guy."

"Vex," says Cruella, "Zelda probably just took a vacation. Which, by the way, I think we could all use. Why don't we go to Mexico?"

"Why Mexico?" asks Vex. "It's not because you think I speak Spanish, is it? Because I don't!"

In Avalon on Catalina Island, where they've been for a week, Zelda is cavorting by the shore while Vince takes pictures of her. She fluffs out her limp blonde hair and wears a halter top fashioned out of a couple of his bandannas. When they go for walks she carries an umbrella, careful not to let the sun taint her fair skin.

They're staying in a cramped house with Tim, a friend of Vince's from college. Zelda delights in hearing Vince tell her how Tim would fly in to school in Long Beach three times a week, but Tim doesn't add much to the story. He spends most of his time casting sidelong, suspicious glances at Zelda that make her certain he listens at their door while she and Vince are having sex. Or maybe Vince had told him how they'd gone below on the glass bottom boat and he'd put his hand up her dress even with people around.

A few nights later, heavy with red wine and Italian food, moments before she falls asleep in his long arms, Zelda decides to accept Vince's marriage proposal. He's attached a stipulation like a codicil: "I don't want you to work. I just want you to be waiting for me all soft and warm at home when I come back from road trips."

The next day while Zelda's taking a bath Vince tells Tim about their engagement. "You're a lucky guy," Tim says. "She is HOT. I saw her bit in that porno film!"

Vince feels his muscles constrict but maintains an outward calm. "Oh, yeah? Which one was that?"

"Shit, who remembers the titles?"

When Zelda finally comes out of the bathroom Vince tells her to pack her things, they're leaving.

Back on the boat, she asks him if he wants to go below deck again but he says no, so she goes by herself. When she's there she's reminded of a recurrent nightmare she'd had as a child—that she was skating and she'd fallen through the ice. When she'd wake up screaming and gasping her mother would tell her she was foolish and that, unlike her, Zelda had never skated on anything other than an artificial ice rink.

They arrive back at Zelda's apartment and after she gives Whitey some fresh food, Vince throws her against the wall that the bed's now entombed in.

"You goddamned bitch! You sleazy little whore!" he screams as Whitey, who's been eating, scrambles and leaves pieces of dry cat food spinning like jacks.

"Thank Christ I never married you. I just wish I'd never touched you." He spits in her face, now streamed with viscous tears, and leaves, slamming the door.

When Zelda regains her composure she notices one of Vince's aluminum baseball bats. She starts to tuck it into the closet next to a pile of broken-heeled stilletos but then holds onto it, thinking it might come in handy when they break into Marilyn's crypt.

IX

The Mexican sun in Rosarito Beach has shined a little too harshly at least for Orange, who's in great pain in the hotel room he, Vex, and Cruella are sharing. He's taken to applying tequila (which Vex won't touch) to his blistered shoulders with a white terry washcloth.

"Maybe you can find me some drugs," Orange moans to Cruella as she's about to leave with Vex to have seafood. "Go to Ensenada if you have to."

Cruella is skeptical that their worn-out El Camino will travel one more mile but assures Orange she'll do her best. "Just try to sleep," she tells him. "Before too long your skin will toughen and then . . . " She starts to giggle.

"What's so fucking funny?"

"Oh, Orange, I'm sorry, it's just that you'll be peeling."

Vex, coming in the front door, starts to laugh too.

"Leave me alone," says Orange, turning away.

In the cantina, after she and Vex politely give their orders, Cruella says, "Considering our names, you and I are such nice people."

"Yeah, well, it's not my real name."

"No!" she says with mock horror. "Guess what, neither is mine."

"What's your real name?"

"I'm not going to tell you."

"Mine's Asunción. It means 'to go up.' " Vex blushes as he tells her this, turning the color of the suspicious wine they're drinking with their abalone.

"I won't tell you mine," repeats Cruella, "but I'll give you a hint. It's the month I was born in."

"I wish I was never born."

"Oh, Vex, you're thinking about Zelda again. That's so romantic."

"Don't—don't say that word. When people say they're romantic I think what they really mean is they're cruel."

"I don't agree. I think Orange and I are very romantic. I really love him. I'd kill anyone who came near him, and if that's not love, I don't know what is. He used to be in a band a long time ago and they were called Frieze. The first time I saw him he was onstage holding this knife and I thought, that's it, that's the guy for me. So the next time I went to their show I wore this leopard skin coat—it was really rabbit that was dyed, but it looked real—and nothing underneath. I stood in front of the stage and just, you know, flashed him."

"What happened to the band?" Vex asks.

"Oh, you know, who knows? I mean, I guess a lot of them work in clothing stores, or they're married. I don't think it's glamorous, being in a band. All that waiting around—it's a lot like being in movies, really. Having our own store is so much better."

"I don't miss my band. I don't think Zelda really liked the idea, anyway."

"Zelda doesn't like the idea of anything except getting that diary. I mean, I can understand if she wanted to sell it."

"I don't think she'd ever do that, considering what Marilyn means to her."

"But that's so silly," says Cruella. "I can't understand idolizing anyone, dead or alive. It's just like being their slave. You might as well work for them, pick up after them."

"I cleaned houses for awhile," says Vex. "It's worse than being a chauffeur."

"We should go," says Cruella. "I didn't realize how long we've been here."

As they leave the cantina Vex feels a sharp pain in his stomach. By the time they're in a swirling, dusty alley in Ensenada he has to throw up.

"Go on ahead," he tells Cruella. "Go get the drugs. This should be happening to you, not me! I'm the Mexican here. You're the one who should be getting sick."

Cruella goes in an arched doorway and meets a fat, tanned American with an authentic 1950s flattop haircut. When she finds she hasn't enough money, she brings him out to see Vex, who's doubled over against a low wall. "Zelda," he says, wet with sweat. "Where is Zelda?"

"I knew a Zelda once," says Fred. "We were married right here in Mexico."

"No," says Vex, before he passes out.

X

Zelda and Cruella ride up front with Vex in his black 1962 Cadillac, in the middle of the night and right down Wilshire Boulevard. Vex turns off Wilshire for Westwood Memorial Cemetery, which is tucked behind tall buildings and parking structures.

"I know one thing," says Cruella, "if we really do find this diary with her, it's a damn good thing she wasn't cremated."

"She would never have been," says Zelda.

"Was she Catholic?"

'No—just not the type to burn."

"I wish I could say the same for us," says Cruella. "We'll all be keeping each other company in hell."

"I believe in hell now," says Vex. "I still don't believe in heaven, but I'm sure there's a hell."

He parks the car in the alley and looks up at the barbed wire that crowns the cemetery's chain link fence. "I've seen worse," he says.

"I think we should check the front gate first," says Zelda, walking toward it. "Oh, look, come on, it's just a little lock. It's like the one Sid Vicious used to wear around his neck. Vex, you could break this easy."

"How do you know about Sid?" Vex asks. "And if you liked him, how come you never liked me?"

"I love you," she says, without much conviction.

"Let's unload the car first," he says. Zelda gets Vince's baseball bat and Vex struggles with a sledgehammer.

"Where'd you get that?" laughs Cruella.

"From a set I worked on."

"It better not be a hero," says Zelda, remembering the prop Vex had shown her when they were new to each other.

"Don't laugh," says Cruella, holding a huge knife. "This isn't mine—it's Orange's."

Vex toys with the lock and then pushes the gate open.

"This guy Richard Conte's buried here, too," says Cruella. "He had this big belief that the afterlife was here on earth and there's a bunch of stuff about it on his tombstone. I hope I can find it."

"I don't know, Cruella, maybe he picked it up when he came back," says Vex.

"Very funny. And Natalie Wood is here, too. Did you know that the evangelist, Aimee Semple McPherson, was supposedly buried with a live telephone? Bet Norma Jean wishes she'd thought of that one."

"Probably it would be bugged," says Zelda.

"Or full of bugs," says Cruella, smiling.

"Hey, Cruella," says Vex, "I never knew you were such an expert on graveyards."

"I guess it's all that death-rock," she shrugs, pulling up her black cobweb stockings.

Zelda enters the cemetery's Hall of Tranquility and stands before Marilyn's eye height crypt, made of marble white as moonlight. She runs her hand across Marilyn's golden name and reverently wipes off some of the greasy red lipstick prints with the hem of her full white skirt. Carefully she removes the fresh flowers from the tomb's vase and places them in her open purse without altering their arrangement.

"How weird about her dates," says Cruella, walking up. "Look how it says 1926 to 1962. It's like they're mirror images."

Vex joins the two and is completely poised, standing rigid and straight as he'd once done when he was in modeling school. He lifts his sledgehammer and starts to hack at the vault. Zelda covers her eyes because flecks of marble are scattering like charged dust.

She goes over to Cruella, who's standing guard at the edge of the Hall of Tranquility. "I went to Elvis Presley's grave," says Cruella. "He's buried by his twin who was supposed to have been stillborn, but I have this theory that the death of the twin was a hoax and he's still alive and is really David Bowie."

Zelda walks back to the crypt where Vex has made great progress in breaking through the two feet of cement that barricade Marilyn's casket. A corner of the coffin is visible now (like the hole left on a table by a missing piece of a jigsaw puzzle). Zelda helps Vex clear away the remaining bits of concrete by using the silver baseball bat, and soon the end of the coffin is completely exposed. "Cruella, come and help us," calls Zelda.

Together, the three lower the casket to the ground as Zelda nudges her purse out of the way with her foot. There's a red velvet and satin sash tied around the coffin, and Zelda thinks it looks like a big screen version of the shoe box she's been seeing in her visions—a sure sign that the diary is inside. Cruella uses Orange's big knife to cut the cord and to pry open the coffin's lid.

They cover their mouths and noses as a pungent odor consumes the air and Cruella quips that they couldn't really have expected Marilyn to have had time to take a bath. They stare at radiant white bones and a sparkling diamond necklace that's loose around the skeleton's neck. A couple of shreds of platinum hair rest on the red satin pillow, and fragments of green material from the Pucci dress Marilyn was buried in are here and there. Tucked beneath her feet by a portion of a plex-iglass shoe is a little red book, settled in a pool of sand.

Zelda picks up the diary and in her hands it feels like corn silk, like gossamer. It reminds her of the residue moths leave in her palms when she rescues them from her apartment and puts them back outside.

She opens the diary slowly, worried it will fall apart like the string on a strand of antique pearls. "Life," it says on the first beige page in narrow, slanting letters, "I am both of your directions."

Zelda closes the book and then the coffin's lid and the three solemnly return the casket to the dark horizontal hole. Cruella jumps as a rat scurries across the concrete slot. Zelda and Vex replace the golden pla-que that is smaller than a vanity plate—there's still a big gap from where the marble was. Vex thinks they should keep the nameplate but knows better than to suggest anything like that to Zelda, who seems to have frozen in place. She finally puts the diary in her purse, after removing the flowers and placing them intact at the right side of Marilyn's crypt.

Vex and Cruella start to go toward the front gate—then see ghostly headlights turning into the cemetery. They call for Zelda and the three run, hurdling over tombstones, to the southeastern corner of the graveyard where they climb the chain link fence. Zelda snags one of her nylons on the barbed wire.

As they drive back across the city, Cruella continues to ramble on about graves. "Now, Sid Vicious *was* cremated," she says. "And I think it's kind of mean that he's not buried with Nancy. They're not even in the same country. I don't think F. Scott and Zelda are together either, but I'm not sure. Scott died here in Hollywood—maybe we can go past the funeral home on Santa Monica. He was eating a Hershey bar. It's true. And Zelda, poor Zelda. I guess there was no question about whether to cremate her and she was a Catholic. I think. Or, wait, maybe it was just him."

"Cruella," says Zelda, "shut up."

"Oh come on," defends Vex, "Zelda, that's uncalled for."

"Sorry," she says. "It's just that I realized I left Vince's bat back at the grave."

"Don't worry about it," says Vex. "At least you didn't leave the diary. Did you?"

"No," says Zelda, touching it in her purse.

It's started to rain by the time Zelda asks to be dropped off alone at her apartment. She cuts short her goodbye kisses when she hears Whitey protesting low and mournfully from her doorstep. "I'll call you when I wake up," she tells Vex.

Whitey, all wet, looks like an albino laboratory rat. As soon as Zelda opens the door he tries to run for the food dish but Zelda grabs him to dry him off. He wriggles as she uses her bathrobe on him.

She opens her fat purse before she places it down on the settee. When she takes out the diary she finds it's gotten wet, not so much from the rain as from the filmy water left by the flowers at Marilyn's grave. Zelda puts the diary open faced on her formica table so it can dry. When she gets in bed she is unable to sleep until she realizes that for the first time in her life she's not alone because Marilyn is with her for good.

Downtown, contemporaries of Marilyn are sleeping beneath copies of the late edition of the *Herald Examiner*, its banner headline a red hem to the mottled-blanket newsprint. "MARILYN MONROE'S GRAVE BROKEN INTO," it says: "REST IN PIECES, NORMA JEAN."

When Zelda wakes up it's still raining as if night never left. She finds clumps of platinum hair on the pillow next to hers and leaps up to run to the bathroom mirror, filled with the terror that her hair's falling out. When she touches her scalp and finds it more or less okay, she wonders what's going on. Marilyn's face appears in her mirror, like the lady caught beneath the ice.

"My diary," she says. "Please take care of it. It's the only thing that ever belonged just to me, that no one else tried to grab little pieces of."

When the vision fades, Zelda walks back out to see the diary. She picks it up and closes it, its pages refusing to meet because they've dried unevenly. They are stuck with white cat hair since Whitey slept on it. Zelda holds the red book to her heart, knowing now she must cherish it, treasure it, but never, never read it.

Vex lies in bed and looks at his t.v. screen which is mostly obscured by party streamers and confetti decorations that have fallen from his ceiling. The news has been covering the break-in and most broadcasts end with the perplexing conclusion that nothing was stolen. "Even the precious necklace specially designed for the late film goddess by artist William J. Fox was untouched," explains a baffled newscaster.

The police chief of Fairmount, Indiana, appears the next hour with the theory that the grave robbing is part of a series of crypt-thefts that includes his own city's James Dean's. "We found Dean's pink granite tombstone recently after it had been stolen in 1983," he says. "It was behind a fire station in Fort Wayne, just lying there out back by where they burn trash. We recovered it and replaced it, but it was stolen again three weeks later. My feeling is that it's some sort of weirdo Hollywood-relics operation and we in Fairmount are going to work very closely with Los Angeles on this one."

Another expert presents a scenario that involves teenagers, a satanic cult, missing household pets, and heavy-metal music. "This is very plausible," explains a priest affiliated with East Los Angeles' Calvary Cemetery. "We've come to expect a lot of disturbances here from Latino gangs who have fallen away from the church to worship the devil and practice ritual sacrifice. It's only logical they would take the next step to blaspheme the graves of famous movie stars."

When Vex hears this he runs to the telephone but Zelda has taken the receiver off the hook. Hurriedly he dresses to go over there, wearing a cowboy hat as a disguise.

"We've got to get out of here," he tells Zelda, who's gone back to sleep. "And the sooner the better."

"I know," she says, rubbing her eyes and smearing her eyeliner. "Do you have a passport?"

"No, and with my record, I'll never get one, either."

"Don't worry. I'll call my friend, Cute, and he can fix it. He has everything fake." She takes the phone on its long cord into the bathroom so she can call in privacy, but Vex listens at the door. He hears Zelda arrange to meet her friend at Woolworth's on Hollywood Boulevard the next morning at ten A.M.

When she opens the bathroom door he's back across the room, looking out at the courtyard through the slats in the blinds.

"Everything's okay," Zelda tells him. "You should try to relax."

"Maybe I'll take a shower."

"You can't. I mean, my shower doesn't work. You can take a bath, though."

"God, Zelda, why doesn't your shower work?"

"How should I know? And who cares, anyway? Really, Vex, what's your problem?"

As he's filling the tub he says it's not so bad after all. "At least this way the mirror doesn't get all fogged up. Do you think I should re-dye my hair?"

"No, no, just keep slicking it back. It looks good like that."

"I think that's the first compliment you ever gave me," he says, struggling to take off his cowboy boots.

Soon Vex is up to his neck in a bed of bubbles. "How'd you meet Cute, anyway?"

"He was handing out flyers at a club." The phone starts ringing and Zelda waves it off.

"You should answer that. It could be Cute."

"No, not even. I can tell by the way it rings. That's how close we are."

"You were in love with him." Vex pretends like he's going to sink.

"I love you," she says.

"No, you don't."

Zelda shrugs. "Have it your way. I'm going to go watch t.v."

When she opens the bathroom door, Whitey runs in and jumps onto the rim of the tub.

"He's fascinated by the bubbles," Zelda says.

"What are you going to do with that cat when we leave?"

"I don't know. I'll think of something."

Vex comes out wearing Zelda's bathrobe over his ripped tank-style t-shirt. Zelda is immersed in *Death Takes a Holiday* which is on t.v. He sits next to her. When the movie is over she takes the robe off him but he squirms away from her attempt to remove his t-shirt.

"I want to leave it on," he tells her, and she suspects it's because he dislikes the tattoo of a block-like cross emitting blue rays that he has over his heart.

"It's too bad you can't shed skin like you can images," he says. "But I guess there's no getting rid of stuff that's been burned into you."

When the phone starts to ring again Vex gets up to answer it. "Don't you dare," warns Zelda.

"But it might be Cruella."

"That's what I'm afraid of. I don't want to talk to her. I don't trust her." It rings three times and then stops.

"Is this the diary?" he asks, picking up a worn-out address book that was by the phone.

"No, I put it away in a safe place."

Vex gets into bed and Zelda joins him. "Be thinking," she tells him during sex, "what name you want to use on your passport."

The emaciated image of Saint Martin of Tours springs to his mind so he decides it will be Martin something.

"It has to be serious," says Zelda, running her stiletto down his spine. "You can't use a really phony name or it's more suspicious."

"I never thought of it before," says Vex. " 'Suspicious' rhymes with Sid Vicious."

"There was a young man named Sid Vicious," begins Zelda.

"Who acted so highly suspicious."

"He took out a knife . . . "

"And ended his life."

"Now, no one's left doing the dishes!" laughs Zelda and Vex, too, until he says gravely, "Except for one thing. Sid didn't kill himself. Only Marilyn fell for that suicide routine."

Before he has a chance to regret saying 'only' he sees that Zelda has fallen asleep, looking happy.

In the morning Vex looks at himself in the mirror and sees this drawn, pale guy that looks like a centuries-old conception of a vampire. He thinks it's due to the early hour or because the light coming in from the tiny bathroom window is murky and grey. It's still raining.

Zelda has decided to wear a black wig and thinks it makes her look like Jane Russell or Liz Taylor. In reality it's more like Vivien Leigh in her depressive phase.

In Zelda's Valiant they drive up to Hollywood Boulevard and go into Woolworth's, which smells like cheap five- and ten-cent individually wrapped candies mixed with cut-rate household cleaners. Zelda picks up a striped hand-basket and starts to fill it with travel- and trial-size shampoos and lotions.

Vex leaves her and wanders over to the underwear department, which is near the souvenir shelf. He is fingering the filmy women's panties when Zelda approaches.

"Now you know why I'd never wear that stuff," she sneers. She brightens as she picks up a scarf branded with the word HOLLYWOOD and little klieg lights reaching skyward. "I'm going to get this."

"Where's your friend?" Vex asks, agitated.

"He'll be here." She spies Cute in the dishwares section; his bleach-blond dreadlocks look like styrofoam packing material.

"Zelda!" he says. "Sorry I'm late. The rain, you know. Have you been waiting long? I thought you were never on time."

"This is Vex," she says, and the two shake hands tentatively.

"You look like a million," Cute tells him.
"That's rude," says Vex.
"No, man, you misunderstand. It's a compliment. A million looks, a million ways to do things. Comprende?"
"I don't speak Spanish."
"Yeah, man, well, neither do I. Now, what can I do for you two? Zelda, it's so good to see you."
"We need passports," she says.
"No problem. Do you have the photos?"
Because they don't, they go into a tiny photo booth in the store where two passport-size photos cost one dollar. Then, to work out the rest of the details, they go to a nearby bar that Zelda doubts Marilyn was ever in, for it never could have been even marginally nice.
The martini she orders tastes dirty, like the glass it's in. Zelda looks down at it and away from Vex and Cute as she sinks into her thoughts. All along she's believed the diary was her ticket out of her life, but now she isn't so sure.
"What?" she says to Cute, like one of those soap opera characters lapsed into vivid daydreams that are so real they're no different from the actual story. "What did you say?"
From the bar Vex phones one of his former band members and asks him if he wants to stay in his apartment for a while. "Rockin'," says the guy. "I just got kicked out of the loft." Vex thinks about calling his father to say goodbye but hangs up after he's dialed the area code.
"I've finally figured out who you look like," Cute tells Vex as they stand outside the bar, squinting in the harsh daylight. "A silent movie cowboy."
Tom Mix, Vex thinks to himself and then decides on the passport name of Martin Mix.
"I like it," says Zelda, a little drunk. "It sounds almost like a martini."
On the way home they stop at the monolithic Home Savings on Sunset and Vine and Zelda closes out her savings account. She does need the money after all, on this rainy day.

XII

There's a guard standing in front of Marilyn's grave now, but not one that can't be persuaded—before the cemetery opens again—to let a freelance photographer who says she's from the *National Enquirer* remove the coffin and snap a few pictures of the skeleton for the highest bidder. Before leaving the gravesite, she notices the baseball bat and takes a picture of it, too.

While Zelda, Vex, and Cute were oblivious in the bar, the coroner was holding a press conference downtown in which he divulged (1) why he was being demoted, (2) his connection with an underworld figure named Toby, (3) who broke into Marilyn Monroe's crypt, and lastly, (4) why they did it.

In her apartment Zelda is putting anything of personal value in her closet, where she had hidden the diary in a shoe box. She takes it out of the box, wraps it in the tissue paper the shoes came with, and adds satin ribbons taken from tap shoes so that it now looks like a birthday present.

She is preparing to mail a check for three months' rent to her landlord when she sees Whitey sitting on the windowsill. Zelda picks him up and holds him close before she places him in his travelling case and takes him to her car. She drives to Rat/s/tar knowing that Cruella and Orange won't be there that early. Her plan is to leave Whitey with Steve, the shop assistant, and see if Whitey can be kept as a store cat until she gets back.

But Rat/s/tar is completely lifeless; the only sign of motion is a "Wheel of Misfortune" in the window that promotes a new album. "DEATH," it says, "DRUG ADDICTION," "BANKRUPTCY." "DESPAIR." All this goes around and around, continually escaping the aluminum foil arrow that tries to linger at each.

Zelda turns up a side street to avoid a traffic signal that's broken. On the left-hand side of the road is a Victorian house with a small, worn lawn—an orphanage. On impulse, Zelda goes to the door, where a short middle-aged woman answers and eyes her suspiciously.

"I have this cat," Zelda explains. "He's a good cat. He likes people, and kids, too. He's like, he's my closest friend, the only friend I ever had . . . "

"And I'll give you some money for his food," she continues.

"Does he have all his shots?"

"Yes, oh yes." She gets Whitey from the car and starts to hand him to a little dark-haired boy who is playing in the yard. Whitey's claws cling to Zelda's white blouse and his purring slows and descends like a zipper as they're pulled apart.

Bedraggled in the curving line that contains the standby passengers are Vex and Zelda, who are waiting to hear the names Martin and Maggie Mix—brother and sister to Zelda, but husband and wife to Vex. "I always wanted a brother," she tells him. "It's so boring being an only child." Vex doesn't reply. Instead he pushes his suitcase along with the tip of his steel-toed boot.

When they get their boarding passes and take their seats on the flight to London, they are completely unaware that Orange and Cruella are one flight ahead of them, finally embarking on their long-planned working vacation to the U.K.

Zelda puts her bulging purse next to the window seat. She feels for the diary which is down at the bottom in a Woolworth's bag next to Kleenex, lipsticks, a cuticle pusher she's never used, and an eyebrow pencil without a cap because Whitey loved to bat it around on the floor.

"Did you bring the diary?" Vex whispers.

"What do you think?" she replies, annoyed.

"You didn't send it through in the luggage, did you?"

"Please."

They have to change planes in New York, and Vex waits while Zelda runs to buy a magazine. Staring at her is the *New York Post* which outbid the *Enquirer* for the photograph, a full front page, of Marilyn's remains. "LOVE GODDESS' GRAVE(N) IMAGE!" screams the headline. The *Post* also features a story about the mysterious baseball bat, which is now missing from the grave site. "Was it a gift from second husband Joe DiMaggio, the Yankee Clipper, who only recently stopped sending his daily quota of roses to his beloved former wife?" the author speculates.

"Lady, does this look like a library?" the man at the cash register asks.

"In a way," says Zelda as she buys the paper and puts it in her purse.

"You won't believe what I have to show you," she tells Vex, who's been waiting back at the gate. "This country is really sick. I'm glad we're leaving."

She tells him she'll show him the paper but not until the lights go out and the in-flight movie begins. Zelda swallows a sleeping pill with her martini but Vex doesn't take one, as he never has any trouble falling asleep on airplanes. He has, however, taken the window seat from Zelda because he wants to look at the sky. When he raises the plastic window shade he sees a startling reflection.

"Zelda," he whispers, "I think someone is following us."

"Who?" she asks, groggily.

"Don't turn around until I tell you, but it's this man. He was on our other flight, too."

"Big deal. So was everyone else." She leans her head on his sharp shoulder.

"No, I'm telling you, I've seen him before. You can look now."

But Zelda has fallen asleep. Vex turns to look at the man, who is wearing what is obviously a wig. Its curly red hairs make him look like a fat Malcolm McLaren, a thought that makes Vex very nervous, considering the kinship he feels with Sid Vicious. If it is Malcolm, he thinks, then I'm going to die. I'm going to be pushed into it, as surely as Sid was. Vex feels himself falling but jumps awake before he hits bottom, relieved to find he's only on a plane and not on some rooftop.

Vex reaches into Zelda's purse and takes out the newspaper. He reads, in the semi-darkness, an article on the inside page about the search for the thieves. He is fascinated by the descriptions of Zelda and Cruella and reads them over and over: Zelda is "a curvaceous but rough-edged bleach-blonde in her early twenties," and Cruella "a dazzling red-headed spitfire of a similar age." His own description further unnerves him, since he's painted as "a sultry, emaciated but handsome young man who bears a certain resemblance to the late punk-rock killer, Sid Vicious."

He folds the tabloid and puts it in the crevice between him and Zelda. Because he's calm, Vex is unable to sleep; he flips through the in-flight magazine but stops before reading the emergency safety card. He needs to read something thought provoking, something that will jar him to sleep. Something like Marilyn's diary.

He fumbles through Zelda's purse for the diary, identifying the pocketbook-shaped item as it. He carefully removes the ribbon but resists tearing the tissue paper. Zelda stirs as the diary falls open.

"I knew I'd have all that I wanted," Vex reads, "because I was dreaming the hardest."

He rapidly puts the diary back, unwrapped, as a flight attendant approaches with the serving cart.

"Would you like a nightcap?" the steward asks Vex.

"No," he replies, going out like the tiny egg-shaped ceiling light above his head.

XIII

After they pass through customs in Heathrow Airport, Vex sees the mysterious man again. "Zelda, come with me," he says. "I have to ask him who he is."

"Excuse me," says Vex to the man, "but haven't we met before?"

"Not that I know of," says Fred.

"No, I'm sure I know you. My wife thinks so, too."

Zelda kicks him. "I'm your sister," she says, gritting her teeth.

"That so? Well, kid, maybe you came into my shop one time. I have a little business in Santa Monica called the A-1 Lock and Safe Company. Here, have one of my cards."

"Thanks," says Vex as the man walks away. "This just can't be," he says to Zelda. "I mean, I've never needed a locksmith in my life."

"It's even weirder than that," says Zelda, feeling through her purse. "The A-1 Lock and Safe Company was Marilyn Monroe's locksmith." Her hand finds the unwrapped diary. "Vex, how did the diary come undone?"

"I don't know. Maybe it happened when we went through customs."

"That's impossible. I watched it. You didn't let anyone see it, did you? And you wouldn't have read it?" She pauses. "God, I've got to find a safe place for this diary. I've got to find one fast."

"There should be a safe in our hotel."

"That's not good enough." Zelda sees a courtesy desk and runs up to it.

"Yes?" asks a grim young woman.

"How do I contact Lloyd's of London?"

Her stern face shows no emotion. "They're shut now."

"They went out of business?"

"No. They're closed because of the hour."

"When do they open?"

"Sometime tomorrow, I should think."

Zelda storms away. "People are so rude here," she complains to Vex as they make their way to the crowded tube train.

They take the Underground to Gloucester Road, where Vex has heard there are cheap bed and breakfast places. "There's a Bowie song about the Gloucester Road," he tells Zelda. "It's called 'The Prettiest Star.' " He starts to sing it to her: "Cold fire / You've got everything but cold fire."

"What album is it on?" she asks, to stop his singing.

"*Aladdin Sane.*" As they exit the Gloucester Road station the air outside feels permanently cold. A boy with high black hair walks by. He wears a velvet suit and carries a flower that has been dyed a luminescent violet.

Their hotel features an enormous number of stairs but no elevator. Zelda collapses onto the bed and pets the heavy velveteen drapes that cover the window. "At least it'll be dark enough for me to sleep," she says.

"I'm going to take a shower," says Vex. "Won't you join me?"

"No, thanks. And why are you talking with that dopey English accent?"

The shower is no bigger than a phone booth or an upended coffin and Vex wonders what Zelda will do, considering she doesn't like showers in the first place. While he's cleaning up, Zelda's carefully rewrapping the diary and hiding it beneath a slender bed pillow.

"Maybe we should go out," suggests Vex, rubbing his hair violently to make it stick out.

"I couldn't. I'm just so worried about the diary."

"Don't worry," he says, kissing her stiff platinum hair that still smells of cigarette smoke from the airplane. "I'm sure we weren't followed." He pauses. "Can I ask you something?"

"What?"

"Well, what is it you plan to do with the diary?"

"What a stupid question! I'm going to guard it with my life. It's, like, the only thing I ever had that ever really belonged to me, was meant for me."

"Have you read any of it?"

"You don't understand. I don't have to. God, Vex, I can never love you if you keep asking me questions like that. It just shows me how far apart we really are. I don't think I can ever love you."

"Don't say that. Don't ever say that."

"Okay, then leave me alone. Let's just forget it. You're right—maybe we should go out."

They travel east to Soho and join a colorful line of people waiting to go downstairs into a club called Earnest.

"This is the most humiliating thing about rock 'n' roll," says Zelda, "the waiting in line."

"This ain't rock 'n' roll," replies a girl, mimicking Zelda's American accent.

"I hate this country," says Zelda, smoothing out a wrinkle in her skin-tight lamé dress.

It's dark inside the basement club but the clientele provide the illumination. They're Day-Glo variations of a modern-day Aesthetic Movement. There's no music inside because, as the coat check girl explains, "all music is useless." By the time Zelda has ordered a poorly-mixed martini, however, someone has put on a record.

Zelda goes back to the bar to complain about her drink but is cut off by a boy with brilliantine yellow hair and royal-blue eyes. "What she really wants," he tells the bartender, "is a glass of absinthe."

"How do you know what I want?"

"I can tell just by looking at you. Allow me to introduce myself. My name is Brill."

"Zelda." He kisses her hand.

"Zelda, dear Zelda," he says, staring at her cleavage. 'Some friends and I are leaving in a few minutes for supper at the Café Royal. Why don't you join us?"

She thinks for a moment. "Okay. Just let me go and get my coat." Zelda looks around for Vex but can't find him. When she gives her ticket to the coat check girl she's told, "Do you know who it is you're leaving with? That's Brill. He's a member of the Royal Family."

Zelda thinks it must be a new rock group but surmises it has to be a pretty big one since Brill has his own bodyguard. When a taxi pulls up to take Zelda and Brill to the restaurant, Vex watches from the shadows of an alley, where he's been leaning against an old and battered Sex Pistols poster that's been torn both by fans and time. Vex walks slowly and numbly back to the station where he gets the last train to his hotel.

When Vex's head hits the limp bed pillow he feels something beneath it, something as hard as a jewelry box. He lifts the pillow to find the diary. Vex knows he must do something with it. If Zelda will withdraw herself—the only thing he ever loved or wanted—from him, then he will take this from her.

He puts on his black velvet cloak, picks up the diary, and leaves the room. Vex has no sense of where he's going; he just keeps walking and walking until he sees a church, lit softly from within by candles. There is a priest about—unusual for this late hour.

"Father," asks Vex, impulsively, "will you hear my confession?"

The priest nods and motions for him to follow. Vex kneels in the cramped confessional which is as small as the hotel shower or the photo booth. "Bless me, father, for I have sinned," he begins, but he can't think of anything else to say. He's aware of how his too-tight suspenders are cutting crosses into his back.

"Why don't you open the prayer book you were carrying?" says the priest.

Vex realizes he means the diary and leaps to his feet to run out. Before disappearing into the night he frantically stuffs the diary into a poor box in the church's vestibule.

Over coffee in the Café Royal, Brill asks Zelda if she plans to visit the Tower of London. "I should think you'd like to see the Crown Jewels at least; you're such a shimmering thing."

"There's jewelry there?" asks Zelda, who seldom wears it.

"A bit. Only some of the most valuable stones in the world."

"They must have some safe!" says Zelda, taking another sip of brandy. "Say, if I had something I needed to hide, could I put it there?"

"I suppose," says Brill, watching himself in the mirror as he puts his hand down the front of her dress.

Photographers, reporters, and a crowd that includes Fred are waiting outside the Café Royal for the prince to leave.

Zelda and Brill rush to the taxi. When Zelda says, "I have to go back to my hotel to get something," he replies, "Nonsense. We'll send someone for it."

"No, no. I have to get it."

Brill, soon tired of waiting outside her hotel, tells the driver to go on to the palace.

XIV

Cruella wipes the glue off the edge of one of her long fingernails as she sits at a low table in her and Orange's holiday bedsit flat. "Did you find the address?" she asks Orange.

"I don't know. Which did you want, *Daily Mail* or *Daily Mirror*?"

"*Mirror*, I think. Orange, I asked you to bring that article with you."

"Sorry," he shrugs. "I guess I fail to see what the reward money for Marilyn Monroe's diary has to do with us."

"You haven't been listening to me," Cruella sighs. "Orange, don't you remember?"

He shakes his head painfully. Wincing, he realizes for a moment there's been a lot that doesn't make sense ever since Vince beat him on the head with that baseball bat.

Cruella presses down one final letter of her ransom-style note and prepares to send it. "I KnOw WHo Has the DIarY," the note reads, and she smiles.

After leaving the church Vex walks and walks until he's back in Piccadilly. He sees the boy with the high hair and the painted lily that he and Zelda saw earlier. "I'm Childe," says the boy when he notices Vex staring. "Who are you?"

"Martin. Saint Martin." He goes to shake Childe's hand but Childe offers him his cheek.

The two boys spend what's left of the night having sex in a Soho alley that holds the phone booth David Bowie is pictured in on the back of the *Ziggy Stardust* album. When Childe points it out, Vex goes in and kisses its filthy floor.

"But Bowie's horrible now," says Childe.

"Yeah, but he'd never be in that phone booth now, either. I did that for what was."

At dawn, Vex and Childe have breakfast at McDonald's in Oxford Street. As Vex is swallowing coffee he sees Zelda's cleavage—not her face—on a folded newspaper. He grabs the tabloid out of the reader's hands.

"THE PRINCE AND THE *SHOW*GIRL," announces the *Sun*.

"I've got to go," Vex tells Childe.

"Meet me tonight at the Yellow Book."

Vex runs down Oxford Street toward Hyde Park.

There's a knock at the hotel room door but Zelda doesn't get out of bed to answer it. When she hears the skeleton key turn in the lock, she pulls the covers over her head. A man and a woman enter, carrying batches of flowers which they set around the room. Dahlias, daffodils, carnations, lilies, daisies, edelweiss, and tulips are placed on the floor and on the bureau. Violets and gardenias obscure the mirror.

"Where shall we put these?" the man asks the woman as he strains to carry an immense bundle of roses.

"Why not just plop them on the bed?"

Zelda, still hiding beneath the sheets, feels she might collapse under the oppressive weight of the flowers.

Vex runs through Hyde Park to Kensington Gardens and on toward the hotel in Gloucester Road. He runs up hundreds of steps and uses all his strength to push open the room door, which is blocked by masses of geraniums.

"These stink!" he says as he topples them.

Zelda, pushing off what she can of the flowers, cowers in bed, clutching her pillow.

Vex hits what's visible of the mirror with his fist and slams down a crystal vase that has violets in it. He takes a chunk of the crystal and holds it to Zelda's neck, planning to slit it but instead making two pin-pricks.

"Goddamn you," she says softly. "What have you done with my diary?"

"Nothing," he says, yanking the sheet off Zelda to expose her nude body to the cold, cloying floral air. "Nothing at all."

Vex pushes down his black spandex pants, still sticky from the night in the alley, and rapes Zelda. In his hand he holds a shard of glass and, thinking of Sid Vicious, he carves on Zelda's chest.

"Gimme a fix," he writes, because that's what Sid wrote. Moving several floral arrangements to open the closet, Vex gets his suitcase and leaves.

An editor from the *Sun* has been frantically trying to find out how he can reach Zelda because he wants her to pose for his paper's Page Three: the British institution of a topless girl, alive in bleary news-print, alongside the day's headlines.

XV

A few days prior to the opening day of baseball season, a strange wave of conscience overtakes the man who has been guarding Marilyn Monroe's grave. He decides to turn in the baseball bat, which he'd been keeping at home by his fireplace, to the police. The bat is dusted for fingerprints so that when opening day rolls around, a surprised rookie pitcher for the Dodgers is arrested just as he reaches the mound. The event is seen on national television, but blacked out in Los Angeles.

Vince's arrest for the defaming and defacing of Marilyn Monroe's grave makes a mockery of the coroner's assertions of blackmail and scandal, and casts speculation as to the sanity of Heaven's Hollywood Agent. It is thought that there will be another demotion for him and this time he might even be sent to Orange County.

Still, celebrity grave robbings persist and many cemeteries that harbor luminaries install security patrols and beefed-up alarm systems. Forest Lawn in Los Angeles boasts a gang of vigilantes known as the Cryptics whose slogan says, "We Bust the Head of any Moron Messing with our Famous Dead."

A copycat break-in at Graceland in Memphis has made headlines. It also featured an unusual twist: neither Elvis Presley's nor his stillborn twin brother Jesse's coffins were opened; they were merely switched.

I would've opened the coffin meself," says an English boy at the bar in the Yellow Book.

"Go on—what for?" asks his friend.

"To see if he was still fat."

Vex's sharp eyes grow dim as he eavesdrops while ordering another pint of Guinness.

"Vex!" cries Cruella, nearly toppling him off the chair.

"Cruella—what are you doing here?"

"Well, this club is the place to be, isn't it? Oh, you mean here in London . . . remember, I told you, a working vacation. Is Zelda here?"

"Are you kidding? She's probably with her prince."

"Big deal. It's better to be with Prince than with a prince. I can tell you from experience it's much harder, too."

"Yeah, well, can we talk about something else? Can I get you a drink?"

"Oh, yes. I've fallen under the spell of absinthe, since that seems to be the drink this go-round. I guess it's like, absinthe makes the heart grow fonder."

"Where's Orange?"

"He's back at our flat. He's been acting really weird. Like, we're supposed to go to Belfast in a couple of days to check out this new band called Cross Section and now he's gotten all freaked out and refuses to go with me."

"Why?"

"It's ridiculous. He's paranoid. He thinks that because of his name he's going to be killed by the IRA. It's the stupidest thing I've ever heard. I mean, I've got his plane ticket and everything."

"I'll go," says Vex, waving off Childe, who rushes past.

"Who's that?"

"This guy, Childe. He doesn't want to know about girls."

"That's cool," says Cruella, "the way you've picked up on the British way of saying things."

A few hours later Cruella takes a taxi back to Chelsea, still tingling from the effects of the absinthe. On the low table in their flat she finds a note from Orange, who, oddly, has gone out.

"Cruella call Mr. Oliver from the *Mirror* tomorrow a/m/. I am out. I always loved you."

He's really losing it, thinks Cruella, as she peels a sequined star off her face. She half-considers going out to look for him, but realizes he could be anywhere and besides she has to prepare for her phone call in the morning.

Mr. Oliver's Cockney accent sounds fake and it is, for he's really Fred, who's been offering the reward money for the diary for some time now. He and Cruella agree to meet and they recite a series of possible places: Westminster Abbey, the Tower of London, Harrod's, the National Portrait Gallery. But it's Highgate Cemetery that they finally decide upon, in front of the huge granite face of Karl Marx.

Cruella wears a shiny red plastic skirt topped off with an ornate velvet top. She looks like the interior of a Cadillac and sports a black dahlia in her fierce red hair.

"Hello, ducks," greets Fred, whose face looks like a pinched red balloon. "You got here all right, did you?"

"Save all that," says Cruella. "Let's get right to the point. I know who has what you want but it will cost you more than the sum you've been offering."

"I expected that," says Fred, "what with all the recent publicity."

"Yeah, well, it's even better than all that."

"How so?"

"Not 'how so.' How much. How much is it worth to you?"

"It's worth more than life itself."

"Forget metaphysics—what about money?"

"I'm prepared to offer you one million pounds. One-fourth when you tell me who has it and where they are and the rest when I hold the diary in my hands."

Cruella and Fred walk away from Marx's tomb since a group of tourists are approaching it. "Sid Vicious is buried here somewhere, too," says Cruella in a hushed voice.

"You know a lot about graveyards, luv. Makes me think it was you who broke into Marilyn's crypt."

"That's ridiculous. Anyway, they caught that guy. Don't you read the papers that run your ads?" Cruella lights a cigarette and leans against a headless angel. "Now, what about the money?"

Fred takes out an envelope stuffed with ten- and twenty-pound notes, which Cruella grabs and crams into a deep pocket designed to hold whips inside her skirt. "Her name's Zelda," she says, "and she's staying at the Savoy Hotel now. She goes around with the prince."

"A pleasure doing business with you," says Fred as he offers his hand and then grabs for her skirt. Because the skirt is slippery she's able to lunge away and run out of the cemetery's south side and across the road to the other side of the graveyard. She hides behind the marker of Christina Rossetti's grave until she hears the voice of a tour guide.

"And over here we have the grave of the pre-Raphaelite poetess . . . "

Cruella leaps up to make a getaway and a woman screams, "Her ghost!"

"No, madam," says the guide calmly. "Street urchin. I'm afraid they didn't die out with Dickensian times."

XVI

Cruella plays with her hair as she sits next to Vex on the short flight to Belfast. She's gotten burrs in her hair from hiding in the graveyard and they are impossible to remove, so she has augmented them with hair extensions, pitch-black curly ones that cloy like Shirley Temple's but make Cruella look like Dante Gabriel Rossetti's favored model, Jane Morris.

"Don't go to sleep," she reminds Vex. "It'll throw you all off when we land."

So Vex, trying as hard as he can to please her, falls fast asleep, only he thinks he's still awake. He is sure he's looking out the tiny window at the clouds, which for him in this moment are sexual and anything but reassuring. The clouds take on the sinister shapes of his former girlfriends—the Nancy Spungen one, Zelda, and his mother, too. The clouds are like the horrid insides of each of them. Then they mutate into the predictable snow to remind Vex of Cruella as Ms. Snowfall.

As the plane skids onto the runway he thinks of the harsh faces of his boyfriends, from band members to the more recent Childe. Waking, he looks over at Cruella and jumps when he thinks, for a hazy instant, that she's Orange.

The borders of the Belfast streets are trimmed with barbed wire and there is a lot of broken glass outside the pub where Cruella and Vex are waiting to go in to see Cross Section. The crowd that has gathered is as quiet as the drab gray and olive-green tones they wear. They disperse silently after a man comes outside to make an announcement.

"Where are you going?" Cruella asks a boy.
"Home, I guess. The show's been cancelled."
"What? Why?"
"Fear of riots, I think."
"But, damn it, I came all the way from L.A."
"Sorry for the strain," smirks the youth.
"I guess people really take that band seriously," Cruella says to Vex as they pass through the metal detector in their hotel's lobby. "I mean, all that stuff about hating governments and religions and work."

Vex doesn't reply but casts a longing glance at the front desk, where his steel-toed boots are being held for security reasons until he checks out.

"And it's doubly stupid now, too, that Orange didn't show," Cruella continues in their room. "He could have at least called me to let me know he was okay."

"Maybe he isn't."

"Oh, he is, he is. I have a feeling he's just on a drug binge. He does that every now and then even though he knows I don't approve. But so help me, if he really decides to leave me, he's not getting Rat/s/tar, that's for sure. It was my idea and I'm keeping it."

"I didn't know he was that much into drugs," says Vex, lying back on the bed.

"He feels guilty when he isn't." She hands Vex another bottle of Guinness. "But, anyway, I wanted to ask you, when Zelda walked, did she take the diary? I mean, she must have, right?"

Vex smiles and pushes back his slick black hair, which he has branded with a thick red streak.

"Vex? Where is it?"

"Let's just say the Catholic Church is a little richer now."

Cruella screams when she hears about the poor box. "You Catholics are all alike. Don't you know nobody ever checks those things? They're just put there for effect. Thank God I was raised Protestant—I know better than to believe in some little ritual or whatever you call it, like that."

"You mean 'sacramental,'" laughs Vex, drunk.

"Wherever. I'm sure the diary's still there, safe and sound. It's brilliant, really; probably the safest place in the whole city. Now all we have to do is get it back." She smears the streak in his hair with her lip.

In a pool hall just off of Old Compton Street in Soho, Orange buys ten pounds' worth of heroin and injects his purchase to the sound of someone's pool stick smacking the hard white cue ball. Later the police pick him up in the Virgin Records Megastore and charge him with possession of a deadly weapon, a knife.

Zelda lolls around the Strand's lush Savoy Hotel, where Brill has arranged a suite for her. She hasn't let a maid in for days, and doesn't wash—her platinum hair has gone gray with all the grease. She spends a lot of time looking at picture books of baby animals that she's ordered from Hatchard's Book Shop.

She's numb with hatred for Vex and thinks of him as a shell of a person. At least her identity remains consistent. But the diary seems an almost impossible attainment—it will be hard to outfox him. No, not hard. Impossible.

Another cable from the *Sun* arrives, and Zelda decides to open it, using a badly-bitten fingernail as an opener. She reads the cable—a request for her to appear as their Page Three girl. Zelda picks up the phone to agree to it. She's told a cab will be sent for her but she has time to bathe and do her hair.

When she gets into the tub the scratch marks surface on her chest like invisible ink. She decides to leave her hair stringy.

Zelda plans to send a copy of her photo to Vince, as he must feel pretty bad being in prison for a crime he's never even heard of. Maybe, too, the photo would make him proud of her. It wasn't like the pornography that had so infuriated him. Instead, she assured herself, it would be very tasteful, "the sort of thing she could show to her mum."

The cab arrives and the driver is talkative but Zelda doesn't feel like saying anything. "What is it with you?" the driver asks angrily. "What makes you think you're so special?"

"I feel so much I feel nothing at all," Zelda finally replies, handing him a twenty pound tip.

Zelda takes off her clothes for the shoot and the photographer calls for a makeup artist to work on her cuts. But Zelda refuses, saying, "This is who I am." For props in the photo she chooses a 1950s radio and a bottle of Chanel No. 5, which she pours out into a little pool beside her.

Writers brainstorm the photo caption while the pictures are being taken, firing questions at Zelda as quickly as the flashing lights. "The luscious Zelda Zonk, whose appeal is messy Marilyn Monroe on ice, indulges in long bubble baths and Chanel No. 5. 'I always knock the bottle over,' she says dizzily, 'because I get confused where to put it on.' The Z's in her name may have been stolen from a certain member of the Royal Family, who's reportedly losing sleep over this American beauty." A writer asks, "But, dear, what can we say about the scratches?"

"I wish you wouldn't say anything about them, or Brill, for that matter," Zelda answers.

"Better specify that in your contract."

Zelda takes a cab straight back to the Savoy, where she finds a string of messages from the *Daily Mirror*. She mistakenly assumes they want her for their version of the Page Three girl.

She desires sleep but knows she can't have it so she takes a careless handful of Nembutol. She sees Marilyn, stark as she leans against a sticky telephone pole. "It's the end of everything," she whispers to Zelda. "It's nothing but blackness."

When Zelda wakes up she's in King's Hospital, where she has had her stomach pumped. A nurse brings the *Sun* to her but Zelda screams in protest when she tries to deliver flowers. Zelda opens the paper to page three and is horrified to find only a trace of Marilyn in her haunted face.

Hours later she returns to her suite in the Savoy where she finds a note from Brill attached to copies of two papers, the *Mirror* and the *Star*. Zelda reads the papers first. The *Star* shows her being carried out of an ambulance and says, "The Prince and the Pill Popper." Well, thinks Zelda, at least I look like Marilyn in this one. But the *Mirror* is more unsettling: "Brill's Girl Has Monroe Diary Says Sultry Dominatrix," it reads.

XVII

As if I were a dominatrix," Cruella laughs. "I mean, if that were so, Orange would still be here instead of pulling that vanishing act." She adjusts the black mantilla on top of her head, using the hair extensions in place of hatpins.

"You Protestants have some funny ideas about being Catholic," Vex says when he sees her. "Even my mother never covered her head when she went to Mass."

"I'm just not taking any chances. Is it close to five o'clock yet?"

Kensington's Saint Martin of Tours church is dimly lit and only a handful of darkly-clothed parishioners are inside. No one stirs as Vex breaks open the poor box and Cruella reaches in amongst the shillings and pound notes to retrieve the diary. They run out of the church, but not before Vex dips his fingers into the holy water font, splashing the diary that Cruella holds tightly.

I haven't had this much fun since I interviewed the Sex Pistols," the talk show host tells Zelda, who slumps in a pod of a chair in the television studio. She is live on the air and her eyes crack like ice when he asks her again if she has the diary.

"I told you I don't," she says, "and it's the end of everything."

"But you know who does."

"I don't," she says.

"Let's talk, too, about the speculation that you're really possessed by Nauseating Nancy, of Sid Vicious fame, what with Sid's messages appearing demonically on your breasts."

"I don't know what you're talking about." Zelda turns from him and looks straight into the camera. "I have an announcement to make." She purses her rouged mouth. "Brill and I are going to be married. I'm giving up my career for him." Her monotone is like Kansas.

"COMMON HER?" asks a headline writer from the *Star*. "THE WOMAN HE LOVES," notes a *Mirror* scribe.

In the darkness just offscreen, Fred watches.

"WHO'S GOT IT THEN?" ponders the next morning's edition of the *Sun*, in reference to the diary.

In Los Angeles, the deported Orange stands outside Rat/s/tar and looks in the window at a kitten who's sleeping in a manger—part of a promotion for Cross Section. Orange goes inside his store hoping that Cruella has come back by now.

But she hasn't. Cruella is speaking on a black phone in London's stately Browns Hotel where she and Vex have been staying and spending some of the money she received from Fred. She's calling Fred now, to arrange one final meeting.

WE'VE GOT IT!" says the *London Times*, "And we'll be spotlighting it in our Sunday Magazine. A mystery man has come forth and given us an exclusive peek at Marilyn Monroe's diary." An accompanying photograph shows a torn fragment of the diary that displays, in a slanted, florid hand, the words "The end of everything." Fred has retained the diary and copied portions of it for the *Times*, the highest bidder.

Cruella waits in the lobby of Browns Hotel until she sees the limousine roll up. She motions to Vex, who is seated across the room, and they exit. They quickly duck into the limo and ride the distance to Gatwick Airport without saying a word.

While they're waiting in the airport's satellite terminal, Vex feels queasy, uncertain of Cruella's feelings for him. Instead of confronting her, he finds a telephone and calls Childe at his squat in Camden Town. No one answers so he dials the Savoy Hotel and asks for Zelda.

"I'm afraid I can't put you through," the switchboard operator tells him.

"Who are you talking to?" Cruella asks as she pulls on his sleeve. Vex hangs up, reassured now that Cruella does care. She has sought him out.

"I just dialed the Speaking Clock," he explains. "I love to hear the way they announce the time: 'At the first stroke . . . ' You know."

"You're giving me a heart attack," says Cruella, without smiling. "Come on. We can board now."

Their flight across the Atlantic is long, and Vex is repeatedly unable to ask Cruella what will happen when they get to New York. Each time he tries, a flight attendant appears, pushing a clanging trolley and making Vex very nervous.

The plane finally lands at Kennedy Airport and Cruella heads for the ticket counter. "I have to see Orange," she tells Vex as she stuffs her boarding pass into her bra. "I can't be without him. I know that. It's like I'm breathing artificial air when I'm on my own."

"That's not fair!" says Vex. "Cruella, wait. What about me?"

"That's just it, Vex. You'll be fine. That's the thing about you and Zelda. Neither one of you needs anybody else. Your own personalities are enough. It's not like that for Orange and me. I guess that's why we have something."

"You can't leave me here."

"Well, maybe I'll see you in Los Angeles eventually." She hugs him and walks away.

Vex takes a taxi to the Chelsea Hotel where, from a cold basement room, he watches the wedding of Brill and Zelda being televised live from Westminster Abbey in London. He sees Zelda in a tight sleeveless dotted-Swiss shift that blends in with the snow on his t.v. He quickly kisses the glass over Zelda's face. He knows he'll soon fall asleep for a long time but one that will never be long enough.

Brill appears at the wedding dressed in a satin brocade suit with military braiding. He joins the disheveled Zelda. As Brill and Zelda are about to finalize their vows, Fred hurdles over a sarcophagus and rushes to the head of the church, waving a book in his hand.

"From the direction of Poet's Corner," notes a reporter.

"Stop! Stop!" shouts Fred, holding the diary above his head. He hands it to Zelda, who turns to the right and skips out of the church, toward the cloisters.

Zelda runs the entire distance to the Savoy, clutching the diary in one hand and swinging her basket of bridal flowers in the other. Once she's safe inside her room she throws off her dress and nestles into her dingy white robe. She calls room service to order champagne. With it, the young man also brings several newspapers which Zelda scatters to the floor.

She pours herself a glass of champagne which she holds in one hand, the diary in the other. Zelda walks across the room, her heels putting bullet holes in the newspaper headlines. "MONROE DIARY A FORGERY," says one, "No more authentic than a rubber-stamped autograph." But Zelda knows better. She smiles as she takes a sip of champagne and then raises her glass to Marilyn, who's smiling from the corner.

On a record-setting cold day in Los Angeles, Cruella wears a bulky fake leopard coat to Orange's black mohair as they wander alone through Westwood Cemetery. The walls and hedges seem worn and decayed since Cruella's last visit. She and Orange stop in front of a soft new grave that has just been given a tombstone bearing the name of Richard Conte.

Cruella starts to read from the marble marker: " 'Fly with joy that I may greet you on the wings of our friend the bird of blue / May the fates surrender in our next life.' That's weird," she says. "Almost as weird as the question mark after his death day." She sighs and then continues, "People are stupid who imagine quiet slumbers." Orange doesn't reply, just keeps rubbing his upper arms, stopping now and then to play with his hair.

"My god!" he exclaims, finding an icy wet spot in his ratted part, "It's starting to snow!" And it is—thick snow is falling everywhere, over every bit of the graveyard: the walls, the gate, and the other side.

WALLPAPER

Plus One

I became condemned to live my life twice. There were things I could have done to prevent this. I could have changed my handwriting so that I didn't keep crossing the t's downward. Or I might have collected monogrammed shirts with irrelevant initials and letter sweaters from schools I'd never heard of—and claimed them as my own.

It was frequently suggested that I change my name, Alma, but I resisted that, leaving it alone to be different. Besides, my mother was constantly telling me how it meant "soul" and, while that fact never really spoke to my condition, I did use the title "Gothic Soul" for a concert review I wrote when I was living in England. But still, my name had troubled me ever since I realized it was nearly the same backwards as forwards—it hastened my double doom.

Back when I was living for the first time, I knew this girl named Mariah, which was pronounced the way they call the wind. Mariah favored the silent movie actress Louise Brooks and had that same silky bob except hers was not all black.

Mariah and I made this world of two in which everyone else was wallpaper (a term I learned from the late Sid Vicious, who told me that was how he referred to the girls who used to come to the early punk-rock shows). All was well for Mariah and me until we starting going out with boys, and it really fell apart when we knew the same one—Mario.

I tried to rationalize our friendship, to explain it away. I knew Mariah was a tormentor, a tyrant. I talked about this aloud to myself. I recalled all the times she'd socked me or broken my records. She'd even thrown projects I was working on out the window and when I'd run outside after them she'd slammed the door and locked me out.

Mario moved in after I moved out (I should say ran out) of Mariah's and my walkup apartment above the Rat/s/tar record store which was called the Ice Age back then. The shop was run by Orange and Cruella, and Cruella was always going around saying things like "Nature adores a vacuum," especially when Mariah was upstairs cleaning. I never could stand Cruella.

I made efforts to reconcile with Mariah but she would have none of it. She told me as much in this poorly written note that I stared at and read and reread, hoping the bad grammar and misspellings invalidated it. According to Mariah, I had no real interest in being her friend, I was just after Mario.

It was then that I knew I had to do something drastic, so I got another boyfriend.

I found him at this party and he was kind of Mario-like, a cross between Sid Vicious and some faded and fated old movie star. We met in a hallway but I talked him into going outside where he held the Joy Division t-shirt I was wearing and whispered how much he'd loved them, a band he'd never been able to see.

I explained I'd gone to several of their shows when I lived in England and started to tell him about the article I'd done on them but he cut in and said his name was Patrick and he wasn't happy about it. I came up with the idea of PX for him, which he liked a lot. He was from a military family.

At first I thought it was cute how he never stopped talking about himself or his band. I also forgave his habit of extending a metaphor too far, something I thought he did because he wasn't that good at sex.

But that was at first. Soon it was different, especially because Mariah still wouldn't speak to me. I knew I ought to give PX more credit, as it's not many people who can bridge punk and death so successfully. But sometimes, like when he'd sit in his room "composing," I really couldn't stand him. Mario and Mariah shared the common thread of heroin (something Mariah had described to me as "the fountain of youth" when she stormed past me in a club one night), but there was nothing for PX and me. As a musician he knew he'd always be the one people wanted to hear about; it's the nature of rock. It made no difference how famous or failed he was, nor did it matter what I'd accomplished. It would always be him. One day he asked me to give him an earring I'd designed, with the justification that he'd "even wear it onstage." As if that validated me! No—thank you very much. I did what I did on my own, for my own reasons.

I worked on two projects at once, considering one to be the gin and the other the tonic, yet I didn't drink nearly as much as my friends. Plus, unlike most of them, I'd had success with my endeavors. I sold a necklace I'd made of miraculous medals and fishing tackle to Prince and that got me in *People* magazine. My painting of a crucifix with syringes for nails won a prize. A magazine called *Better than Nothing* printed a story of mine, which I was particularly proud of because I hadn't even changed any names.

My plan was to send a copy to Mariah, since everything I did, I did for her.

And then one night PX asked me, as he was adjusting his bat-black suspenders, if I shouldn't be getting ready.

He roused me from the velveteen sofa, smoothed my crimped platinum hair.

"What gallery?" I said.

"Gallery? It's a record release party. You know that."

As usual, it was because of me that we were invited. I was sure that if I ever married him, our wedding invitations would read, "Alma + 1."

"No, no way," I replied. "I can't, PX. Those twins." The band being showcased was fronted by twins.

"Come off it!" he screamed. PX was so tall he only stood straight when he wanted to make a point, as he did then. "I am so sick of this phobia of yours—this double business. Really, you should see someone."

"Besides," he continued, "they're not really twins, anyway. They don't even look alike."

I picked up my stack of magazines from the boomerang table and walked to my room. I shut the door and started to get ready very deliberately, very slowly. When I was finally done I addressed a nine by twelve envelope to Mariah and seriously considered staying in.

The next day I had tea with my mother, who bored me with details. I wanted to tell her what was on my mind, how much I hoped the pre-release party was the last gathering I'd ever be dragged to. I'd left the party early: as soon as I saw the specter of the twins wearing t-shirts depicting each other's faces, I knew it would have been bad luck to stay. I felt like I was seeing my own funeral—my body all laid out and my face as heavily made up as those of the twins. I could hear everything I'd done being recited, with me inert, unable to defend myself.

I knew then that I had to become more famous so that the people who always smiled blankly and kind of ignored me would come crawling and I could overlook them. I needed to concentrate on one field, on one of the things I did. I needed to live alone. After my fifth cup of tea (an excess of mine that my mother finds in the worst of taste), I decided to give PX this news when I got home.

I unlocked the apartment door and saw his room door closed; he was still asleep. The previous night's talk of rehearsals and recording sessions had worn him out more than a world tour could. I went in his room. He looked so cute asleep, wearing just a white t-shirt with the sleeves and collar torn off. I laid down next to him and whispered in his ear, "I'm moving out."

He opened his gray-blue eyes so quickly I doubted he had really been sleeping. He pleaded something like Mariah did when I left her, and he asked, "How will you be able to be close to me?"

"We'll still be together and we'll talk all the time," I explained. "Besides, if I want to know what you're feeling, I can always watch 'One Life to Live.' " This was a daytime show that defined PX's existence as much as his guitar did. I'd always found the accessories of a person's life to be more revealing than their personalities. For instance, once Mario went back to writing pornography reviews, I read his stuff and felt closer in spirit to him than I had ever felt in person. It was no big deal, though. I never loved Mario.

PX stared at me and his pale eyes were the color of tears.

I moved into a studio apartment that leaned over Hollywood Boulevard and offered me a great view of the mannequins' cleavage as I looked down into the front windows of Frederick's of Hollywood.

Living alone taught me two things very quickly: I really loved PX, and I did want to write. I chose writing like a contestant makes a decision on a game show. There was always a chance, too, that it would end my duplicity problem by adding a third and charm-like dimension.

I fell into a pattern of working every morning and all morning long. I always wrote in pencil because I liked to watch the words on their sides disappear into pencil shavings. It intrigued me in an ashes to ashes kind of way plus it made me feel productive.

With practice, I finally learned to write in the first person. I'd also do little introductions for most of the stories so the reader could feel more a part of things.

PX and I spent less and less time together and as a result he focused even more on his band, which had finally managed to book some studio time and was cutting an EP. I wasn't sure if the band was getting any better: I found it impossible to judge local groups, always preferring their British counterparts.

I stopped by a recording session one night and the band members were all messing around and eating fast food. I was talking to the bass player and telling him how this guy I'd gone out with in England played a bass that had all four strings made out of the thickest E string material.

"Is she telling her Sid Vicious war stories again?" PX interrupted, and I was not amused. I felt he was trying to trivialize me so I left. In an attempt to make amends he called me the next day and asked if I wanted my name on the record jacket's liner notes or etched in the record itself, in that little pool of black vinyl at the end.

"You shouldn't have to ask," I said. "The vinyl, like a tattoo." PX, a veteran of several tattoos, had no reply.

After I hung up I got ready to go out to a club. Just as I wrote in the morning, I went out by myself at night to any club that would put me on the guest list. From a dark corner I would watch people and write down ideas on the backs of flyers whose faces promoted anonymous bands.

At Exoskeleton that night I saw this girl, Scottie, who was most notable for having been Mario's first girlfriend. Now she was like a perverse born-again, except she went Catholic. Somehow our conversation got around to PX, as it always did, and I told her how he had this habit of sitting on top of my electric blanket, like it was such a defiant gesture. Relating the story made me miss him.

At once Scottie turned all serious. "That kind of behavior denotes the devil," she said. "You should stay away from him." Well, this kind of diagnosis might have been appropriate for Mario who, after all, was Catholic too, but it would never fly with a Protestant like PX. I felt sorry for Scottie and wondered if there was a place for her anywhere, like some sort of distorted convent or something.

When I got home that morning there was a note stuck with gray-veined electrical tape to my door. It was from PX. The point of it was that he had started seeing someone else and that he never meant to hurt me. Really, he was no better a writer than Mariah.

That day a manuscript I had mailed off ages ago was forwarded to me from the dead letter office. Receiving it made me think how the Postal Service was more powerful than religion: it could provide an afterlife while maintaining that it couldn't. Dead letters were supposed to be dead. I made a mental note to mention this whole episode to Scottie (whose father was, I believe, a mailman) when I saw her next. Also, because I had mailed my story to Mariah, I got it back, too, with "RETURN TO SENDER" written on it in drippy red ink. I was sure that this must have been fun for her to write, to live out a song like that, much like I had to when I heard PX's band on college radio. It was like having one's own personal soundtrack.

I got another letter as well: an acceptance from a publisher for a collection of my stories. It was true: after receiving various rejections (including one with a rationale that featured strange people, none of whom appeared in my manuscript), I sent the work to a major rock star. I selected one who is respected because he acts, too, and collects Lalique crystal. He liked my style and so he arranged to have my book published.

Still I missed PX and probably loved him. I thought of him during events that weren't even remotely tied to the two of us. I saw his name—a name that, after all, I created—in local gossip columns and how pretty it looked in print! I felt sure he would be the first to come back to me when my book was published in the spring. Mariah would be the second.

And now that I'd solved the problem of my double doom by adding a third and written element, I had the new and stunning fear that I'd created characters who might outlive me, and that was something I never intended.

True Money

Each time Halloween crops up I'm filled with the same horror. I think it's profoundly sad to see people dress up in ways that they could any day of the year (if they possessed the nerve) and then go out this way, with a vengeance. I know the frantic malevolence has everything to do with their identities' expiration date—a lull as timely as Cinderella's—but the whole thing seems so stupid to me.

I got around the issue this year by staying in and answering questions about what I was with the reply of "a latchkey kid."

No persona or identity, however ephemeral, can match that of the True Money Girls, two legendary scenesters whom everybody knows but few have ever met. There are some who think that, like Lana Turner's malt, the Girls never existed. I know the Boy no Wonder, and pretty much trust his story, although he may have invented it to establish his credentials. Most people don't believe him, especially today as he wanders around, addressing his Wildean fear of not being talked about by only going out with girls who are strict Catholics, comfortable that his name is whispered at the very least in their confessions.

True Money

Until now, the Boy no Wonder has been placated.

He's gone to parties where everyone was earthbound. Their shoes were all scuffed.

By chance tonight he stumbles into an underground club called the Assumption, where most people come in costume. There are pirates, high priests, beauty queens, and Highlander madmen. And there, back in the corner close to the bar, are two glorious flappers. These are the True Money Girls.

The True Money Girls like to do things like have sex in bank parking lots. The thrill for them is in being that close to the money in an offbeat sort of way. They adore what they know of two luminaries from the 1920s, Sara and Gerald Murphy; they understand F. Scott Fitzgerald, and hate Hemingway for his flip remark that the rich are different because they have more money. Whether or not he ever said it. Their motto is "Better the Platinum Card than Platinum Hair," although between them they have three of the two things. It doesn't matter yet which and where.

The Boy no Wonder is walking around, feeling a little out of place in his jeans and leather jacket. The only way he got past the door was by offering the Beau Brummell bouncer some speed.

The Boy overhears the True Money Girls discussing writing checks versus using credit cards. "Whatever," the taller of the two concludes. "But I do think one should always cross the dollar sign twice."

There's really nothing introductory the Boy can say that won't be a non sequitur, so to the tall one he says, "You look like Louise Brooks."

She fails to respond but he doesn't give up. He's drawn in like opium from a velvet box. "What are your favorite movies?" he asks.

The ice cream blonde answers, "I like *Sunset Boulevard* while Louise here likes *Whatever Happened to Baby Jane?*"

Boy thinks he's found the rhythm now. He leans into the blonde, here called Thelma. "I get the feeling you're very complex. Like if I stripped layers off you, I'd just find more layers."

"I don't know what you're talking about," she says. "I wear garters. Not the belts but the real twenties kind. You know." Thelma pulls up one side of her dress to reveal a circle of unadorned elastic wrapped like a simple ivory bracelet around her very white thigh.

The Boy no Wonder thinks he might faint.

"You're not leaving?" he asks skittishly as the girls turn to walk away.

"I don't drive," says Thelma.

"She has this thing about fumes," Louise says. "Particularly carbon monoxide."

To close the club that evening the deejay plays a song called "Bela Lugosi's Dead," to which most everyone moves too fast, like they're dancing on graves of hot sand. But the True Money Girls are slow, close, and in synch with the beat. They command attention the way any sole, slow dancing couple does.

"We're going to Malibu tomorrow," Thelma whispers to Boy as they're about to leave. "Louise loves to wear long strands of real pearls at the beach."

Boy feels abandoned when they don't invite him, but a couple of days later his feet are on their welcome mat. The TM Girls have an indoor entrance to their Old-Hollywood apartment. The Boy is all spiffed up: his new patent leather shoes are at least as glossy as his dark hair, the blood in his veins, and whatever other fluids he has to offer. He'd given them his phone number—"Don't you have a card?" one had scolded—but wasn't sure who had called him or exactly which one he was taking out. Still, he'd followed her directions to number 1929.

Thelma, now an accelerated blonde, opens the door. She's wearing a long silk kimono and a bass guitar. "Hiya."

"I thought you guys were probably in a band. What's it called?"

"Called the Spats. We never play, though. Anyway, come in."

Their apartment looks like an opium den. It has all the trappings: a low-slung couch smothered with fringed velvet pillows, beaded doorways, a huge and ornate Oriental carpet.

"Hi," says Louise, who appears framed by the hallway eaves.

Boy is stunned by her, all in black except for a long strand of viscous pearls. She looks like she's lit from behind by a chorus line of steady candlelight.

She snaps shut her beaded bag and picks up her cashmere coat. "Are you ready to go?"

Boy and Louise go out to dinner at the oldest restaurant in Hollywood. She pays. "I know you're poor," she tells him softly, "while I have lots of money."

"Do you want to go to a club?" Boy asks at dessert.

Her eyes are so big they elicit and emit sorrow. "No, no," she says. "I want to go home now."

When they get there Thelma announces she's purchased some heroin cut with Vitamin C. "I'm on a health kick," she shrugs. "The only thing is, I had to sell some Depression glass to get it."

"Goddamn it, Thelma!" Louise throws her bag across the room, narrowly missing a shelf of glass figures. "I liked that stuff!"

"Maybe I should go," says Boy, and he does.

Now Boy is smitten. He buys new clothes. During his Contemporary English History class he sees how many words he can make out of the first letter of Louise's name. First among them of course is "love" followed by "lonely." His scribblings become an obsessive cryptogram. He's transfixed, stares off and sees how Louise looked in that hallway. He stops by a church on the way home to light a candle for her even though he's not Catholic. The altar is still and dark except for this one light reaching up dizzily all day.

"Louise isn't here," Thelma tells him when he arrives at night. "She had to go home to see her mother. She's sick or something."

Boy isn't disappointed because it's enough to be close to Thelma who's close to Louise. "You might as well have these," he says as he hands her some daisies dyed black which she puts in an art nouveau vase. She drops an aspirin into the vase to make the daisies last longer. Boy sits down on the sofa and Thelma sits next to him, close enough so that he is enwrapped by her perfume, Shalimar.

"Are you still going out tonight?" he asks. It's Monday and they were all supposed to be going to the Assumption.

"I don't drive." She kisses his neck. Her white skin, he notices now, is a lot powder.

If he has to, he'll say she put something in his drink.

"It's okay," Thelma says. "Louise won't care. Besides, I lied to you.

She's not really with her mother. She went out with Steve Strange. He's famous."

He kisses her rose, cupid's-bow lips and with his eyes closed sees the morning candle blown out, its smoke rising like a genie.

The next day he doesn't remember that much about their sex except for one detail. Her pubic hair was shaved in the shape of a heart and dyed platinum blonde.

"It was the rage among sophisticated women in the twenties to sculpt and color this hair," she'd explained, pointing to it. "The most popular shapes were the heart and the brown derby. I've never had the hat, though. I don't think it suits my image."

"I put henna on it once," she giggled as he touched her there as if she were a velveteen candy box and his fingers, ribbon.

The heart is all Boy can see as he drives to school. He sees it on bumper stickers, on billboards, and in drugstores. He thinks it must be close to Saint Valentine's Day. That, or his love for her has driven everything else from his mind.

He has to make Thelma believe in love because she told him the reason she and Louise idolized the Murphys so much was that, while scholars and everyone thought they had this true love, what they really had was true money.

"Fitzgerald sort of wrote *Tender is the Night* about them," Thelma had said. "Gerald was a painter and Sara was just beautiful. They made it chic to go to the south of France; they started it. But all this money enabled them to live apart—on separate continents, even. Love is all money and separation, you know."

"Where do you get your money?" Boy asked.

"Louise has a trust fund. She's very nice to me but sometimes I like to pull my own weight. That's why I sold the Depression glass."

When Boy slept with her he had dreamt of Thelma as a chained white angel—a sorceress like Joan of Arc, but with a big pile of money burning at her feet.

For days later he calls their number and leaves messages. Their answering machine overloads. Its message music, "Pennies from Heaven," becomes a sleepy slur.

Boy hears a rumor that the True Money Girls went to London or Berlin and before too long he starts going to the seedy Ascension Club which has taken over from the now-displaced Assumption. It has the same owners but the patrons wear black and don't bother to brush off the lint.

Contrary to Popular Belief

What happened to Scottie," the joke goes, "shouldn't have happened to anyone: she converted to Catholicism." I'm not so sure that she did, and prefer to think that she fulfilled her ambition of creating her own hybrid religion.

Scottie would perhaps be best off in the kind of secular life that involves assuming a new identity. For one thing, she would have an excuse to shed her name, which she's often complained of having to live up to. "I was named after F. Scott and Zelda's offspring," she told me. "But my parents were only vaguely literate. What were they trying to prove?"

Contrary to Popular Belief

Rule #1: *It's a myth to think that people from your past don't come back.* They do. It's like Mario's grandmother used to tell him when he was a little boy, "Dream of the dead, hear from the living."

Mario tends to get into things too fast and then find out they were forced on him, and that he can't get out. His first date, Scottie, was his first love. They went out, he got drunk, and he threw up on her. It made Scottie like him more.

I'd bleed for you, Scottie had said, like it was purely a stigmata matter. She was alien to Mario, at once a homecoming queen and cheerleader to a shy boy who'd gone to an inner-city, all-male Catholic high school. She was as foreign as Miss America.

Mario was certain he didn't want a girlfriend. His idol was, and is, Sid Vicious and he hated how that stupid bitch Nancy had ruined him; he would've killed her, too. Mario has pictures and posters of Sid all over his apartment—Sid falling down off Mario's bedroom wall and shooting up in his kitchen. Mario affects Sid's looks and sees himself as a version of the Sex Pistols' bass player.

Scottie stayed with Mario against his wishes. He constantly worried that she could be pregnant even after she'd had three or four periods, as if the blood didn't wash anything away but rather enhanced and fed it.

He tried to avoid her by unplugging the phone or having his roommate say he wasn't home. Often he wasn't: Mario was working in the arboretum at the college he attended and he'd stay in the tiny plot of a park for hours after his shift, even if it was cold, drinking and smoking pot.

When he came home, he would write video reviews for a hard-core sex magazine. He couldn't show them to his mother, but he reasoned that when he told Scottie about them, he'd offend her feminist sensibilities and she'd leave him.

His plan backfired. "I'm so proud of you, Mario," she cooed. "Pornography's the only honest art form." He felt sick, and stopped writing the reviews.

Around the time they first met, Scottie was in Mario's mother's car, pretty sure religion and sex were just metaphors for each other because Mario kept telling her she was wafer thin. She pictured this communion host while she was eating greasy, salty potato chips and moving on him. Her elbow knocked the magnetic statuette of the Virgin Mary off the dashboard while Mario was saying this is wrong, this is really wrong.

For Scottie, that was the point of conversion – the first time she had sex with Mario.

It wasn't, however, the first time she'd had sex. That was a few years back, when she was still in high school. After practice, she and her football player boyfriend drank beer in the visitors' stands at dusk, in the dark except for across the field where a group of boys were playing basketball by car headlights.

Scottie had pushed her boyfriend away afterward and insisted on walking home alone. She put on her camel's hair coat that extended just beyond her ripped cheerleading skirt to a few inches above her grass-stained knees. Scottie walked back on the right side of the road – she was a pretty girl so she moved in the same direction as the cars to avoid meeting drivers' eyes.

Before she turned down her street, she stopped in a convenience store to buy a Coke and some magazines. At home she headed straight for her bedroom.

She flopped onto her bed, feeling leaden. She began sifting through the magazines, one of which was a rock music monthly she hadn't meant to buy. Buried in its pages was a column from Britain about a new group called the Sex Pistols. They were beyond pub-rock, the writer said, and into something called punk.

Scottie looked at the accompanying photo: four boys pushed together, their clothes torn and safety-pinned. One of them had his eyes closed because an opened can of lager was spraying globules all over, especially in his spiky, disheveled hair.

Just like that, something in her snapped—like the screen door in summer. Scottie went to her vanity table, got out the scissors, and cut her long, dyed-blonde hair severely short.

Her new look made her feel better and got hostile reactions. "They're making me retreat," she'd insist to her family as she justified why she now lived in a world populated solely by this band. She'd quit the cheerleading squad and attended school only for the required hours.

Soon after she graduated, Scottie moved to a tiny Hollywood apartment. One night at a club, she met Mario, who was influenced by punk-rock, Catholicism, and drugs. And, for a time, each became the one person in the other's life. Everyone else was flat on a poster, or voices.

As punk-rock faded and mutated, Scottie began to feel the extravagant draw of religious conversion and much to Mario's dismay, she took instruction to become Catholic. "What's happening to you," Mario told her, "shouldn't be happening to anyone." He felt that Catholics should be born that way and believed her conversion to be an affront to the faith.

But Scottie proceeded with her lessons. On her Day of Recollection she was asked to write her thoughts about converting. She sat on the grass outside the tiny parochial school and listened to the sound of children playing basketball—the dull bounce-bounce followed by the jangling chain hoop like rosary beads against a cassock.

She wrote,

Dear Father:

These things all smell alike to me: damp cement floors in old buildings, dry ice at the Sisters of Mercy concert (in the art deco Palace on Vine Street), rain on London taxis, amyl nitrite, luminaries in churches, stone markers in Westminster Abbey, and old city snow.

Also mirrors and the air after a funeral. The Sisters of Mercy played in Hollywood on a rainy night, a long way from their native England. A storm got the street stars wet. Greasy slick puddles illuminated the names and for a while they shimmered as intended. Inside the club, dry ice affected the humidity.

Spilled drinks on old tweed jackets smell like worn patterned carpet and compartments on a train.

Forget it. I haven't been ethereal enough. I'm too possessive, too attached to the things of time. I only want to lie in my narrow bed with cotton in my ears so I can't hear anything except the absence of sound maintained by snow falling on taxis, dry ice muffling the Sisters of Mercy, and English flowers folding in slow motion, in a cathedral.

When the priest came to collect what Scottie had written, she told him, sorry, she couldn't think of anything.

On the night of her baptism, she looked out across the church and thought she saw Mario in the vestibule, leaning. Looking again, he wasn't there.

He was in Pasadena with a friend of his brother and the next morning Scottie went to visit him. On her way, she stopped by a liquor store. Inside, less real than any cardboard standup advertising vodka, was Johnny Rotten, once the lead singer of the Sex Pistols.

"John, Johnny," Scottie stammered. "My name's Scottie. Maybe you remember. I've written to you." Rotten, who wore contrasting plaids and thick-soled shoes, gave her a puzzled look. His blue eyes were the precise color of the sky in stained glass.

"I've wanted to tell you," she continued, "I converted because of you, became a Catholic mostly because of your song about bibles being full of libel, and sin being a kind of hymn."

Johnny paid the clerk and, bracing the paper bag from the bottom, picked it up. He looked straight into Scottie's eyes and said levelly, "I think that's pathetic of you." As he exited, the security bell rang once.

Scottie didn't go to see Mario but stopped at a park, where she sat in the shade. Mario read her all wrong anyway, she decided, since he believed she had converted completely out of love for him and wouldn't forgive her for having been a cheerleader, as if wearing that outfit branded her. Never mind, she thought, taking a drink of vodka. She had her religion now.

R*ule #2: Never do anything substantial in a bar. It won't stick.* At the end of summer Mario knew he had to get rid of Scottie so he took her to a bar with a Tahitian motif, thinking the bamboo decor and the fluorescent drinks would set her on edge. He sat far from her in the booth and started talking to the guy behind him about baseball. He could tell Scottie was bored. She picked up and put down her empty glass at least a dozen times, as if doing so would make more liquid appear.

"Listen, Scottie," Mario finally said, "I'm not going to go through life with you."

"So?"

"So I may do things you don't like."

"Like what?"

As hard as he tried, Mario couldn't think of anything, except for maybe going out with someone else, which even he couldn't say, for fear it would destroy her.

"Maybe you should write down your feelings and then send them to me," Scottie suggested.

"For Christ's sake, Scottie, this is goodbye, not a fucking ransom note." Mario walked out.

They also serve who sit and drink, thought Scottie as she sat in a marginal bar that had a dirty floor, two pool tables, and a half-dozen scattered and freestanding booths added as an afterthought. It was finally November, her and Mario's favorite month, a month that seemed equally divided between living and dying.

The jukebox in the corner was exclusively country, and the longneck beers cost sixty cents. Scottie had never walked into a bar alone before, but it was like second nature. She curled the soft dollar tightly in her hand, toyed with her straggly blonde hair, and got the bartender's attention.

When she sat down, she realized it was no big deal to be in a bar alone. A Marine approached her and she liked him because he was far from home, in a hostile world but with a ready-made identity. "Would you like to hear a song?" he asked, giving her a glimpse of the silver coins in his hand.

"Yes. 'Jolene.' "

He played "Jolene" for her six times and didn't come back but drifted away like a spirit sent just to grant her that one wish. The song burned into her like impressions on a tintype, and as she drank she searched deep for things to commemorate.

Pretty soon she went into the bathroom where the light didn't work and then proceeded to the centerpiece of all bars, the pay telephone.

R*ule #3: Never answer the phone after midnight. It's always bad news.* On the first of November, Mario dreamt about Scottie. Later that night, she called.

"I'm calling to tell you not to call me anymore." He hadn't called her in months. Mario could hear "Ring of Fire" playing in the background, so he knew she must be calling from a bar. "I know you're seeing someone else and I don't want to know about it," she said.

"Maybe I should see someone else too," she continued. "I could, you know. There's this guy. This guy named Gerard. And he's a good Catholic, Mario—not like you. I thought about it. Gerard, you know. The patron saint of pregnant women. It will make having sex more nerve wracking . . . "

"Scottie," Mario broke in, "I don't care. No matter what." He sighed. "Look, maybe we should meet tomorrow and end this in person."

The next day they met in a park. Mario refused to walk with Scottie through the rose garden, feeling it was too romantic, too religious, and too strong a reminder of his time spent in the arboretum during college.

"I'm not seeing anyone," Mario lied. "Well, I mean, I might be."

As if she were talking to herself, Scottie said, "I don't think I could love anyone I could believe because so much of it is mystery, anyway."

Scottie seemed so fragile that Mario took her back to his apartment where she sat and stared at a poster of Sid Vicious. The poster was called "From Beyond the Grave" and it showed a tiny Sid-doll rotting in a little coffin.

"How can you stand that poster?" she asked. "I think it's really cruel. It makes me think you never really understood the Sex Pistols. They weren't about death."

"Listen, sweetheart," Mario said, "Don't tell me about the Sex Pistols. At least Johnny Rotten never called *me* pathetic. At least I never converted to a religion that didn't want me."

Scottie ran out in tears and Mario realized it was the only time he'd ever seen her leave an unfinished glass of wine.

"I'll call you tonight," he shouted after her. But he didn't. He worries now about when she'll reappear like an unwanted vision—Elizabeth to the Virgin Mary or Nancy Spungen to Sid again, now that he's dead.

Arson

It used to be my fashion to disparage Chris, a nineteen-year-old too beautiful to live. I dismissed him because I thought he drank for no other reason than to escape the ordinary decor of daily life. One night, however, he smelled excessively of medium-priced after-shave and I asked him point-blank why he drank.

"Because if I don't," he replied, "I see ghosts."

Well, I think the play about the invisible rabbit Harvey is really a metaphor for the beauty of alcoholism, and is also symbolic of the potential for religion in each of us. Because Christ couldn't be with us in person, he worked the miracle of transubstantiation. Wasn't that some kind of a hint?

Help me I'm drowning help me I'm converting but somehow I know the thrill is in the ascent for air and never in the safety of having reached the top.

Looking for faith is like twisting the radio dial and encountering only static and dead air between the familiar sameness of the stations. I'd hoped for a nice transition, although that's like fostering a false sense of emancipation, a tease that you're actually free from what went before.

Anyway, get ready for a play on morality, a passionate pastoral, and a cautionary tale. It's left me longing to be buried in London's Highgate Cemetery, right between Dante Gabriel and Christina Rossetti, nearer in spirit to that most cartoonish of punk-rockers, Sid Vicious.

My conversion was maybe an act of cowardice; I don't know. I do know it took a lapsed Catholic—a former altar boy who is Mexican, and therefore a clobbered Catholic—to give me the final smack that sent me reeling toward redemption. But I can't call him a scoundrel and I can't call him a creep because if someone leaves conversion in their wake, aren't they acting as an instrument of God? I mean, aren't they as good as a saint?

You see, the boy just may have loved me. We had a brief grace period together. In the end, though, he had a greater love for drugs.

Of course, maybe loving drugs, like loving people, is not a conscious choice. You just DO and hopefully you do so with complete surrender, perfect abandon.

The story begins in a dry club on a rainy night in Los Angeles. Mario was brooding at the bar which served only fruit juices and herbal teas. He walked over to me and facetiously asked, "Can I buy you a drink?" Later that evening I replayed this scene hundreds of times, only each time I'd reply "No," and that would be that.

But instead I laughed and we began to talk. We left the club for a while to stand in an alley and drink vodka and malt liquor. Mario dropped a cigarette and I stepped on it, my foot lingering like a kiss. He suggested we go have something to eat but I said no, I'm tired, and besides I have to go to work in the morning. When I returned to my cramped Hollywood apartment I uncovered the typewriter and wrote:

He is six foot two but even his height seems tentative. He is tall, to be sure, but his presence is so erratic he may just disappear at any given moment. He's Mexican with extreme—as perceptible as great temperature discrepancies—good looks, like Montgomery Clift but Catholic. His dark eyes have a bright sadness, his sexuality is ambivalent. He plays basketball and all sports gracefully and fiercely, his eyes narrowing to win. He's the formerly dutiful altar boy who now won't set foot inside a church for fear his soul will be claimed again. He's had as many jobs as years on earth, drifting yet never leaving the state. And get this, he likes Jack Kerouac. He watches scavenger birds circling in the sky, safe in the knowledge there's something dead just below. He can be mean in person; he can be kind—at the prescribed distance.

Finished, I got ready for bed and before I finally fell asleep I concluded that at last I knew someone I wished I'd never met.

A lot of mornings and nights came and went until the two of us finally went out, driving the straight-line Pomona Freeway. Overpasses entangled with ivy sped dizzily over our heads. I munched potato chips and kept eyeing the Virgin Mary magnet on the dash of his mother's car.

"Today when I was getting my watch repaired," I said, "I noticed they sell rosaries and cigarette lighters in the same glass case."

He laughed. I couldn't look at him.

"When I was little," he said, "I used to be a pyromaniac. I'd take things into the street and set them on fire."

"I think it means you're gifted."

"What does?"

"That, setting fire to things."

"Huh," he dismissed. "I thought it just meant you liked to set things on fire." He drank vodka and orange juice out of a cup and when he set it down I loved the cup, too.

We went to a bar in Monterey Park. It wasn't the kind of place you'd find trendy young people (he had blue-black spiky hair and I wore too much color) but was more of a cocktail lounge. I felt comfortable there in a deep, genetic sort of way.

I ordered a beer. Mario had something hard and straight, like the British meaning of the word "neat." He smoked one cigarette after another, as he had the night we met, and I told him they made him look very film noir.

"I love you," he said, and he whispered the word like a regret. "And I've never said that to any girl. Like you know how many girls I've even been with?" He connected his thumb and index finger as if he were okaying another drink.

"It doesn't matter," I announced proudly, but he didn't hear me. He was totally absorbed in his own story.

We got up to leave, walked out on the stained red and black velveteen carpet, and then drove away. In front of my apartment he said, "Well," and then kissed me goodnight and it was as if all the stars were sucked right out of the sky and with them, all sources of light.

"Thank you for telling me all that you told me," I said, but he looked confused like he'd already forgotten what was said.

Imagine being so highly-strung for a person that when they finally concede to touch you it's like skin-popping something very fine, to say the least. That's how I began to feel with Mario and it infuriated me.

It made me as mad as when I'd see pictures of Jesus Christ suggestively pulling apart his swinger's muslin robe and pointing to his pierced and sacred heart. I'd want to scream and tell him to stop it, to quit being such an exhibitionist. We get the idea. Or in the Stations of the Cross when he falls not once but two and three times, so inept, so clumsy. I mean, if he can't go through it smoothly, how can we?

I'd been told by a priest that the non-believer is in fact very close to faith. It's called the Dark Night of the Soul and is a very status-ey sort of thing. What I wanted, however, was (as they say in Alcoholics Anonymous) the wisdom to know the difference.

The days weren't all dark. One was as bright and as cheerful as enveloping angels' wings or cool, ironed sheets. It was a Saturday in May (jacaranda trees were blooming) and Mario and I met for lunch at the Ambassador Hotel.

I remember getting bread crumbs all over the oppressively thick white tablecloth and how far you had to walk from the street before you even approached the hotel.

The street is a pew and the long, flat hotel is an altar, obviously.

We looked at *Playboy* in the gift shop to see Bo Derek with another girl and then went into the Cocoanut Grove, which was dark and silent and an embarrassing anomaly in the daytime. Little lights lit the floor like candles in bags. I tried to conjure the spirit of Montgomery Clift but decided it was cruel somehow, like a child trying to will something: "I want this NOW!" and stomping her feet. I guess if they appear at all, ghosts prefer to be seen out of the corner of one's eye, glimpsed as true stars and not propped up like the tacky wax corpses that leer and primp for any camera.

Mario and I stopped by Elysian Park on the way back and then went to my apartment and made love. It was so hot later that afternoon that I removed the sweaty sheet from my bed and flung it over a chair, where it hung lifeless until a Santa Ana wind came up and made it flap like an invigorated shroud racing through a window toward heaven.

I'd always admired both William Blake and Elvis Presley because each created a religion to suit themselves. Is traditional faith, then, lying in wait for those who aren't too good at anything else? Just like the big drugs?

It started to dawn on me that Mario was just a nice boy who wanted nothing so much as to be very, very cruel and drugs were the means he used to go from innocence to sleaze with no purgatorial middle ground. I mean, one day he walked shyly into my bedroom and asked, "Is it all right if I sit on your bed?" and the next it was all emotionless pornographic sex.

I saw all the drugs he took as little plastic skeletons hanging and dancing from rearview mirrors. And believe me, there were enough of them to resemble a Tijuana cemetery on the Day of the Dead.

The last time I saw Mario I gave him a novena card of Saint Gerard Majella and joked about having chewed the bubble gum. He chastised me for "applying baseball metaphors to life." When he finally called me it was from a panelled doctor's office in Woodland Hills.

I knew once and for all I'd been upstaged.

I have some things of his that I've saved: a strand of hair, a page of doodling (all circles), and a matchbook with two bent and soft matches beneath its tattered cover.

I call him and there's no answer. I call friends I used to know. They don't answer either and I feel like Marilyn Monroe on her last night, that sinister telephone cord in an umbilical beeline to her deathbed.

And when I go to Mass and the priest utters something particularly offensive I jolt my head up. Our eyes meet and it's just him and me. And I hate him, Him, and him, hate them with all my might.

It's fortunate, really, that Sid Vicious was cremated. It gave his veins relief. He left some jarring, so-so songs that, true to all lullabies, have no audible end.

It's fortunate, really, that Sid Vicious was cremated. It gave his veins relief. He left some jarring, so-so songs that, true to all lullabies, have no audible end.

The Social Secretary

People are starting to ask me to define my writing style and I've come up with a patent response: "I write romance stories about people who can't love." I'm left alone after that—it's not something you can sip wine over.

Of all the characters I've met I envy Cheri the most because she won't do anything. This is a real achievement (though she'd hate me putting it that way!) in an environment where you are pressed to create. Like me, Cheri was shadowed by the twins but she shrugged it off in a fairy tale fashion.

The Social Secretary

I wasn't much of an office worker. I couldn't type—my fingers kept leaving the home keys. And I didn't like to temp, either. The very word made me queasy with freedom.

On my last job I was fortunate enough to be laid off, qualifying me to receive unemployment benefits. I went over to the unemployment office one dreary morning that seemed itself to be part of the plot to keep me from my money. Aware that the unemployment office exists to break you, I went prepared. I wore my mother's pearls—the only thing I had of value and one that would surely pass for fake. I was glad that my dead mother couldn't see me because this would have killed her for sure.

By some grace I breezed through the process and even saw a lot of familiar faces there, people I'd seen as ornaments at rock concerts or decorations in clubs. I'd always wondered what they did during the day.

It took a few weeks but I got my first check, and then another and another. I spent my time getting caught up in my favorite soap opera and waiting for the mail. I didn't go out much—I couldn't afford it—but I made an exception one night because my favorite band, Gene Loves Jezebel, was giving a concert.

I worked hard all day planning my outfit. I'd lay one out on my bed, try it on, hang it back up, try something else, add some jewelry, and so on until everything fit. It became leopard print tights and a big floral shirt. I crimped and ratted my hair, the heady smell of hairspray filling the bathroom. This is about as close to an artificial high as I get because I hate drugs and alcohol. They make your personality seem sponsored.

I went deliberately late to the concert. The opening band was called the Skeleton Crew and since I can't stand any allusion to work I had to miss them. I waited outside the Palace until they were safely offstage and then went in. Gene Loves Jezebel is fronted by identical Welsh twins, boys wearing oodles of makeup, and they are dipsy, daring, and enchanting. In the foyer after the show I saw a guy I'd met at the unemployment office. He was passing out flyers advertising a party to be held later that evening for the band.

I passed time drinking tea in the Snow White Coffee Shop on Hollywood Boulevard, and when I got to the party the twins were already there, surrounded by admirers. They were like the center of a bouquet. Up close they were tiny, highly-painted marionettes or wooden soldiers. I asked for their autographs ("To Cheri," they wrote twice in this strikingly similar scrawl) and asked one, Michael, if it was less lonely having a twin. "We're not very much alike," he replied, "although we do surprise people by saying the same thing at the same time sometimes."

"Did you ever work a regular job?"

"We're working now," the other twin said somberly.

I thanked them and started to walk around the two-story club. Guess who I saw coming out of the boys' bathroom? Trinity Jones, who was pretty famous and had some hits in the pre-punk years. She still looked beautiful—long, ravishing black hair, deep blue eyes, black leather skirt, fishnet blouse—but she was also pale and a little out of it. Her real name was Camille and I never understood why she changed that and left the Jones part. I was about to ask her for her autograph when she spoke.

"Are you a lost party?" Her accent was transglobal, really affected.

"What?"

"Never mind. It's just that when I see someone looking confused I think they must be lost."

"Oh. That's funny."

"I love these 'A' parties, don't you?" Trinity purred.

"I don't know what you mean." I didn't. Anyone could come to this party. You just had to get a flyer.

"Oh, yes you do. All the right people. The 'A' crowd. You must be part of it."

"I guess," I said. "If 'A' stands for 'alone.' " I told her I spent a lot of time by myself and she asked me if I had a job. When I said no, she looked thoughtful.

"Do you know how to cook?"

"No way."

"Good. People who do just scare me." Trinity lit a cigarette. "What sign are you?"

"Gemini. June eleventh."

"Me too! June twelfth."

I already knew that because one year David Bowie had thrown a birthday party for her here in town.

"I've been looking for a girl," she continued. "Someone to help out, you know, keep records for me and tell me where I am supposed to be when."

"For money? You'd pay someone for doing that?"

"Sure. For money, and if they'd live in, too. Are you interested?"

"I-I'm not sure I want a job."

"But don't think of it as a job, darling. It's more like an adventure."

I shook off the cliché while Trinity drove me to her place, a big house in the Hollywood Hills. On the way there we passed a building and I remarked that I used to know two girls who lived there. "They had lots of money and they dressed out of the 1920s. I could never figure out where they got the money from. Maybe they were prostitutes or something."

"Sometimes just to go on living is a form of prostitution when you don't feel anything," Trinity said.

I didn't get it but then she is a good deal older than me.

Well, it wasn't too hard to give up my closet of an apartment. Once I'd started having to stay in more at night I'd realized it was a place only a vampire could love. The Hollywood Hills was a definite improvement.

Initially my main responsibility was feeding Trinity's two cats, Noir and Victim. Poor Victim was one because the striped bully, Noir, always picked on her. They had to be fed in separate rooms.

Trinity spent most of her time talking on the phone or going clothes shopping. She still got a fair amount of mail, which she asked me to answer. As much as I liked her I couldn't bring myself to do it, so I was secretly stashing it all away in my closet, which was starting to resemble a sorting office.

One night she sent me out to pick up some Thai food and also some Seconal. I refused to do the drug part and I think Trinity was kind of shocked but she let it go. When I came back with the food she was already up in her room. "Cheri," she called, "I want to eat up here."

"You can join me," she said. MTV was on with the sound turned off and her heavy velvet curtains were drawn. We sat cross-legged on the bed and ate like at a wicked picnic.

"I'm sorry," I said, "I'm getting crumbs all over your comforter."

"Don't worry. I can't see how I'll ever fall asleep tonight anyway."

"When I can't sleep I try to remember lullabies."

"Oh, Cheri, sing one for me!"

"You're the singer," I protested.

"No, no. Singing's like work for me—it won't relax me. Please."

I sang one that my mother used to sing for me, a riddle about a baby with no crying and a cherry without a stone.

"I'm glad you're here," Trinity said, kissing me. As we leaned back onto the bed I hoped I'd remembered to close my room door because if Trinity got up in the night she might look in and see the stacks of unanswered letters that I hadn't hidden in the closet yet.

I stayed with her all that night and then got up first to feed the cats. Noir, I'd noticed, hadn't been his usual voracious self lately. In fact he'd barely nibbled his food. Still I wasn't prepared for what I found. Noir was in the pantry, his head submerged in his water bowl. I rushed to wake Trinity, who became hysterical.

"Cheri, please hurry and take him to the vet's. My vet's on Highland. Hurry!"

I put Noir in his travelling box and left. There was a guy at the vet's who was really cute but a little strange. He worked there as an animal attendant. His name was Mario and he asked me if I wanted to go on break with him and have a donut. "To calm your nerves," he offered.

"I've seen you around," he said, "but not lately." We went to Winchell's and he began telling me about himself. He said he'd taken the job at the vet's because he needed money to buy a bass and had found that the soap vets use is really good for sticking out your hair.

"I'm not too good with animals," he confessed. "I used to work in an arboretum when I was in college and we had this pet cat there called Squeaky. All the hippies loved him. It was part of my job to kill these gophers with this pellet gun that put poison pellets down the gopher holes where they'd eat them and die. One day I didn't notice that the gun was broken and the pellets were dropping on the ground." He stopped and laughed. "I guess Squeaky ate some and died."

"Why are you telling me this?" I was mad.

"Don't get upset!" he said. "Sid Vicious killed a cat."

Now this is the sort of thing stupid druggy people say and drugs are probably the real reason this guy was working at a vet's.

I went back home and saw Victim first thing, sulking like a guilty ghost, like she was the wrong one to be around and healthy. I remembered I hadn't fed her and started to when I heard Trinity on the stairs.

"What happened?"

"The vet's going to call us later today. He's running some tests."

"Did you speak directly to him?"

"Yes," I lied.

When the doctor called the news was bad. Noir had feline leukemia. Without belaboring, Trinity decided to have him put to sleep. "I can't stand a slow death," she said.

I was relieved. My mother had died slowly and it had been a drag.

Victim continued her slinking shadow routine for days. Maybe she felt lonely without her tormentor. She'd walk in a room all low to the ground and keep looking around while she ate.

One morning I was putting the mail away when I noticed a letter from *Bold Face*, which was my favorite magazine. It was published in London. I like London: the best thing about it is that hardly anyone works. I had my hair done there once, dyed magenta. The guy who did it wore just a leotard and a leather jacket and when he answered the phone in the salon he just said "hello" like it was his home or something.

I opened the letter to Trinity and saw that the editor wanted her to come and do some modeling for their "In/Famous" section. Hey, I thought, Trinity must be back in vogue. I left the letter out where I'd remember to tell Trinity about it and then sat down to watch "All My Children."

Trinity came in laden with shopping bags and looking like a black artificial Christmas tree with silver jewelry for tinsel. "You got an important letter today," I told her at the commercials. She picked it up from the table and studied it like a script.

"Can you get London on the phone for me?" she asked. "It's 8:30 there now. I don't think it's too late." It took a few moments to make the call and Trinity got a little aggravated. "Cheri, couldn't you do long distance any faster? Isn't that something you should do?"

After that phone call, my life changed. "I'm going to London," Trinity announced. One of her singles, "Sweater Girl," had been rereleased there and was doing pretty well. That was why she wanted to go and why *Bold Face* was interested. I sat there hoping I could get unemployment again until Trinity said, "I want you to come with me."

"There's a lot to do," she continued. "You'll have to close things here and arrange for Victim to be quarantined."

"Huh?"

"I want to take her with us and I know there's a quarantine requirement but I don't remember how long it lasts."

Six months, I found out when I picked up our tickets.

On the flight over we rented headsets. Gene Loves Jezebel had a song on one of the programs and Trinity nudged me when it came on to remind me that that was where I came in. "I think a lot about the twins aspect," Trinity whispered. "You know, I consider you to be something of my soulmate, my other half."

I thought it was ironic that out of eight programs we were listening to the same one, but apart from that I never considered us to be very much alike. Trinity worked for her fame and I avoided it. Besides, I think of twins as being more like Victim and Noir—one dominating and one cowering and both never forgetting.

The editor of *Bold Face*, Nick O'Rourke, had provided Trinity with a garden flat to sublet. It was in posh Hampstead, north of central London. The affluent village atmosphere suited Trinity. I mean, a squat in Euston might have been okay for struggling new romantics like Boy George but it never was for her.

Trinity liked to walk in Hampstead Heath and I did, too. Once we saw a bare tree which had dropped a little branch that looked like a wishbone. Trinity and I broke it and she won but I persuaded her to tell me her wish. It was that we'd always be together.

Trinity's "In/Famous" shoot was coming up and it was to be done in Highgate Cemetery. I didn't go along because I felt ill that day, I think because of some french fries I'd eaten at McDonald's the night before.

"Cheri, there's something I've been meaning to talk to you about," Trinity said before she left. "It's something Nick mentioned." Trinity and Nick had been seeing each other—meeting for lunch usually at the Tate Gallery, which was on the Embankment where the paintings provided a relief from the unrelenting gray. "He said he thought they'd pulled off quite a coup getting me to come here. When I said I didn't understand he told me countless magazines had been after me, phoning and writing but getting no reply. Do you remember anything about it?"

"Not at all," I said as I pulled the covers closer to my face.

"I'd better go or I'll be late," Trinity said.

I imagined the photo session, saw the overgrown grass, the broken headstones with green moss veins, and Trinity reigning in black and glitter.

Nick suggested Trinity do a concert that would be her comeback show. When she agreed, posters went up in Soho alleys and down the Kings Road. She was hot. Her record company even sent over two boys to help around the flat but I couldn't see what they did apart from answer the phone and bring in the milk.

I hardly ever saw Trinity anymore but when I did it was as if the cold climate had brought her back to life. Her cheeks looked like Snow White's apple, poison or no. She was on a mad schedule of rehearsing and going to interviews, teas, and parties.

I wished England had "All My Children."

The night I was getting ready to go to Trinity's show I realized I hadn't been out since Gene Loves Jezebel back home. I got dressed and caught a cab to the packed club. I spotted the Jezebel twins huddled in a corner and also saw the two 1920s money girls whose apartment I'd been to once. But I didn't feel like talking to anyone.

Trinity was great and got rave reviews. "HOLY TRINITY!" said the *NME*. "NO SWEAT," sighed *Melody Maker*.

A few days later, Trinity called me into a room and thanked me for all I'd done. Then she asked if I'd go pick up Victim. It was my first errand since our arrival six months ago to the day.

I took a cab to Heathrow airport, a wonderfully long way away. I saw bricks, rain, gray, roundabouts, dark overcoats, and smelled exhaust mixed with morning tea. When I thought we were almost there we were only in Hammersmith.

Victim didn't seem to know me. As I waited with the cat in the taxi queue I felt in my pockets for my passport. A cab pulled up and the driver lowered his window halfway. I looked in. "Would you deliver this cat?"

"Just the pussycat, luv?"

"Yes."
"Going to a mews, is she," he joked and I laughed.
"Going to Hampstead to see about a nightingale," I smiled.
I went into the airport terminal and bought a ticket home.

History and Past

Miserable was always drunk and what annoyed me most about her was that although she perceived herself to be very outlandish and unusual, she really just fit it. For example, she'd go out to a concert or a bar and complain of all the "bad vibes" she was getting from people who didn't notice her; people for whom it would be a strain to affect even apathy.

She must have been something in her day when, no doubt, platform shoes really highlighted her (she claimed to be five-foot-one but she was shorter than I am).

History and Past

Shyly at first, Miserable is explaining why she likes to be hit. "It's the moment of pure attention," she says, gaining confidence as she caresses a bruise on her broomstick-like arm. "It's when you're one-hundred percent alive. All your senses *feel*." When one boyfriend threw her across a room, she lingered mid-air in that split second when she thought she could fly.

Miserable has a strand of lovers stretching back to the glitter-rock years of the early 1970s, but her presence is so eerily weighty it seems like she couldn't have carried another soul. She would have sunk.

Because she's older—in her mid-thirties—she doesn't go anywhere that has fluorescent lights. She has the drugstores deliver and works in the vaguely-hued children's section of a branch of the Los Angeles Public Library. The thick makeup she puts on exaggerates the fine lines on her face and makes it look like the gilt edge of a closed book where the pages meet.

To work she wears a gray vintage dress and her thick blonde hair pulled back in a sober ponytail. When she walks across the library's wood floor her black velvet flats make a dusty, muffled sound. She helps a ten-year-old locate *A Wrinkle in Time* and returns to her desk to see Jordan come in. His heavy bother-boots have metal shin guards that rattle as he walks up the stairs. Miserable can't think of where she's seen him before. It couldn't have been a club because he looks about fifteen.

Jordan knows without asking that Miserable has this other life outside of her job, one with aspects that might approximate his dreams.

When he says hello to her, she can't see her outline in his cornflower-blue eyes.

He waits for Miserable on the stone steps in front of the library and they go to her apartment. Jordan is impressed by her collection of rock posters and memorabilia (mixed in with real antiques and rarities), especially the things from the glitter era. He points to a pair of pink platform shoes which are nailed to the wall. "Did you walk in those?" he asks, believing that if she did she must be ethereal, able to walk on clouds.

"Sure," she replies flatly. Miserable never smiles, she just shows teeth. "I was dancing when you were probably just taking your first steps."

"I'm sixteen," Jordan answers, indignant. He refuses the drink Miserable offers him, explaining, "It's my 399th day of sobriety."

"God," she says, "that sounds like vampire-years to me."

"I don't get it," he says, grinning.

"The thing about the glitter days," Miserable continues, "is that there were fewer people then. It was a very brave and in-crowd thing to run around wearing lamé pants and having pink hair. I mean, there were less than thirty people in all of Los Angeles who did this, unlike now when it's almost the norm. Early punk-rock was the same."

"Punk-rock was like glitter?"

"No—well, yeah, in a way. All the people who'd finally caught on to glitter and glam weren't about to let it go. But what I meant was that it was very exclusive. I mean, the boys and girls who are aware enough of any trend in the very beginning always number very few, and they're the ones who count. But things were better then. Not now."

Miserable is at the bottom of her fifth drink and the room is spinning like a warped record. Jordan says he has to go but refuses her ride home, walking to the bus stop instead.

Miserable arranges to meet Jordan the next afternoon at the top of the parking structure by her work. It is a hot late-summer sunset and Jordan's huge silver radio rests on the concrete ledge and blends in with L.A.'s downtown skyline. Jordan walks toward Miserable and kisses her amid the cluttered solitude.

"Let's go for a drive," she suggests, and they get into her late-sixties model Volvo and drive east, out the San Bernardino Freeway.

"I go this way whenever I start to feel that there's about to be a premium on sadness," Miserable says. "Going down Melrose Avenue or the Sunset Strip it's so falsely glitzy and all the poignant reminders—dusty old vacuum cleaner shops or wooden bus benches—are just vanishing. Out this way there's really tall and precarious fast food signs and sticky motels, you know, dingy old thrift shops selling broken refrigerators . . . "

"I've never been to a motel," says Jordan. When Miserable doesn't look at him, he adds, "I've never had sex, either."

Miserable drives into the parking lot of a gas station/truck stop. "Let's get something to eat," she says, *sans* emotion, "and then we'll head back."

She leaves their booth to go to the ladies' room and when she returns Jordan shows her his wrist, where he's written her name in blue ink. The words look like filigreed veins. She takes his wrist with her left hand, and with her right dabs a paper napkin into her glass of ice water. She rubs the ink and skin on Jordan's arm until they mix into a shade of purple.

"I'm not going to take you to a motel, either, if that's what you're thinking," she tells him as he's finishing his fourth cup of coffee. "I don't want the responsibility of being your first, you know. I don't. I don't want to be remembered."

"Then why do you collect things?"

"To bury myself."

At the cash register, Miserable asks for a book of matches to save and the one she's given has a blank white cover.

Back in Los Angeles, Jordan asks Miserable if she'll drop him off at his A.A. meeting, and she does. "I'm going out to a club later," she says. "I could probably get you in if you wanted."

"Yes," he says. "I can never sleep after I go to my meetings, anyway."

The club, Snappy Re:Party, is set in a Chinese restaurant on the wrong side of Chinatown. In the line outside Jordan holds his fake ID uncertainly, like it's an indifferent talisman. "Put that away," Miserable growls, already pretty drunk, "it'll only betray you."

The doorman lets them in without question; he's seen Miserable around for years and doesn't care to check who the latest boyfriend is. Miserable goes straight to the bar and Jordan looks around at the club's hanging plastic plants that obscure video monitors. He enters one room that is filled with phosphorescent-like paintings for sale, only it's so dark no one can see them.

"Miserable!" calls Cruella from the far end of the bar. Cruella's husband, Orange, is the club's deejay. "Miserable Mary!" Cruella walks up to toy with the edge of Miserable's black lace blouse and asks, "What's with the widow's weeds? This is a happy club, Mary. There's no punk- or doom-rock anymore. Besides," Cruella pauses and then stage whispers, "you don't look to be in mourning if you know what I mean. Still, I have some advice for you. Having a teenage boyfriend gets old fast. You'll see."

Miserable orders two rum and Cokes and laughs at Cruella. "You know, Cruella, you think you're really something with your bitchy persona and shopping mall wit. You think you'll last forever. Well, maybe I've got advice for you . . . " She turns to look Cruella in the eye but by then she's halfway across the room. Downing one drink, Miserable orders another and goes to find Jordan. "This is for you," she tells him, holding out the drink.

"Is it just Coke?"

"No, rum and Coke. It's not going to kill you. It's just like candy."

"I can't."

"What do you mean you can't? What did you come to a club for—and who do you think you are? I don't believe this." She stands closer to Jordan, waits for him to push her.

Taking a step back, he says, "I may not know who I am, but I know who I want to be." His pale eyes reflect the club's darkness now. "And I figured out a long time ago that if I kept drinking I'd be dead by now."

"So what?"

"So, I don't want to be. So, there's stuff I want to do, like be in a band. I don't care what other people do. I don't care if you drink."

"Sure."

"Don't you want to do anything with your life or do you just feel like everything is against you?"

"Once you give up yearning," says Miserable, "you give up the feeling that everything is against you."

"That sucks," says Jordan. He takes a piece of folded-up notebook paper from his pocket and writes down a phone number. "I'm going to take off now," he says, "but call me later. This club is too boring and arty."

Miserable takes the paper and goes to order a beer. She sees a guy from a band she used to know and they spend the rest of the night making out by the bathrooms.

Kissing is not feeling, Miserable thinks as she's driving home on the

Hollywood Freeway. She crumples up the paper with Jordan's number on it and throws it out the window. When a highway patrolman stops her for weaving, she agrees to go with him to a motel off Van Nuys Boulevard.

"I've never been with one of these punker-girls before," he says, and then he hits her before she has a chance to explain that there isn't punk-rock anymore.

Fixation

I like the style more than the references," was something I was starting to hear again and again about my work. I decided it might be a good saying for an epitaph. I have no idea what the gravestone for Sid Vicious says (or even if there is one), only that I wanted to tell a little bit about someone who became such an oblivious symbol. Sid means a lot to many people, most always for reasons they invented.

Fixation

It occurs to me that after your first love, it's all just revenge. I think this thought a lot, especially as it applies to Sid Vicious.

You might say the earth moved for Nancy Spungen, the late Sid Vicious's even later girlfriend. It shifted to make room for her just south of Philadelphia where she's buried intact save for a shallow knife wound and some needle tracks. Her death was about displaced love, I think, but I don't pretend to know if she loved him, or he, her. It is certain that, if love is suicide and suicide, murder then their chain of events began unbreakable, as linked as a skull and crossbones charm bracelet.

Sid was an awkward and shy boy who, if left alone, would rather listen to lightweight European pop music than rock and play with his Action Man toys than socialize. The former John Beverley went from spots to spotlight when his friend Johnny Lydon invited him to be in a band, the Sex Pistols. Lydon suggested Sid use the name he'd been calling him: Sid (after Johnny's pet hamster) Vicious (he was anything but).

Within two years the irony would imprison them both.

John Beverley lived with his mother in a small flat by tracks, probably tired of trains. He wasn't a wayward, haunted child, he just wanted to spend all his time with his best and only friend, Johnny. On any school day you'd find them in a damp bathroom, smoking and talking together while others passed in the halls.

Johnny Lydon was devoted to reggae and obscure music and, therefore, so was Sid. And, at fifteen, Johnny was already showing signs of the brilliant rebellion that would soon stir the music world.

He had this image: deliberately ratty, matted dyed-red hair, fluorescent-white skin, electric blue eyes, and this sharp wit and harsh temper that merited his nickname, Rotten. His long, thin arms were dotted with cigarette burns. "What about them?" he'd challenge. "Pain doesn't hurt."

When a teacher suggested that Johnny buy a new suit, Johnny asked his mother for the money, bought the clothes, and then shredded them with scissors precisely to be salvaged with scores of visible safety pins. He wore his creation like armor replete with an anemic-looking polkadot tie to school the next day.

He was sent home, which wasn't a bad place to be once Sid joined him there. The two sat in Johnny's room listening to records while Mrs. Lydon was downstairs cleaning.

Mrs. Lydon, passionately Catholic, was dismayed that her son was no longer in parochial school. He'd been expelled for drawing something sacrilegious during art. Still, in his new school Johnny wasn't doing that poorly and Mrs. Lydon was assured he would graduate. He might even read for an A-level in English Literature because he liked Keats's poetry.

Sid stared at the crucifix that was for the moment hung upside down on Johnny's bedroom wall. "Do you ever wish you were still in Catholic school?" Sid asked.

"God, no! All they'd done was, like, teach me religion. They didn't give a damn about your education, like, that's not important, is it? As long as you go out being a priest. I mean, imposing ideas on your mind like that when you don't want to know is, like, bound to have the opposite reaction."

Sid and Johnny would leave the house each afternoon to walk around north London's Finsbury Park which, despite its name, had no trees. It was gray and chipped and, as Johnny would write, "a side of London the tourists never see." Other people, unless they were Pakistani, would jeer at the two figures as they'd walk the streets and then go into a chip shop where they would buy identical large orders smothered in vinegar and swaddled in scandal-smeared newsprint.

If his mother lived for Sundays, Johnny existed for Saturday mornings when he and Sid would take the Underground to Chelsea and parade down the Kings Road to the SEX Shop which was run by Malcolm McLaren, who'd been to America and once managed a glitter-rock band. Among the racks of 1950s clothes and bondage gear, Johnny, Sid, and a cluster of like-minded youths would gather, sensing the stagnancy of the current rock scene and its congruent excitement: pop culture would change and they'd be a part of it.

Johnny was becoming the figurehead of this collection that the press christened punk-rockers. When McLaren suggested Johnny sing for a band he was overseeing (to be called the Sex Pistols), Johnny auditioned in front of the SEX Shop's jukebox, screaming his own words over the song.

Sid soon fancied himself a singer as well, and tried to gather his own group to be named the Flowers of Romance. They never happened, though, because Sid was always with Johnny, watching each of Johnny's rehearsals and shows. The two would ride the last train home at night, Sid sitting opposite Johnny. Sid's feet were covered in thick black boots and chains, and planted on the seat next to his friend. Sid would ride that way and just stare at Johnny.

Johnny constantly protested that he couldn't work with Glen Matlock, the Sex Pistols' original bass player, until McLaren finally asked Rotten if there were any alternatives.

"My mate, Sid."

"They were really close," Glen explained to the press with a shrug. "After Johnny joined the band when I was still in it, he didn't have so much time for Vicious because now he had the Sex Pistols. Vicious used to be ringing him up all the time and Rotten just really put him down and I think Sid felt a bit left out. That's when Sid started beating people up."

So now Sid, who'd previously peered out of the corners of newspaper photos of Sex Pistols fans, was a Sex Pistol, front-page material. Only, except to Johnny, he didn't know what to say. "What do I have to do?" Sid would ask reporters. "What happens now?" He responded to one rock journalist by hitting him with a bicycle chain.

The compelling, articulate Johnny Rotten wanted nothing so much as to be taken seriously. He conceded that a person can't speak truly, honestly, into a microphone but sighed, "Never mind. Some of the wisdom will get through." He condemned the monarchy, the white-supremacist National Front, and consumerism. He lashed out against the "star trip" and hoped—but didn't promise—it wouldn't happen to him.

Johnny's views appeared in the papers buried beneath updates on the latest exploits of Sid Vicious, who could fight anything except the image the media imposed on him. Feeling undermined, Johnny started to turn against Sid. One night in a pub Rotten told Sid how he felt. "Look," Johnny said, "you have no reason for living, yet you're determining my life."

Sid left the pub that night to link marked arms with Nancy Spungen, an American groupie much detested within the Pistols camp. Too starstruck to be a punk, Nancy might have made a romantic anti-hero save for one detail: she didn't photograph well. She was good at heroin though, and soon Sid got to be, too. Nancy needled him, hauled him around, and told him to sit up straight while he stammered to the press about how much he loved her.

During the Queen's Jubilee Week in London, the Sex Pistols' "God Save the Queen" was the Number One record. Its place at the top of the charts was acknowledged by a few moments of silence because the song had been banned from the airwaves. "God Save the Queen," went the lyric, "she's not a human being." Posters promoting the single were plastered everywhere like blackmail wallpaper. They depicted Queen Elizabeth with a safety pin through her lips. Another picture gave her a ransom note for eyes.

To celebrate their success (won against great odds as the Pistols had been dropped by two record companies and prohibited from performing live), Johnny went to a pub in Highbury. When he left he was beaten up in a car park, thrown to the ground and cut with glass. After being released from hospital, he went home and listened to a reggae record, *Black Star Liner*. His attempts to reach Sid were pointless—Vicious was nodded out on junk.

At the turn of the year, with no place to go and nowhere to play, the Sex Pistols came to America for what was, with the exception of San Francisco, a Bible Belt tour. The band's publicity preceded them like a barker's cry—They Spit! They Drool! They Vomit!—and Sid obliged the carnival atmosphere by hitting a fan with his bass, getting tangled up in his (usually unplugged) guitar cord, and appearing onstage with "Gimme a Fix" etched on his skinny chest, dried blood providing the ink. "Big, tough Sid Vicious just fell down," Johnny would announce in a tone tinged with sarcasm and disgust.

Nancy had been prevented by the Pistols' management from joining the American tour, and relationships within the group (and between Sid and Johnny) were strained as well. When the Pistols appeared at a honky-tonk in snowbound Tulsa, evangelists warned the huddled crowd waiting outside to save their souls and avoid seeing the Anti-Christ. Inside, the sound check collapsed in apathy. After the show that night, Sid sat on the edge of the stage in silence as the other band members prepared to board the tour bus. Sid missed the bus in favor of leaving with an impossible blonde—a drag queen—who tottered precariously over the six-foot Vicious.

The Sex Pistols broke up after playing their largest show, in San Francisco, and they quickly headed in different directions: Johnny went to Jamaica while Sid combined Valium with alcohol and collapsed on a flight to New York. He was revived in a hospital in Queens.

Months later, Nancy and Sid left London to return to New York, where they stayed at the Chelsea Hotel until he cut her. When Sid was released on bail, Mrs. Beverley (in New York to be with her son) brought him his last present, and he wrapped it with string because it was more heroin.

Nancy had given Sid a heavy lock that he wore around his neck, a lock that's now in the possession of his mother.

"I loved him," Johnny says today from his oceanfront home in California, but he won't elaborate.

Sex-Gang Children

I *can't.*

Sex-Gang Children

PART I

A young seminarian, Gabriel, dies during an explosion in a shed behind his parents' home as he's inhaling twenty-five cents' worth of gasoline from a milk carton. The family cat races across the yard. When the paramedics arrive, there's nothing left except for Gabriel's black shoes.

At his funeral Mass are two friends from high school, Mario and Orange, Orange's wife Cruella, Alma with Mariah, and Mariah's boyfriend, the Boy no Wonder.

All these people like to wear black anyway.

Mariah and Alma are basically just attracted to tragedy and didn't really know Gabriel except in passing at clubs. Boy is along for the ride—he goes where Mariah goes.

Boy hates being in a church almost as much as Mario does, although Boy doesn't know Mario yet. They'll never become friends because only Mario takes drugs, and stuff like this tends to separate men.

Orange wears a myriad of crucifixes and a broken rosary held together by safety pins. Chrysanthemums are everywhere—the flowers of necromancy.

When the Mass is ended a cortege is formed, with Mariah and Orange's cars looking kind of odd, being a bright pink Morris Minor and a red T-Bird convertible, respectively. Mario has a dark, beat-up

Chevrolet that at the moment won't start so Mariah calls out, "Come ride with us."

Mario says he's worried about his car, that he'll get a ticket for leaving it in the church parking lot or that it will get towed away since it looks so abandoned.

"Don't worry," says Mariah. "Get in."

He hops in the back of the fuchsia-colored car and sits next to Alma, who introduces herself and holds onto his hand tightly as if to console him. Mario wonders how they knew Gabriel but doesn't ask.

A mixture of priests and seminarians, family, friends, and intruders are on hand for the graveside ceremony. The priest who said the Mass adds a few words over the casket as it perches above the freshly dug earth. Then he sprinkles holy water, which beads up on the coffin's heavily-waxed lid.

In the car on the way back, Mariah and Alma ride up front together because they're best friends. They amuse themselves by demonstrating how they can accurately complete each other's sentences. Boy feels nervous, perplexed by the show of religion he's just witnessed. "What was that thing the priest shook?" he asks. "It looked like a tire gauge."

This sacrilege rattles the already shaken Mario, who struggles to be Catholic. He removes the beret he used to mat his customarily spiky black hair. A trail of black dye on his hairline looks like asphalt.

"Would you like to stop by our house?" Mariah asks Mario. Mariah, Boy, and Alma all live together in a two-bedroom apartment over the Ice Age, a record store owned by Orange and Cruella. The three like the novelty of a storefront apartment—something not easy to find in Los Angeles.

Mario declines because he's still worried about his car. "I'll give you a ride to the church," Alma offers, and they transfer to her orange Volkswagen. When they get to the church Mario says thanks and opens the car door. Alma turns off the motor and gets out too. She sits in Mario's car with him and notices a crumpled letter on the floor which he pushes aside with his boot. "I know that must be a love letter," Alma tells him as they start kissing and holding each other.

PART II

Boy no Wonder is up in the apartment shining his shoes while Alma and Mariah are downstairs in the Ice Age. Alma holds a quart of milk. Orange and Cruella are both working and Orange asks Mariah how she knew Mario and Gabriel. "I still can't get over how Gabriel died," Orange says, shaking his head. "Like spontaneous combustion."

"I'd seen him in clubs a couple of times," says Mariah. "He was always really nice."

Alma adds that she knows Mario and that they are really good friends. Mariah glares at Alma who suddenly feels like she's standing in the shade during winter.

"You know what?" Cruella asks, her vivid red hair falling in her face. "I notice as I'm filing these records that there's always four of everything. Four original band members, four music categories, you know, four plates, four chairs at a table."

"Great, Cruella," says Orange. "Like you'd think it was the mystical number instead of three or seven."

"Four in a family," adds Mariah.

Alma waits for Mariah to finish looking around so they can go back upstairs where Boy is now watching MTV. Mariah orders him to turn it off. To Alma she says, "Let's invite Mario over to watch videos."

"I-I don't know," Alma answers. "I was going to go over there." Mariah follows Alma into her room, which features a collection of brightly-colored souvenir scarves that sag voluptuously from where they are pinned to the walls. "Alma," she continues, "come on, ask him over or I'll do it myself. What's the problem?"

"There's no problem, Mariah. I wouldn't even be hanging around with him if it weren't that you were always with Boy."

"I'm not."

Alma is afraid to say no to Mariah. She remembers the last time she did, and how she'd found herself outside the apartment wearing just an antique slip as she retrieved jewelry she'd designed that Mariah had flung out the window. The glittery pieces had landed on shrubs and looked like Christmas ornaments. Alma is shy, too, of Mariah's beauty and of her silky 1920s-style haircut. Like Mario, Mariah dyes her dark hair black, except for a wedge which is rose-pink as a flapper's headband that has slipped to rest around the nape of her neck like a threat.

Mario comes over that evening and the four watch videos. They drink margaritas, take Quaaludes (except Boy), and eat quarter-pound hamburgers. As it gets later Mario says, I'll be going now, goodnight Mariah, bye Boy. Alma says, I'll walk you to your car.

When Alma finally comes back Mariah and Boy are waiting up, Mariah's blue eyes burning into Alma.

PART III

The phone rings early the next morning and when Alma answers it she learns she's landed a part in a Prince video. Alma dresses in velvet and brocade, satin and paisley lace, and wears her favorite clear Lucite slippers. She rushes around and leaves an excited note written in lipstick since she can't find a pen.

When Boy gets up to go to school he finds the note and considers telling Mariah the good news. Then he thinks better of it and decides to let her sleep. He throws the note away—his palms are smeared with lipstick from having crumpled it.

Mariah awakens a few hours later and goes into Alma's room to look through her things. She finds Mario's number and dials it only to learn that his line is busy. When it's busy again she asks the operator to do an emergency cut-in.

Mario releases the line. "I was talking to my mother," he lies. He was calling in sick to work. Yes, he says, I can come over. When Mariah hangs up, she unplugs the phone so Mario can't cancel.

Mario stops in the record store before he goes to see Mariah, to say hello to Orange and Cruella. "Great, Mario," Orange says. "Gabriel's mother called me at home last night. She wants to get in touch with you."

Mario feels a chord of terror that's deeper than the death-rock soundtrack being played in the store. "I gave her the number upstairs," Orange continues, "because I thought they know you."

When Mario sees Mariah he nervously waits for her to mention the call but instead they make love, crushing the imported rock and fashion magazines that cover the bed like a patchwork quilt.

"I drank too much last night," he tells her, "because I wanted to be with you so much."

"Me, too," she says, "but what should I tell Alma?"

"She doesn't have to know."

Boy no Wonder, whose class has been cancelled, is on his way up the stairs to the apartment. He unlocks the door.

He sees Mario and Mariah. He yells and screams and throws a heavy vase at the wall. Flowers shower the carpet and water runs down the wall. Chips of terra cotta are crunchy underfoot.

"Get out!" Boy tells Mario who runs quickly out the back, down the rickety fire escape. Boy turns to Mariah who's crying a little. He asks her to explain. She says, please, just hold me. It was all a mistake. All his fault.

"You're so much bigger, anyway," she tells Boy during their sex. "But one thing. I don't think we should tell Alma about Mario being over here."

"I won't," says Boy, burying his head in her armpit.

Later that evening Boy goes out to the school library and Mariah heads straight for the phone just as Alma walks in. "Shit," Mariah whispers.

"Hi, what's up?" says Alma, cheerfully. She notices but doesn't mention the flowers on the floor.

"Nothing, nothing," says Mariah. "What's new with you?"

Alma gets some mineral water from the refrigerator. "Did you go out today?" she asks.

"No, no, just stayed in and read magazines."

Alma waits for Mariah to ask her how the video went but knows better than to bring it up. "Oh, yeah," she says, "let me run downstairs. I want to buy a new album that comes out today."

In the record shop Cruella asks Alma if Mario's still over. "Huh?" she replies, feeling a chill. When she is back upstairs, Alma asks Mariah, "Why didn't you tell me Mario was here?"

"He wasn't."

"Mariah, Cruella saw him. She asked me if he was still over. I know he was here." Alma starts to cry, mumbling that she's really tired from the day-long shoot. She goes into her room, gets out her two suitcases, one of which is completely round. She begins stuffing her clothes and scarves into the square plaid case and then, like a pre-schooler working out a shapes puzzle, forces the records into the circular carrier.

"You're my best friend, my only friend," says Mariah, who's pushed open the door to Alma's room. "You can't go."

"I'm sorry," says Alma, crying as she walks. "I'll get the rest of my stuff later."

"I love you," screams Mariah as Alma goes down the stairs.

Driving back from the library Boy no Wonder runs a red light and is hit by a car making a left turn. He's not seriously hurt but he calls Mariah from the emergency room.

Her line is busy. Once she'd plugged the phone in, it rang. It was Gabriel's mother who held a letter with Mario's name on it.

"Mario's not here," says Mariah, hanging up abruptly to call him.

PART IV

Alma sleeps fitfully on her friend Jade's leopard print couch. She dreams she's being chased through the snow and only Prince melts the mood by appearing and then vanishing in a tropical light.

Boy no Wonder returns to the apartment the next morning and Mariah tells him to collect his things, Mario's coming over for good.

"You can't do this," Boy cries.

"Yes, I can," she replies. "It's Alma's and my apartment."

Boy goes to his father's guest house where he thought he and Mariah might live one day.

When Mario arrives with some of his clothes and his bass guitar, Mariah asks him if he's called Gabriel's mother.

"Yes, I did," he lies.

"I'll be back in a minute," she says. "I've got to run downstairs to get another copy of the Sex Gang Children album. Alma must have taken mine when she packed her things."

"Mariah, great," says Orange. "Gabriel's mother just called for Mario again and I'm getting sick of it."

"Did she leave her number?"

"Yeah." Orange writes it down for her and Mariah marches upstairs to call.

"I'd rather speak to Mario," Gabriel's mother says.

"That's not possible, but don't worry," assures Mariah. 'We'll both come over tonight."

Gabriel's family lives in Rosemead. Their home is filled with colonial-style furniture and appointed with lace doilies and religious knickknacks. His mother offers them tea and keeps the pot warm with a tea cozy.

"To begin," she says, "our cat, Lady Jane, still sleeps in Gabriel's room. We've been trying to uproot her, you know, since we'll be painting and redecorating the room. But she insists on sleeping in there in a box of my son's mementos. In moving the box . . . " Gabriel's mother starts to cry and places the delicate corner of a crocheted handkerchief to the edge of one eye.

Mario stares at the living room's sliding glass door.

"Mario," Gabriel's mother continues, "the box had letters from you to my son."

"So what?" says Mariah, but Gabriel's mother doesn't acknowledge her.

"I thought you might like to have them," she tells Mario. "It's too late for me to ask questions." She hands him the packet of letters, now held together with knitting yarn.

"Thanks," he says.

Mariah drives a short distance from Gabriel's home and pulls into a gas station where she wrests the letters from Mario. She reads a portion of one and shoves it back at him. "You're going to burn these letters," she tells Mario, "and I never want to hear about them again.

"Don't even mention his name," she says as she drives onto the freeway onramp, "or I'll kill you."

Mario sits up straight, says he won't, he promises. He looks away, off and down into the blackness that is just outside the car window.

Later than Night

As a child Mariah held fast to the chores assigned her. She would rake the few leaves she could unearth in her family's southern California backyard and then sit despondently on the porch, certain that somewhere in the world there were more leaves to rake. This was not due to any religious notion; Mariah was simply more concerned with eternity than with life.

Mariah was big-boned and healthy, and she went through her youth pretty much without incident or exception. She was neither outcast nor most popular, neither bully nor victim. To her parents she presented few problems and they let her come and go through the kitchen door to the outside world without asking questions.

Late one school night Mariah came downstairs to return a ball of string to the kitchen cupboard. Her mother, who was reading the newspaper at the table, looked up over her slipping bifocals and gently teased her daughter. "Mariah, dear," she said, "you know you could have kept that string in your bedroom until morning."

"I know," Mariah replied, "but it's just that one thing leads to another."

Mariah's mother continued to think about her daughter's response long after Mariah had gone back upstairs. The strange logic, expressed so matter-of-factly, had to be a warning signal for a deeper problem, she was sure. While Mariah was in her bedroom writing in her journal, her mother was deciding to start her off with psychological counseling.

We're dropped here on earth, Mariah wrote, *to what do we cling?*

Having to articulate her emotions to another person forced the fifteen-year-old Mariah to drink. She drank before her counseling sessions, before homeroom, throughout the day. But her drinking went undetected because nothing about her changed. She continued to get adequate grades, see the same friends, and wear her long, straight hair parted in the middle. When purse styles got smaller, she bought an antique flask to hide her liquor.

I keep hearing voices every night, but when I say, "What? What?" they don't answer me.

Mariah got out of high school and enrolled in a community college where she met Alma, a diminutive but powerful girl. It was Alma who, upon seeing the flask in Mariah's purse, insisted Mariah adopt a 1920s look. With her large frame and flat chest, Mariah felt she had found an image destined for her.

Alma also convinced Mariah that they both belonged in Hollywood with other misfits, rock 'n' rollers, and starlets. Unequipped to argue, Mariah moved north into the city and began to amass for Alma the sullen venom reserved for rescuers.

Mariah and Alma lived together for several years, through at least three pop-music trends. Alma flitted from one artistic endeavor to another, a practice Mariah found annoyingly convictionless. Once, when Mariah was cropping a concert photo she'd taken of David Bowie, Alma snatched the black borders and created her own work that she dubbed *The Darkness that Surrounds David Bowie*. To Mariah's horror the black collage was exhibited in a downtown art gallery.

Mariah was embarrassed by the feelings Alma aired in her work so she took to hiding Alma's things and trading in her favorite records. It was when Mariah was doing the latter that she met a boy who immediately told her he had a thing for the Jazz Age.

"You look like Louise Brooks," he said as the cashier handed Mariah a credit slip.

"I don't really," Mariah replied as they walked out the door together. The boy, who was called Boy no Wonder, stared at Mariah's profile until he tripped on a crack in the sidewalk.

It occurred to Mariah that if she asked this guy to be her boyfriend, it could help to further distance her from Alma. When Mariah told her he was moving into their apartment, Alma had no recourse but to pick up a withdrawn and dark-eyed boy named Mario.

The first night Mario came over he told Alma, Mariah, and the Boy no Wonder how he had worked at a drive-in dairy in the San Gabriel Valley when he was a child. He explained he'd gone through Catholic school feeling completely frantic but never showing it or letting on, and when Mariah heard this she knew she'd found both a soulmate and a person who could cleanly snap Alma's hold on her. For the first time in her life, she felt the ethereal strength of determination.

Mariah and Mario moved together to the Hollywood Hills and Mario, who played bass guitar, continued his tradition of half-heartedly auditioning for local bands. He joined one group for a day and its lead singer offered him heroin. When he told Mariah about it she was very interested—she no longer trusted alcohol because of its failure to transport.

In heroin they believed they'd found the one thing that could reverse the pain and they became more and more reclusive. Mario would write love songs about the drug while Mariah admired it in a way she had once admired the Northern Lights when travelling with her mother.

Going out to a movie one night, Mariah and Mario stopped at the concession stand. The sight of the licorice, rope-thick and drooping, suggested their veins aching for a shot and they turned to leave. At the door were two old friends, Orange and Cruella. "Well, well," said Cruella, "here's living proof that even junkies can roll down the hill. You see, Orange, nuns aren't the only ones who wear habits." Looking at Mario she continued, "I didn't know anyone still wore those black zippered pants."

Mario and Mariah, who'd always maintained the trendiest of appearances, looked silly and out-of-date. The heroin had made it impossible to keep up.

Orphan Story

Mariah is late getting home on the evening of the Sex Pistols' ten-year reunion concert and Mario occupies himself by getting ready. From where he stands in the bathroom he has to strain to hear the Sid Vicious record he's playing. Mario adds more Vaseline to his hair, on top of the baby oil which he knocks over onto the floor. He ties a rubber tube around his upper arm, seeks and finds his favorite blue vein and shoots up, wincing slightly.

Mario checks his hair again and decides he wants it frizzy so he puts talcum powder on it. Picking up Mariah's lipstick he writes "I did it my way" on the mirror while miming the words. As he skates in his black silk socks, he slips on the shiny floor and cracks his skull on the porcelain toilet bowl. By the time Mariah finds him Mario is as rigid as any medieval effigy.

Scottie is one of the first to arrive for the concert at the Hollywood Palladium. She wears special anniversary-edition bondage pants, an original SEX mohair sweater, and a dozen miraculous medals next to her skin. Looking around for her ex-boyfriend Mario, she doesn't really want to see him or Mariah, his girlfriend; she wants to know which parts of the hall to avoid.

Maybe Mario's dead, Scottie thinks. I wish he'd drown. But he can't—he's too hollow, too shallow. But even if he did sink like Percy Bysshe Shelley, she knows she'd ask for his heart, too, and save it all pierced and sacred in a jar.

The Palladium's balcony is exclusive, open only to VIPs. Trinity Jones is up there with Angela Bowie; Prince is alone. One Gene Loves Jezebel twin talks to a fashion model.

Backstage, Johnny Rotten is refusing to speak to anyone. He also doesn't allow the opening band, Skeleton Crew, to come anywhere near the Pistols' dressing room.

More people arrive as it gets later, like the Boy no Wonder, Orange and Cruella, and Alma. When Cruella spies Alma, she calls out, "I hear the pitter-patter of little plots!" in reference to Alma's penchant for turning real life into fiction.

Another girl, Cheri, is waiting outside until Skeleton Crew plays their set and gets off. Someone asks Cheri if he can take her picture and she says yeah, but then refuses to sign a release form.

The Palladium is packed. Skeleton Crew goes on and plays songs from their forthcoming album, *Notes from the Overwound*. People don't pay attention to them. Boy waves to Alma and Alma waves back but does not approach him. Scottie wonders if Mario has made it upstairs into the VIP balcony.

Johnny Rotten tells the reporters to get out of the dressing room, which is flooded with flowers. He storms past Glen Matlock, the Pistols' original bass player, who is standing in tonight for Sid Vicious. Johnny looks out one of the hall's back doors into the parking lot which is a seamy sea of beer bottles, dark puddles, plaid, black boots, and spikes. He stares up into a speeding night sky and remembers his mother, now dead.

When the Sex Pistols walk onstage the audience pushes and shoves like pedestrians on a crowded city sidewalk. Scottie is up near the front in a direct line with Johnny. She is moved by his tormented yet eerily hollow stare (which seems more mocking than ever), and she wishes she could be sucked into his manufactured vacuum.

The Pistols play all their old songs like "I Wanna Be Me," "Pretty Vacant," "God Save the Queen," and "Submission." During "No Feelings," the next to last song, Scottie is jostled by someone she recognizes to be Mariah, who wears black leather as she storms her way to the very front. Scottie backs away, feeling suddenly outside of herself. When she reaches the back wall she starts staring at the ceiling.

String of Pearls

I was almost done with the stories and my request to the publisher that the book be printed like a toddler's book, bound in plastic and equipped with squeaks in the appropriate places, was being denied. The result was that I was blocked. I needed just one more story, but I'd told everything.

I tried collecting found pens in hopes they'd give me something else to say. I got out my Barbie dolls and moved them around on the floor. I considered plagiarism.

It was also bothering me that, while I'd told everyone that the book was about to come out, nothing changed. There weren't offers of friendship or declarations of adoration from old loves. There was just my mother, irritating as ever.

Until one day it dawned on me: what if everything I wrote were different? What if my mother weren't who she was but who I wanted her to be? What if I had my own, totally fabricated, history? How much happier I would be.

String of Pearls

A woman I once knew—in fact, she was my mother—had this kind of beauty that was appropriate to one era and touching to another. She was a blonde of Danish and German extraction from Fargo, North Dakota, where she'd spent her childhood downtown in a boarding house. Mother was a man's woman: by the time she was in her teens she had more male friends than female ones, an enthusiasm for sports, a good golf game, and an easy and charming wit. There was also her looks, as if the best of Barbara Stanwyck, Lauren Bacall, Bette Davis, and wartime Marilyn Monroe were combined and made tangible.

My life with my mother existed only in the past. "I'd take you in your stroller around Brooklyn," she'd recall when we lived in California, "and people would stare at the pretty blonde baby. They'd say, 'Oh, you've got a little Marilyn Monroe!' " As she spoke I'd be playing with my hair, which was dirty-brown and stringy as a rodent's tail. This was the only story about married life I ever heard her tell.

Mother had done some modelling when she was younger, usually hand modelling, for her hands were graceful and perfect and the reason my father fell in love with her. They met at a baseball game in Fargo—Father was a recruiting officer stationed at Grand Forks—and they left the brightly-lit sandlot for the darker hues of the Bison Bar. Some months later, he proposed to her there while staring down the funnel of his drink.

This was recounted for me by my mother as she lay ill beneath a heating pad and my grandmother's afghan on our living room's uncomfortable sofa. Dad was at the enlisted men's club drinking what I thought must have been innumerable Shirley Temples. "I wanted to do leg modelling," she continued, "but I had faces in my knees." I pictured the faces like the weakly-scratched illustrations in my book of fairy tales.

I got down our cache of family photographs (which were kept in a candy tin) and quickly cast aside anything from the recent past, as if the full color falsified them. We focused instead on pictures of Mother's old beaus, including one who posed with Joan Crawford. The boy, in military uniform, looked at once playful and scared, and Miss Crawford looked away. In the next photo he was with my mother and they both stood knee-deep in the floodwater that had swallowed up the porches of the surrounding houses. Mother had her hair in a silk bandanna and she wore a suede car coat. She looked as if she was about to start dancing, like she was the 1940s version of Flaming Youth.

I put the photographs back into the tin and Mother said she'd go to bed after she prepared Dad's lunchbox. Because my sister's bedroom door was closed, I went to sleep, too.

When my father came home from work the next day, he was irate because Mother had made a sandwich for him using the paper picture of the bologna as a joke. His anger was too late, however; she was dead. I know that he cried and was grieved but remember more clearly how years later, when Susan Hayward died, he was inconsolable.

My sister and I each have a set of Mother's pearls. One is authentic; the other, simulated. We don't bother to have them appraised and my sister keeps hers on the closet shelf next to the tin of photographs.

NEVER AN AUTUMN BUT ALWAYS A FALL

Male & Female Ghosts

When her age reached two figures, Nicole shortened her name in attempts to disappear. Nic, she named herself, never Nicky or Nick. She always suspects that those who persist in calling her Nicole know the real her. They read her soul.

Nicole was raised Catholic but by 1977 she had adjusted her beliefs to embrace self-destruction, which she felt was the one way an individual could show she was in control. She would argue with her boyfriend, Steve (an indifferent young man and one of a handful in the city who took Sid Vicious for a familiar), and their shouts resounded like doors slamming. When they'd make up, she would toy with Steve's black hair until it stood out nimbus-like around his delicate face.

Angry again, she'd carelessly fasten safety pins to her clothes, sticking herself like a voodoo doll, and go out—not anywhere, just walking—for the night.

Nicole remains uncertain as to how much she cares for Steve, since she views love as being either arbitrary or a kind of transference. Plus, until Steve, all her significant "firsts" had been with people who were notable, people who overshadowed her. She had been baptized by, and received her first communion from, a priest who became Archbishop of Los Angeles, got her first kiss from a teen idol, lost her virginity to a glitter-rock star, and initiated her infrequent drug use with a girl who now leads an organization calling for the ordination of women priests.

It is because of all this that Nicole can never think of Steve as her first boyfriend. Instead she is compelled to constantly come up with ways of making the relationship interesting.

Upstairs in the huge house she shares with her parents in a worn-out suburb south of Los Angeles, Nicole waits for Steve. Her brothers and sister have grown and moved out, leaving Nicole alone with her mother and her father, who is a doctor. Nicole wishes he were dead so she and her mother could be alone.

She hears Steve's car in the driveway, so she runs downstairs to meet him. They are going to visit the grave of an acquaintance, a local punk-rock star who made a successful suicide bid. His funeral had been Nicole's first.

"Dave Vanian of the Damned used to be a gravedigger," she tells Steve as she slinks down into the passenger seat. "When he lived in Hemel Hempstead. He'd go to work on his bicycle. I think about him, you know, gray English mornings, riding over the low hills and carrying his shovel, his hair waving like bat wings. He was the first real English punk I ever met."

Steve says nothing and the rest of the ride to the cemetery is spent in silence. When they arrive, he gets out of the car and says, "I'm going to look around for a little bit."

"I'll go with you." She threads his arm with hers and they walk the perimeter of the grounds.

"Damn, but it's weird," Steve says. "I've been in lots of graveyards but I've never found my name on a headstone." Nicole steers him toward the mausoleum where their friend is buried. She presses Steve up against the cold, shaded marble and kisses him. He brushes her neck with his lips, twists the clear buttons on her blouse. She steps up on top of his boots, rubs against his torn jeans. "Wait," he whispers, "we can't do it here," so Nicole motions toward an alcove—a women's restroom. A sink and counter for the preparation of flowers and wreaths are outside the door.

Nicole leads Steve into the bathroom and props herself up against the basin as she bunches her miniskirt around her waist. She bites her lip as he enters her, then cries sharply and her sound echoes in the emptiness.

As they walk out, she grabs a pair of scissors that are chained to the counter and cuts the tip of her pinkie finger with them. She goes out into the sunlight sucking the blood as if through a straw.

Later that afternoon, they're upstairs in her room. "You can have death without a body," she tells Steve. He is still fretting because he couldn't find his name anywhere.

"You're right," he says. "Maybe I'm a vampire." Nicole is looking out the window at her mother who is lying by the pool, her face covered with an open magazine. The water beside her is motionless.

Steve observes Nicole and thinks how she will never leave home to move in with him. He could never equal this luxurious old house that has all its sharp edges cushioned. Never. He moves closer to kiss her but Nicole pushes him away.

"What's wrong?"

"I don't know," she says. "It's like a blank flashback, like I'm seeing something but I can't make out what it is. And it's the lack of clarity that I can't break away from, like holding on to nothing." She shifts her position on the bed, punches her fist into one of the feather pillows. The impression is a crater on its face.

Steve thinks she is probably remembering her first kiss or something else he could never live up to. He gets up to leave but she grabs the edge of his leather jacket and pulls him back. Slipping her fingers beneath the collar of his shirt, she starts to massage his neck and shoulders, removing his clothes as she works her way down his body. He is slick and wet with sweat beneath the black fabrics.

"I'll call you after dinner," he says before leaving her room. He waves at Nic's mother across the yard, and she waves back with the magazine as if she were shooing a fly.

Nicole stays on her bed, licking her hands that smell of Steve, running them over her breasts, through her lunar-white hair, and finally inside her. She is happy, almost away. When she hears her father on the stairs, her touch becomes rapid.

Driving home to South Gate, Steve wonders how he'll ever get Nic to move in with him or even to go anywhere with him. She'd gone to Hollywood all the time when she was younger. Wasn't she always in Rodney's English Disco on the Sunset Strip back then? Hadn't she seen David Bowie the night she started her period? Or something like that? And during punk-rock, too, wasn't she constantly at the Whisky or the Masque? But ever since 1980 she hadn't been anywhere, and that was five years ago.

Once he's home, Steve makes sure he's the only one there. His father, a long-distance truck driver, is somewhere between here and Tulsa, so Steve is alone. He decides to take a nap, and he talks himself to sleep. When he wakes up a few hours later, his mascara has mixed with sleep and looks like little chunks of coal around his dark brown eyes. He gets up and sifts through the mail. He finds a notice about the annual parade to commemorate the anniversary of Sid Vicious's death. It's held in London, down the Kings Road. In addition to the parade, this year there will be a collector's convention of Sid Vicious memorabilia. Steve tapes the flyer to his bedroom wall.

A few hours later in an alley behind the oldest McDonald's in existence Nicole wraps her legs around Steve's waist, tells him she loves him. She needs the embellishment the words provide to erase the memory of something she'd said earlier over Big Macs. As they sat outside at the plastic picnic table, Nicole stuck two french fries like fangs in her mouth and said, "See, I'm a vampire, too," and Steve got mad.

"It's not funny, Nic. You make fun of everything I do or say." He stood up to leave and Nicole followed him to the back of the hamburger stand, where the last two workers were leaving for the night. "We're closed," one of them said. The air was thick with the smell of grease. "Oh, we're finished," Nicole replied, taking Steve's hand as she watched the workers walk away like tarnished ghosts. She places Steve's hand, slimy from the burgers, in her mouth.

"I hate the feeling when you slip out of me," she says, after he's come. "It makes me sure I'd hate giving birth, like it'd be like losing something." They walk arm and arm to the front of the now-dark McDonald's. Its arches look like haunches.

"I'm sure," Nicole continues, "that everything's a substitute for sex but I'm not sure what sex is a substitute for."

"For everything, I guess," says Steve.

"Nah, no way. It's never that easy. You can't just turn those things around."

As they stand on the street corner a van drives by. "Fuckin' freaks!" the long-haired passenger yells out to Steve and Nicole.

"I hate this town," Nic says. "We should leave."

"We should go to London," Steve says. "I was going to go anyway, to this Sid Vicious convention-thing."

"You were going to go without me?" Nicole bolts to cross the street against the traffic light, leaving Steve on the corner.

"It's just that I didn't think you'd go," he calls to her. "You never want to go anywhere, not even to L.A."

"Get away from me," she screams from the center meridian. She removes one patent leather boot and throws it at him. "How dare you think you can have a life without me!" She hurls the other boot into the street and then turns to walk home barefoot. The street, an image of the sky, is dotted with glass and metal debris.

When Nicole gets home her feet are black so she jumps fully clothed into the pool, ruining her leather miniskirt. She frantically swims laps back and forth, back and forth, and when her mother hears the thrashing she looks out to see her daughter, a spot in a well of swaying ink.

"You must have displaced a lot of water last night," her mother tells Nicole when she appears for breakfast the next morning. "The water level was down below the starfish design on the tile." She cracks another egg.

"Did Dad hear me?"

"Oh, I don't think so. You know how he sleeps."

The sleep of the dead, thinks Nicole, when suddenly her mother gasps.

"What is it?"

"This egg was fertilized," her mother says, covering her eyes with her hands. Then she tilts the bowl to show Nicole the bright red dot, a bull's-eye in a mound of yellow. Her mother pours the mixture into the sink and says, sobbing, "Things will never be the same now." Nicole rushes to hug her, certain at times that she and Marilyn Monroe share the same curse: a parent who is insane.

For the passenger, Pier, the drive through the middle of California is one long, dull strand. Her boyfriend Nestor is driving and looking all around, categorizing the scenery as a darling Los Angeles poet (which he is) would. He has been assigned to write a story for *Sideshow* magazine and his subject is San Jose's Winchester Mystery House, which he has described to Pier as "a massive lump of folk art, lost in a nothing place."

Nestor glances sidelong at Pier, who's using her fingers to twirl pieces of her long brown hair that is crimped and looks like tiny steps.

"You'll see," he explains. "In the late 1800s, this old widow inherited twenty million dollars from the Winchester Rifle fortune—there was blood on her hands, all right. A medium convinced her to build a home twenty-four hours a day, forever, to achieve eternal life while appeasing the souls who lost theirs due to her in-laws', ah, greed."

Nestor looks again at Pier, who looks worried.

"But you'll like the house, Pier," he insists. "It has Tiffany glass windows, hand-inlaid parquet floors, rambling, turreted roofs, chandeliers, fireplaces . . . plus a lot of strange things like upside-down posts."

"Anyway," says Pier, barely louder than the sound of the car, "are there any flying buttresses?"

"Pier, she was into the occult, not Gothic architecture! Pay attention to how many times you see thirteen of things, like thirteen lights or thirteen hooks, and so forth."

"Where are you?" he asks when she doesn't react. Pier scowls, wanting to reply the obvious. "Aren't you enjoying the ride?"

She leans her head against the window. "I feel funny here."

"We're just observers, Pier. No one said we were going to move here. And if anyone should feel funny, it should be I." Nestor points to his head. His shaggy hair is dyed a deep blood-red, which sets off his pale olive skin. He's proud, too, of his bluish-green eyes, as proud as he is of his poetry. His most recent collection, *The Price of Darkness*, was released last week. There had been a book signing at which Pier observed several women giving Nestor their cards which were softened on the back by hand-written home phone numbers. She pretended to believe it was all routine until she found cigarette butts resembling soaked tampons in the ashtray of Nestor's '63 Cadillac.

Pier had tried to bring up the subject of his infidelity but each time she began by saying, "By the way," Nestor cut her off, assuming she was just filling time with her voice.

Nestor calls Pier "The Girl Who Loved Passive Interjections" because she is always pausing and then saying things like "Well, anyway." They met when he was waiting for her to get off a public telephone. Pier noticed him staring, as people often did, but she kept on talking, assuming he admired the way she looked holding the receiver. It never occurred to her that he might want to make a call and, as it turned out, he decided not to. Instead he asked Pier to have coffee with him. "Well, okay," she replied, shaking a little because she'd just finished arguing with her boyfriend.

Over coffee-shop tea Nestor told Pier how he'd been a film student but dropped out when he saw little loops of film on the cutting room floor. "They looked like cul-de-sacs," he said passionately, explaining that he took this as a sign that filmmaking was decidedly bourgeois. It was then that he descended upon poetry.

"Anyway," said Pier as she reached for the check on the tray where his hand met hers to cover it like a blanket. She followed him back to his loft in East Los Angeles. He lived on Brooklyn Avenue near Soto Street, above a pet shop that sold chickens, pythons, and parrots. The talking birds swore in Spanish.

As he undressed her, she wanted to tell him about her phone conversation, about her boyfriend, but when she started to, he took his hands away and covered his eyes.

"I always visualize things first," he told her as he slid his hand inside her thrift store jersey dress. "And I'm always right." She raised her hands over her head as he removed the dress. Had he guessed how beautiful she was?

Pier moved into Nestor's apartment, and when he periodically went away to New York she was the one who sent him postcards and letters, at his suggestion. "You're the one things will be different for," he explained. "You'll be here without me – I'll be somewhere else, so I won't notice."

"In other words," she'd begin her letters. "That is to say, I love you. I mean, I love you even though we have only the intangible in common."

When Nestor flew home the last night in October, Pier met him at the airport. He told her how he'd looked out the plane window and watched it be Halloween progressively across the country until the gray lights of L.A. blotted everything out. The story had made her cry and it is the one she's recalling now as they exit the freeway at San Jose's Stevens Creek Boulevard.

She decides that Nestor would love her and only her if she spoke more cleverly and had deeper things to say. And perhaps this trip would be good for her: she would soak up every nuance of the Mystery House, much the way ghosts absorb the only light in darkness, and then impress Nestor with her observations.

The Mystery House is not what either of them had expected. It is brightly painted and surrounded by immaculate grounds, with little of its Victorian soul apparent. While Nestor explores the Firearms Museum filled with Winchester rifles, Pier strays back and takes her own tour of the mansion. She stares down at a window that was built into the floor, squinting to see it as a vision of hell. The Widow Winchester's penchant for stairs going up to the ceiling, Pier is sure, foreshadowed the fact that there is no eternal life – just efforts to go up.

Pier rejoins Nestor in the Victorian garden, where he is writing things down in his composition book, the cover of which is flecked precisely like his suit jacket. "160 ROOMS," he writes, "CONSTRUCTED 24 HOURS A DAY FOR 38 YEARS." Over tea in the café, Nestor begins to formulate his article. "I think I'll open with their motto," he tells Pier. " 'Discover the World's Strangest Monument to a Woman's Fears.' "

"In any event," Pier says while nervously stirring more sugar into her tea, "I mean, you could compare this house to Graceland and the way Elvis was always redecorating the rooms."

"No, no way, Pier. It wasn't for the same reason. Elvis wasn't building on to try to live forever. He wasn't attempting to appease any spirits whose deaths he'd brought on by his creations. Besides, any allusion to Presley is overused. It's a cliché."

"Whatever," says Pier, softly.

In bed that night, in their sparse hotel room, Nestor tells her he's decided on a title for his piece. "I'm going to call it 'Spirit World.' And my opening lines will be, 'Floors don't meet. Walls aren't upright.' It's a take-off on the Goth classic *The Haunting of Hill House*."

"If it's a take-off, don't you feel guilty about stealing it?"

"You have to understand. Something like that is not like stealing. Whoever wrote that didn't take it far enough. They weren't going to do anything more with it, so I might as well. In a way I'm doing that writer a favor." He kisses each of her palms and starts to make love to her again.

The other beginning was better, Pier thinks as he's inside her. Except they got it wrong. This is the strangest monument to a woman's fears—the act of love.

Steve places Nicole's lone boot on top of his bureau, next to the photograph of his mother. The other boot flaps like a rubber bat in the middle of Lakewood Boulevard. Looking at his reflection in the dresser's mirror, Steve sifts his hands through his hair and wavers his gaze from himself to the boot to his mother, whose wedding ring he wears on his fifth finger. The photo, taken on her wedding day, shows his mom in a long Indian-print skirt, leotard top, and yards of beads. There are dried flowers in her hair. His father had let Steve keep her sand candle—a thing she'd made. He seldom lights the candle, wanting it to last longer than her life did, but he does so now. He wonders if his mom would have loved him with the same conviction he feels for her, and if his personality would have been enough. He knows she read tarot cards for friends—would she have been able to select a card to accurately represent him?

Is it all to do with magic—getting someone to love you? Steve glances around the room again, unsure just who it is he's trying to befriend.

Nicole nurses her morning cup of coffee the precious and tentative way alcoholics caress their glasses. She knows that any moment Steve will call or come by, carrying her boots like an offering. When he doesn't show by the time she's on the screened-in patio having an avocado salad with her mother, Nicole feels a little uneasy.

Steve is nowhere near Nicole. He's on Sunset Boulevard in the Spirit Shop, a place he found in the White Pages. He'd hoped they would help him work some kind of a magic spell, but the shop turns out to be a liquor store/deli so he has a roast beef sandwich and a beer instead.

Pier roams the apartment, remembering the day she went to Olvera Street, certain that the place would teach her more about Nestor and help her catch the most oblique of his references. In one of the stalls she had purchased a packet of trouble dolls that were made in Guatemala. The shopkeeper had explained how Pier should tell her troubles to the dolls before she went to bed and then, while she slept, the dolls would resolve her problems, moving around in a kind of morality play. The dolls are on her nightstand now, still and bashful in the morning sunlight while Nestor sleeps next to them.

Pier climbs back in bed and Nestor says her name. She hopes he's talking in his sleep but knows that his feeling for her doesn't go that deep. "What?" she answers.

"What are you doing?"

"It's the trouble dolls," she explains. "They make me feel guilty, the way I talk at them and then just desert them."

Nestor sighs and reaches his long arm across Pier's neck and then crisscrosses her with his torso. He scoops the dolls into his palm and puts them in the nightstand drawer. "Forget about them. They're defeating their purpose." Pier wants to protest but doesn't, believing Nestor is right. It's his world the dolls are from, anyway.

She falls back asleep and when she dreams that she's suffocating, she jolts awake, worried that she's now taken on the dolls' problems.

The midday light is so unusual, like it's caught in carnival glass, that Nestor decides he's going to paint. "I'll go to some thrift stores, then," Pier tells him as they're in the shower. The sun comes through the shower's pockmarked glass and makes little rainbows in the gray water.

Dressed in a hand-painted *folklórico* skirt and a holey turquoise sweater, Pier waits at the bus stop. Passersby look down at the skull and crossbones buckles on her black boots. She gets on the westbound bus for Olvera Street but realizes that she's missed her stop when she is in Echo Park.

The next time the bus stops moving, Pier exits and starts walking back in the direction of Olvera Street. She passes shoe shops and the 99-Cent Store but stops suddenly when, in the window of a clothing store, she sees inflatable lovedolls dressed in frilly polyester. There isn't much difference between the feel of their pursed lips and the texture of the clothing. Pier stands in place, amazed. Love dolls! The window-dresser must be playing some kind of a joke.

Pier starts walking again, paying attention to the window displays, and she looks through burglar bars at another one. A dish of herbs and dark roots, twisted and gnarly as knuckles, sits in front of an elaborate crucifix. Next to this is a bowl of water, which makes Pier think there must be a cat inside. As she ponders going in, the door flies open and Steve rushes out.

Pier follows him with her eyes, examining his limp black hair and skin the color and consistency of the sidewalk. If she had seen him in a rock club she would have looked and then looked away but because he's here, out of context, Pier wonders who he is.

She goes inside the shop, a *botánica*, and a small, elderly woman behind the counter gives her an inquisitive look. The woman is puzzled by the two strange Anglos who have come into her shop in succession and she assumes they must know each other. She resists addressing Pier until Pier says in Spanish, "*Tengo muñecas.*"

The shopkeeper thinks Pier must be asking for dolls so she points to a baby-sized one with eyes as dark as its skin tone. "No, no," says Pier, "*muñecas pequeños.*" The woman is confused and shows Pier a jar of dried leaves. "These," she says, "help you get a husband, help you have baby."

Pier looks at the contents and wants to say they look like thorns, only she doesn't know how. "*Mi novio,*" she says, about Nestor, "*es muy lejo y tiene pelo roja oscuro.*" Her words are convoluted at best, but the shopkeeper guesses she must be talking about Steve since he, too, had falsely-colored hair and had purchased a holy card of Saint Gerard Majella, patron saint of pregnant women.

"*Yo se,*" she replies, taking Pier's wrist. "Where you meet?"

"*Cuando llamame por el teléfono público,*" Pier announces proudly. The woman takes a tall red candle encased in glass from a shelf. From under the counter she gets a tiny bottle of scent. The label has a drawing of a square-jawed man driving toward a woman, who is waving frantically. Little hearts dot the air—she's blowing kisses. It is a picture of madness that Pier hasn't seen yet.

"He no leave you now," the woman says as she puts the candle in a lunch bag and hands it to Pier. As Pier takes it, the phone rings and the shopkeeper goes toward the back of the shop to answer it. Pier reaches across the counter to look at the bottle of scent but mistakenly picks up one being held for Steve, who had rushed out to go to his bank. This bottle has a picture of a man staring at his reflection in a plate.

The woman comes back to the front of the shop as Pier dangles the bottle by its black cap to demonstrate that she's placing it in her bag. After she pays she shakes the woman's tiny, arthritic hand and leaves. Pier takes the bus back home, comforted by the feeling that her trouble dolls have been replaced.

When Steve returns to the *botánica* just before it closes, he picks up an order that is only half his. The shopkeeper is aware of the mistake but doesn't correct it because she believes Pier and Steve are lovers. "What one desires, the other lacks," she whispers to herself in Spanish. Steve collects the holy card of Saint Gerard, an ecstatic Italian saint who could be two places at once, make himself invisible, and render painless childbirth before and after his death at age twenty-nine. On the card, Saint Gerard is tall and helpless-looking, like an eighteenth-century Sid Vicious. Steve also gets a black candle and Pier's attraction oil.

He drives the surface streets back to South Gate and when he gets home, he notices he's left the radio on in his room. He starts to turn it off but the music gets louder with his touch; the magic must be working already. He empties the contents of his package onto his dresser and wonders for a moment if Nicole has tried to call. No, it's not something she'd ever do. He lights the wick of the black candle and it hisses and sputters like a feral cat before gaining steadiness.

Pier finds a note that Nestor has left for her but decides to read it later, after she's done her spell. She admires her ghost-like reflection in the t.v. screen (Nestor refuses to have mirrors in the apartment) and then sets her red candle on the hardwood floor. She opens Steve's bottle of scent and places it next to the phone. "Angels descend," she whispers. "Devils ascend." She does a ballet step and accidentally kicks over the potion as the phone rings. As Pier quickly saves what liquid hasn't varnished the floor, the phone keeps on ringing.

Nicole sits in the shade by her swimming pool, distractedly writing in her notebook. "Some people feel as nervous around nuns as they do around police," she writes, about religion. It doesn't apply to Steve, who still hasn't called. Steve, who as a Protestant, seems to Nicole entirely godless.

"He's nobody, anyway," she consoles herself. "He's certainly not Robert Smith." She picks up her pen to write about the time she met Smith, the enigmatic lead singer of the Cure.

It was sort of East London, not the deep East, not the hollowed-out part. But in that direction. It was 1979 and the Cure was a new band supporting a Mod act at this dance hall that looked like a roller-rink with a stage at one end. There was some snow outside and not that many people in—the hall was about one-quarter full. After the two bands had played, I went behind the curtain—you couldn't really call it backstage—and talked to the guys. Robert Smith hovered awkwardly just to my left. He was so thin and shy, so unremarkable in his Marks and Spencer "jumper" and corduroy trousers. What made him stand out is how far he was from a musician. I would have felt sorry for him but something held me back. It was like he didn't need the pretense of music; he already had his own world.

He told me he'd purchased his guitar for twenty-nine pounds from Woolworth's and that was pretty much the only coherent thing he said. That he was incomprehensible wasn't due to drugs—it was just that he had this brilliance working for him that did the job like heroin. Somebody else in the band said they all came from Gatwick and that seemed strange, too. I thought of Gatwick as a pretty place jolted by this huge airport, a place both urban and rural. Maybe that's why whenever I hear the Cure I think of two things at once. And perhaps that's what makes genius: the ability to be two contrary things at the same time. Like the saints or poets. I also know that while I could never find that hall again, it will always be haunted. Haunted by me happy.

Nicole hears her mother calling her so she goes toward the house. "Steve's on the phone for you," her mother tells her, but when Nicole picks up the receiver she hears him say hello and then there's just dead air. The doorbell rings and it's Steve, holding a wadded-up red bandanna beneath his nose.

"Who hit you?" Nicole asks and he shrugs.

She hugs him tightly. "Did you bring my boots?"

"No," he says. "I only had one anyway. Don't you have the other one?"

"No! I thought you picked it up in the street." Steve has this forlorn, almost beatific look that Nicole finds touching. She takes the bandanna from him and finds a faint trace of blood. She kisses that part, then stuffs it in his jeans pocket.

Nicole gets her purse and she and Steve leave to go thrift store shopping. At the Children's Hospital Used Clothing Store Nicole and Steve walk up and down the aisles. Babies in strollers stare at Steve and reach their soft and tiny arms up to him. Their mothers smile knowingly. He passes one check-out line and a screaming infant hushes as its father shifts the child to the other shoulder.

Steve finds Nicole in the back of the store, rummaging through the bins. She finds an eggshell-colored satin bra and puts it on over her Damned t-shirt. It draws Steve to her and they start kissing and caressing, oblivious to the other shoppers. As Steve puts his hand under her shirt he feels moisture on his upper lip—his nose has started to bleed again. "I'd better wait for you in the car," he tells Nicole. He tilts his head back and rushes to the store's exit.

Nicole checks out and finds Steve in his car. His window is rolled down as he talks to a Salvadoran woman who has tended to him with one of her baby's Handi-wipe cloths.

"What's wrong with you?" Nicole asks as they drive down Telegraph Road, through Santa Fe Springs' ancient oil fields. Her hunch is that he's a coke freak. "When did this first start happening?"

"I don't know—I was in my room, laying on my bed. Oh, God, Nic, I was thinking of being with you."

"You were jerking off?"

"Yeah. And then . . ."

"Sounds like Catholic guilt to me." She looks out the window at the oil pumps as they slowly repeat the same movements like arthritic praying mantises.

"But I'm a Southern Baptist, remember?" he protests, citing the only religion he can think of.

When Pier hears Nestor on the steps she blows out the candle and runs from the front room. Her shoes sound like claws against the floor. She re-enters—a stage entrance—as Nestor opens the door. He walks toward her, puts his hands around her face as if examining an art object, and kisses her.

"Did you buy anything?" he asks.

"What?"

"At the thrift store. Did you get anything?"

"Oh, yeah. No. I mean—yes. I bought some candles."

Nestor scowls and then smiles. "That's a strange thing to buy at a thrift store. I went out too, to the indoor swap meet. Look what I found." He holds up a tie-dyed t-shirt.

"That looks like the Shroud of Turin," Pier says.

Nestor shakes his head. "The Shroud of Turin's been defrocked. Haven't you heard? Oh, I got something for you at the used book store." He hands Pier a bag. She opens it and takes out two books, *Ariel* and *The Bell Jar*.

"I thought it would be good for you to read them, to better understand the artistic mentality. Even though I've been wavering toward painting. Let me show you what I was working on."

She follows Nestor to his room where an unfinished canvas features money scattered on a day bed in a studio apartment. "I call it 'Emotional Rent.'"

"I like it," Pier says. "But, you mean you're not going to write anymore?"

"No telling. It's just that painting seems more honest to me at the moment."

"Like writing is conjecture?"

"No—that's an oversimplification. You need to get away from jumping to conclusions like that. But anyway," he stops and smiles. "I sound like you now, with my 'anyways' . . . Have you eaten yet?"

"No," she says, mentally going back over this conversation to conclude that she hasn't used a single "anyway."

It isn't often that Nicole goes over to Steve's house but tonight she is compelled to be surrounded by his belongings. She buries her face in the plaid coverlet on his bed, inhaling his scent. When she peeks out, she starts talking to what she thinks is his reflection but he's in the kitchen getting drinks.

He reappears with two goblets of wine. "What? No beer?" Nicole asks.

"I just didn't have the taste for it," he says and follows her gaze to a poster of Sid Vicious nursing a longneck. "I know what you're thinking," Steve says. "I can read your mind. You think it isn't very Sid-like to drink wine. But . . . ."

"Never mind. It's fine. I'm just happy to be here with you."

Steve is positive the spell has been successful: he has obtained Sid Vicious's charisma. He puts on a tape of the Cure, knowing it will please Nicole, who pulls off her Damned t-shirt to reveal the satin bra she has transposed since the thrift store. Nicole pushes down her tight skirt covered in 1920s flapper fringe to bind her ankles. She rolls her t-shirt longways and has Steve wrap her wrists with it. His black studded belt is at his feet. Together they have sex like snakes, no hands or feet, until a thin stream of blood gushes like a serpent's tongue from Steve's nose.

Nicole starts to lap up the blood but Steve recoils. Craning his neck, his eyes toward heaven, he wonders what in the spell has gone wrong.

The last time Pier toyed with the magic, the candle wouldn't go out and she panicked, afraid of what Nestor would do if he found her with it. She fanned the skinny fire with magazines, covered it with a blanket, a scarf, a rag rug, but nothing would make it go out. She finally extinguished the flame by cupping it with half an eggshell she'd retrieved from the garbage disposal.

When she isn't practicing magic, Pier reads the books Nestor bought for her or stares at her reflection where she can find it. She sees her mouth now in the shiny side of a lipstick tube. She and Nestor are going out to dinner one last time before he leaves. He has been assigned to cover the Sid Vicious march in London and, as often as Pier has begged to go along, Nestor has refused to bring her.

They walk hand in hand down Brooklyn Avenue, and as they pass a bank of telephones the phones start ringing like church bells. Pier jumps and insists that they're following her, but Nestor just complains that the phones are a public nuisance, tools for gangs to conduct business. But Pier is shaken, doubly so when at the restaurant the waiter summons her to the phone. She says hello into the receiver but no one is on the line.

Steve has to concentrate his courage to tell Nicole that he intends to go to London for the Sid Vicious event being held on February 2, the anniversary of the punk-rocker's death. But Nicole wants to go along, to be where Steve is. Before leaving, she dyes her hair more blonde, adding so much accelerator that she's blonder than Harlow as she sits next to Steve on their nonstop flight. Her eyes, underscored in boldface kohl, would render black tears if she were to cry.

Rows back sits a very restless Pier, who has decided to follow Nestor to London. Unlike Steve she has brought along her magic supplies which roll around in the carry-on compartment just over her head.

As Pier's plane traverses the Atlantic, Nestor settles into the Cadogan Hotel in Knightsbridge. He had been delayed in customs—for some reason Pier had safety-pinned her trouble dolls to the lining of Nestor's luggage and customs officials had seized them, certain their tiny bodies concealed cocaine.

Nestor is baffled as to why Pier has done this. His puzzlement gives him a glowing feeling so similar to love that he takes to sleeping with her letters. He spreads them to look like autumn leaves on the icy, flat sheets.

On Pier's third day in London it's very windy, a condition she likes because she believes the gales, like supportive spirits, keep her propped upright. That trees were toppled in Kew Gardens is of no consequence to her; they'd stood for so long they might as well lay on their sides like the effigies she had seen in Westminster Abbey.

In her room in Bayswater, Pier lights her magic candle without fear of being caught by Nestor, who is unaware that she isn't in Los Angeles. He would never suspect her of having followed him here, he thinks her far too passive for that. She ignites another candle that she picked up in Portobello Market. This second one is bone white and is supposed to offend evil spirits and keep them away. She feels secure in this, failing to consider the souls of those who were cremated and thereby unaffected by the flame—people like Sid Vicious, for example.

Do you think ghosts have souls?" Nicole asks Steve, who's meticulously hanging his clothes in the hotel closet. She lounges sleepily on the big bed.

"They have nothing but," Steve replies without looking away from his task.

Nicole sits up. "You say that like you're so sure, like you know everything now. There's something different about you, Steve. You're, like, so self-assured and arrogant now. Ever since we stopped having sex."

"Oh, come on, Nicky."

"No—I mean it. I'm not even sure you care about me anymore. I kind of think we should just break up."

"Nicole," he says. Just her name. "You know I love you more than life."

"Big deal!" she says, heaving her pillow at him. "A whole lot that means! Everybody knows you want to die. So you can be with your mother. You're always saying that, 'I wish I were dead. I want to die.' Oh, and another thing. No matter how much you say you love me, you could never, never love me enough." She runs out, leaving him to cradle the pillow like an infant he had caught in his arms.

February 2 is All Sids Day, the anniversary of the punk-rocker's everything but deliberate suicide. There is snow outside the Chelsea Town Hall, a venue that will host the Chelsea Flower Show later in the year. But today it is three-quarters capacity with dark-haired Sid Vicious look-alikes, none of whom are foreign to this Kings Road stomping ground. Curiously, no one, male or female, has come as Nancy. "Oh, nobody wants to be HER," a girl tells a television reporter. "It would be so depressing."

Most participants wear stickers bearing a printed "HELLO I'M" followed by a written-in message of their own design: "HELLO I'M A Mess"; "HELLO I'M From Beyond the Grave"; "HELLO I'M Dead." The ones Nestor can read he writes down in his speckled robin's egg blue notebook. He starts to compose his story for *Acolyte* magazine. "They mill about—tall, gaunt Elvis imitators as seen through a funhouse mirror. They are sexless monsters."

Nestor sees the palest Sid so far, a boy huddled beneath a black tapestry coat. As he approaches Steve, Nestor can read his nametag. "HELLO," it says, "I'M The Last Saint." Steve stops in front of a stall that is selling badges depicting Sid as a guardian angel. "What do I think?" he says to Nestor. "I think the whole thing is a travesty! I think they should all be thrown out on their tails!" He upturns a table and sends the badges shimmering like pearly buttons to the floor. As he heads for the door, he pauses long enough to spit on a lock-shaped crystal being displayed at a booth entitled "Channelling Sid."

A security guard chases Steve but halts when he hears a dull thud coming from the center of the hall, where a boy has fallen over, straight as a tree. As a stretcher is brought in, the boy's girlfriend says, "He kept telling me he was seeing double but I thought he was just trying to hurt me."

A writer from the *Face* edges up to Nestor and says, "Personally I find the entire patina pathetic. It's worse than a fancy-dress Come as You Once Were party." Nestor nods and looks toward the stage where a young man has appeared and is reading a speech straight off his densely tattooed forearms. "I fought Sid," he announces, "beat him, too. But now we're mates. He's loved more in death. So speak well of him. Remember, the dead are more sensitive than the likes of you and me."

"And don't let people tell you you should 'Be Yourself,' " he continues to a crowd that's largely ignoring him, " 'cos rubbish like that is just as fascistic and manipulative as anything else. Goodnight, and *Viva el Sid.*"

Nestor looks across the room and stares at a boy who has dirty gray-pink hair until he realizes he knows him. They went to a barrio Catholic high school together. He remembers how, during closing prayers, they'd show each other the edges of gleaming knives in their pockets as preludes to after-school fights.

"Mario!" Nestor calls.

Mario jumps, then takes another drink from his concealed can of lager. Nestor is amazed at how homely the once-handsome Mario looks, as if he'd willed himself ugly. His dimples are pockmarks on his sallow skin.

"Oh, hey," Mario says, slurring even these two words. "Want some?" He tilts his lager toward Nestor.

"No, thanks."

"I have to do something, you know, so I drink to be taken care of. I kicked heroin, you know."

Nestor never knew he was on it.

"It wasn't easy getting here," Mario continues. "I had to trick my bitch girlfriend. I told her to meet me at a counselor's office so we could talk out our problems togetherlike. Then when she got there I told her the appointment was for her alone. I split." He laughs. "Pretty clever, eh?"

"You make it sound like they took her away in a straitjacket."

"Yeah, right," says Mario, looking down. "Who says there's no such thing as free will?"

When Nestor finally leaves the convention, he doesn't spy Pier, who is outside standing in a gutted telephone box. She follows Nestor as silently as the wet leaves on the pavement, up to his hotel off Sloane Street. Her plan is to wait until Valentine's Day, which is twelve days away.

It's bloody Saint Valentine's Day," Nicole says through clenched, foamy teeth to her reflection in the minuscule bathroom mirror. She rinses her mouth and walks back down the hall to her room in the YMCA. After flopping on the bed, she picks up her spiral notebook and, using a red felt pen, draws a large heart. "NICOLE–STEVE," she writes within the heart's interior. "YOU DETRACTED FROM MY LIFE." She dresses quickly, absently, and heads for Russell Square, where she will leave this message for Steve at his hotel.

Pier wakes up early the same morning and looks out into the road to make sure that her rental car is still there. Then she begins her daily ritual of lighting the candle and dabbing the magic oil on her wrists, her temples, and between her breasts. By the time she leaves for Nestor's hotel the oil is staining the neckline of her eggshell-tinged shirt.

She explains to the desk clerk at the Cadogan Hotel that she wants to see Nestor but he mustn't be informed because it is a surprise. Valentine's Day, she explains. I am his girlfriend, just arrived from America. Luckily for Pier her beauty is persuasive and the clerk waves her on.

Nestor answers her knock. His magenta hair sticks up in two lumps. "What are you doing here?" he demands of Pier and she opens her eyes wider to prevent tears from forming.

"It's Valentine's Day and I thought you'd want to see me."

"I don't. I mean, I do, but not now. I'm working, Pier." He gestures to papers on top of a dark wooden desk. Pier advances toward them.

"The Sid Vicious thing?" She reads the title, which Nestor always writes at the top of each page. "Called 'The Girl Can't Take It'?" She reads on and sees something about a telephone.

"It's about you," Nestor says, grabbing her wrists. "I was going to surprise you."

She breaks free and goes back to the papers. " 'She is Sylvia Plath without the talent,' " she reads aloud. "And that's me," Pier says. "That's your gift to me?" She turns toward the door. "You know what talent is, Nestor?"

"Of course I . . . Pier, wait."

"I don't think you do. Talent is madness, Nestor, a world of your own making. A place you can go for some privacy. Your darling Sylvia Plath wasn't talented. She wasn't even crazy. She was just bothered by her hair getting darker." Pier leaves and lets the sound of the door closing end her speech.

She drives her little car on the side of the road she is accustomed to, and when oncoming drivers honk their horns she thinks it sounds like hundreds of phones ringing, a noise she's gotten used to.

Nestor writes for a couple hours and then goes out to window-shop. He lingers at a display that Nicole is also considering. It shows a female mannequin in a bathtub of red roses and a male dummy at the door. The man wears a brown cassock and holds up a huge, jeweled cross.

"Not much of an advertisement for Valentine's Day," Nicole says to Nestor, who nods agreement.

"They're not much on that holiday here anyway, I take it," he says.

"Oh, you're American too," Nicole says. "An expatriate?"

"No, just visiting. A man without a country."

"Nicole," she offers her hand. "A girl without a boyfriend."

"Nestor."

"I know who you are now. I saw you read back home."

Together they walk the length of Sloane Street toward Chelsea Bridge and the river. On the concrete embankment of the slow, icy river, Nestor kisses her and they turn back for his hotel. As they walk, he tells her what he imagines she's like in sex, in his arms. Nicole smiles as she listens, giving away nothing, and assesses him, her first poet.

When she feels him reach in her, she sees Steve's face before her like the flickering image in a nickelodeon. It alternates with the black background of narrative bordered in white filigree.

"It's painful," she says and he stops moving, "painful holding onto nothing." When she turns away to sleep, she rolls onto Pier's letters, which Nestor had pushed to the vacant side of the bed.

Nicole sleeps heavily and wakes up wet. Her period has started and blood covers the letters like sealing wax. She crawls over Nestor and gets her purse, which she takes into the bathroom. When she returns, Nestor is collecting the letters into a smeary stack.

"I'm sorry," she says but he stops her there.

"I want to see you again."

"Okay," she says. "When?"

"Would you like to go with me to an art opening tonight?"

"Sure." She steps into her black cotton leggings and pulls her torn blue jeans over them. As Nestor gets up to help her with her sweater, the letters fall to the floor.

Back in her communal bathroom at the Y, Nicole throws up. She has drunk too much the previous night and this combined with her period makes her sick. She changes her tampon – the morning flow is always heavy but it will be negligible by nightfall and gone by the next morning. In the shower she thinks about Nestor, whom she feels is curiously without an earthbound soul. Maybe all artists are like that, she decides, remembering Robert Smith. She makes a mental note to write it in her notebook when she is back in her room.

A line has formed on the sidewalk outside the Hangover Gallery in W1. The occasion is an exhibit by a Los Angeles-based artist named Alma, whose name Nicole recognizes from the punk-rock days. Nicole enters the gallery to find the petite, elaborately made-up Alma addressing the press. "I call the showing 'From Rage to Riches,' because that's what I do, turn anger into profit."

Nicole looks at one picture, a mockup of the death of Chatterton in which the dead poet holds a telephone receiver in his hand. The work is called *A Vision of Evil Wires*.

"I don't get it," she whispers to Nestor, who's joined her in front of the painting. He leads her over to where Alma is describing another piece, *Baby in a Bottle*. It shows a child's baby doll encased like a clipper ship in a glass bottle. "It's about science being a hoax," Alma explains. "I defy anyone who's ever claimed to have seen anything under a microscope."

"She knows how to put on a show," Nestor says to Nicole. "I'll be right back." He corners Alma in front of a section called Cotton Matter, where t-shirts of her work are for sale. He introduces himself to Alma who says, "I need platform shoes to hear you," because of the difference in their heights.

"I have an idea I want to discuss with you."

"I usually don't do this without my lawyer, but shoot."

He tells her about Pier's tie-dyed Shroud of Turin idea, claiming it as his own, and Alma stares straight ahead. When he's finished talking, she says, "But it was a fake. Excuse me."

Nestor turns to see Nicole talking to Pier in front of the Chatterton painting. He quickly exits out the front door.

"I don't get it about the telephone," Nicole says to Pier, whom she's just met.

"That's something I can't talk about," Pier replies and Nicole thinks, how strange, all I meet in London are other Americans. She looks around for Nestor in time to see him rushing out the door.

"I have to leave now," she tells Pier.

"Me too. Can I leave with you?"

They walk up to Oxford Street and when a telephone rings, Pier jumps. "That usually doesn't happen at night," Pier explains as Nicole props her up.

"It's okay," Nicole says. "Maybe you should get something to eat."

"I want to go back to my room. Can you help me get there?"

Because Nicole still doesn't know the city very well she hails a cab and they ride the short distance to Queensway.

"I have some beer in my room if you want some," Pier offers, and Nicole follows her into the hotel. She looks around the dingy room and at the candle Pier has lit on top of the lightweight bureau.

"I hope you don't mind it warm," Pier says as she hands Nicole a bottle.

"I'm used to it by now," she says. "You're lucky you don't have a phone in your room since they make you so nervous."

"You knew about it too?" Pier asks. "Does everyone know?" She sits next to Nicole on the bed.

"I don't know anything."

"What do you do for a living?"

"Me? Nothing. I'm a writer, I guess."

"My ex-boyfriend was a writer," Pier says.

"What are you?"

"Nothing."

"You're so pretty I thought you were probably a model." Pier looks up at Nicole who kisses her. Their shadows make a silhouette on the wall before Pier gets up to blow out the candle.

They make love, leaving their t-shirts on. Pier is afraid that Nicole is not satisfied so she puts the glass-encased candle inside her. The remnants of Nicole's period form a lipstick mouth on the candle's shiny rim.

"I hate having sex with boys," Nicole tells her. "They're such sock-doll nobodies." Pier remembers the love dolls dressed up in the Echo Park window.

"I liked my boyfriend okay, though," she continues. "You remind me of him in a way, before he went berserk and lost his personality."

"Do you go out with him at home?"

"No, not out. I like to stay in my room where it's dark. I'm like a reverse moth—attracted to darkness." She kisses Pier's cheek when suddenly Pier sits up and looks wildly around the room. "Things will never be the same now," Pier says and then cries until she sleeps.

In the morning Pier is happy as she and Nicole walk the length of Oxford Street to pick up Nicole's things from the Y. Street noise dims the sound of ringing phones. As they approach the Y, Nicole stops dead: Steve is waiting for her at the curb. The shabby cloak he wears barely disguises his gauntness and dark crust haloes his bright eyes. Nicole doesn't acknowledge him but he starts walking with her anyway.

As they enter the lobby, Pier hears herself being paged at the front desk. "No!" she shouts.

"I'll answer it for you," Steve offers. He crosses the room to pick up the receiver. "Hello?"

"Come here," says a male voice at the end of the line. "I want you."

Steve hangs up. "It was for me," he tells the girls. "I know what to do now. It seems I was born for heaven."

Nicole looks at him sidelong before he grabs her. "Goodbye, Nicky," he tells her and kisses the top of her head. "Remember me."

" 'Remember me'—what's that supposed to mean?" Nicole asks Pier as they ride the elevator up to Nicole's room.

"I don't know," Pier answers calmly, feeling that she finally has someone with whom to share her thoughts without effort. "I think it best to avoid epiphanies."

English Summertime

Sharlott sits gracelessly on a padded bench in the Tate Gallery. She is exhausted; she has walked from Fulham along the river. She raises her head to alternate her gaze from one painting to another and then back to the first, as if she were watching a sport or an argument. The painting to her left, *Chatterton*, seems to soak up shadows—they darken the poet's sinking cheeks. That to her right, Rossetti's *The Annunciation*, is all light: only the Virgin looks doubtful, her eyes averted and focused on what can only have been her final private thoughts. She is giving up, thinks Sharlott, packing it in as plainly as Chatterton.

Later and further east, Sharlott descends into the crypt beneath Saint Martin in the Fields, where she has tea in the cafeteria. Plastic tables and chairs are arranged on top of the gravestones and Sharlott adjusts her tray in symmetry—enamel cup and saucer, and silver-colored teapot. She pours bone-white milk into black tea and stirs it with a tiny spoon that tinkles like a benediction.

After her tray is swept aside with one wing-like gesture from a busboy, she heads for Ladbroke Grove where she is staying with a friend and trying not to dominate his front room. There, her luggage huddles in a tight corner as she prods one case while sitting astride another. Because the flat has no full-length mirror, she unravels a roll of tin foil that she purchased in the market. When the shiny paper approximates her height, she tears it off and tapes it to the wall. Sharlott dresses to go out for the evening, wears a vaguely Edwardian minidress patterned with green and peach mushrooms. Her black tights are splattered with prints of daggers, clocks, and knives, all of which are distorted by the contours of her legs. She assesses herself in the makeshift mirror, grabs her black coat, and leaves.

In the Underground station, she puzzles over her *London A–Z*, cursing the freelance writing assignment that has brought her to London to write about Los Angeles. In essence, she's called to conjure and mentally inhabit the home she wanted to leave behind, and the result is like being in two places at once, and in neither very successfully.

She plots her journey to see a band in a pub over a wine bar. The group is sort of mutant rock 'n' roll—Teddy-Boy children weaned on sci-fi technicolor and musical myth. The female guitar player wears a pink lamé dress perfect for the Grand Ole Opry of two decades ago. Sharlott speaks with her when she's changing in the ladies' room and notices her sizable thighs that seem to have a series of goofballs just beneath the first layer of skin.

When the show is over, Sharlott walks up the road toward Camden to an after-hours club. She lingers outside for a while, trying to determine if it's worth entering by watching who's being let in. A small moon is in the sky—strange for London, a Los Angeles moon—and as she looks at it a boy falls down next to her.

He tugs at the hem of her coat. He has eyes like steel, skin like talc, and a romantic face. His hair is a modified quiff—its natural curl stubbornly resists the rigid style.

"If you're going in," he says, motioning toward the club, "please take me with you. I'm just out of money. Once we're inside, I'll get you free drinks, I promise."

Sharlott considers him, impish and charming as a sprite. She smiles, an attempt at resistance.

"What's your name?"

He tells her as he stands up, "Damien."

"Are you named for a saint?"

"I think so."

"Oh. Are you a good saint or a bad saint?"

He doesn't answer. (Months later, when she is back home, she will go to a religious gift shop to buy his holy medal. When she can't find it, the saleswoman will offer her a cross encrusted with the likenesses of the Holy Family. "They're all you'll ever need," the woman will tell her and Sharlott will think the woman a fool, and dismiss the medal that is as trivial as a handful of leftover holiday change.)

"Do you color your hair?" Damien asks Sharlott.

"Yeah," she says. "Platinum. The *b* at the end is silent." Her joke is lost on him, between her accent and her rapid speech, and they swerve inside the club with a handful of others.

It's obvious that the club is someone's converted basement flat. Damien and Sharlott find a place in a corner of what was probably the sitting room. "Wait right here," he tells her, and she does until he returns with a tall can of lager for them to share. When he takes off his leather jacket, she notices that the cuffs of his white shirt are frayed. He isn't tall—barely taller than she—and a couple of times when she leans in to hear him, her forehead cracks against his. The second time it really hurts and she backs away in pain. Mostly, though, they just converse like old friends, with the difference being that Sharlott is using the background music to envision him. She often feels things as a result of something else, something indirect, like a shadow.

Damien disappears from time to time but he always turns up with partially finished pints of beer that he's found around the club. Normally, Sharlott would be apprehensive about drinking them, but she is drunk and so she hardly notices covering other lip-prints on the glasses' thick rims.

She tells Damien there is no one for her in Los Angeles; she values her boyfriends in accordance with what they can do for her. They could, for example, make free photocopies, get promotional records, or run her mail through their postage meters at work. That's as deep as it gets. Damien is puzzled when he hears this. Although he's certain she is older than he is, he's also sure that unlike him she's never been loved.

"It's been a long time since anyone has stared at me," he tells her. "Like that guy over there."

Sharlott sees an outline through the beaded doorway but can barely make out his features in the darkness.

"He keeps staring at me," Damien repeats.

Close to four A.M. they leave the club, high and drunk.

"Am I going north or south?" Sharlott asks. "I need to go toward Oxford Street."

They keep walking.

"One more thing," she says, leaning on him so heavily he weaves, "are we going my direction or yours?"

He tells her she is welcome to stay in his flat in Camden, but they will have to be quiet since he shares with his mother. He lives in a tower block that's tall and about as stable as Sid Vicious. Sharlott removes her shoes in a filthy elevator that wobbles as they go seven stories up.

What Sharlott will remember about the front room of the flat is that there were a lot of crystal-like objects—lamps, bowls, picture frames—and how they caught refractions of light from the hallway as she came inside.

Damien's room is dark and dusty. A loft-bed hangs above speakers, amplifiers, and black tangled cords thick as snakes or dreadlocks.

Together they sit on the floor, where dirt has become part of the carpet's pattern. As Damien makes a joint out of tobacco and a tiny chunk of hash, Sharlott lies on her stomach to survey his record albums. She sees classical music, acid jazz, reggae, the Clash.

"What a naff record collection!" he says and Sharlott nods, uncertain of the meaning of the word "naff."

"You don't have any Sex Pistols?"

"Nah," he says. "I like to listen to them on the radio." He pulls out a dozen or so records that he has played guitar or bass on, and shows her his name in the credits. She has to ask him for a hit of the joint—it has fully drawn him in by now.

"You can have the whole thing," he offers.

"That's okay," she says. "I don't like drugs all that much. They make you feel things in a false light." She inhales a little anyway and asks Damien if he's always wanted to be in a band.

"Yeah."

He tunes in a reggae station and tells Sharlott he thinks she will be very cold sleeping on the floor—there is no heat in the flat and it is early spring. She climbs up into his bed and touches his cheek when she realizes he has no intention of even kissing her. Then they kiss and explore each other—Damien keeps his eyes closed and his lids are covered in shadows.

"I love the feeling of you touching me," he tells her before he drops into sleep.

Despite the lull of the reggae, Sharlott can't sleep. Every time she starts to fall, a deejay will announce the time in a voice that's at least a decibel above the music. "Good morning London," he'll say, "it's 5:42." Never on the hour or the quarter-hour; unusual times, times like the clock Sharlott had seen earlier when she was in a shop on the Kings Road. The shop had a deliberately slanted wooden floor and a clock with hands that spun backwards and forwards like a plane circling a spinning globe.

Damien stirs and says something about money, if he only had money. Sharlott sees the filigreed pound note symbol whirling gracefully and she nearly sleeps until her pillow falls off the bed, down into a deep morass.

As the sun climbs up the side of the tower block, Sharlott feels very far from home, from her life, from herself, and the sensation is romantic. She climbs carefully from the bed and takes the stairs down from the flat, certain she was not more than one flight up. While she is still descending, she takes out her guidebook to map her way to Camden Lock.

The morning sun is warm and bright, rendering her black coat almost unnecessary. She opens it and views her mushroom dress, stiff now from having absorbed the milk of cum. In his room, Damien wakes, turns over, and screws the impression her body has left in his bed.

Sharlott has a breakfast of egg and chips and then she takes the train back to Ladbroke Grove, where she is alone in the flat. She sleeps the entire day, waking up the next morning to go to Easter Sunday Mass. When she hears the radio announcer give the time, she stares at the receiver in disbelief—it is English Summertime and she has not adjusted her clock. There is a later Mass but Sharlott will miss it.

Damien has been up fifty hours when they say goodbye, coming off speed and drink. The Chinese takeaway they stand in is so anonymous Sharlott manages to feel nothing at all.

"I'll live to see you again," he tells her, and then kisses her cheek before turning to leave with his three band members.

At five A.M. in her apartment overlooking Lake Hollywood, Sharlott is having lunch. She can't adjust to the time change, won't adjust. Her thoughts of Damien make the hands on the clock move ahead and disrupt her sense of time. She pictures how he wore his earrings to bed, wishes she could wrap her tongue around one and draw him deeper into her. She sets her watch to London time.

She comes close to sending him money to come to her, but each time she stops herself. It goes on like this for a season until fall, when time changes and along with it, light.

Anchorites
(A Wilderness of Lost Connections)

In the midst of memorabilia lies an uneasy thought: is there any significance in things burned in effigy?

Honor likes to lounge and write letters. It's the only way she can think. She often designs a logo for each one first, involving words embellished with curlicues, an acid filigree. She draws only in blue and black, the colors of depression, of schizophrenia's better half.

Every letter is a rendition of the same theme, a definition of her love for Robert Smith, a pop star she's never met. Do people still do this sort of thing? Honor thinks not: idolatry, obsession, has been done to the death and it's lucky for her. Other fanatics have gone before, paved the way and then disappeared out of boredom or age, leaving a clearing through a forest of rickety trees just for her.

Honor lives in an apartment that's more like a drainpipe. Music and her thoughts reverberate and bounce in a gray distortion. When she has to, she sells old things to buy postage stamps, but it's harder making food or rent.

She had a date last night, with a boy called Skitz who wore his hair in his face like Robert Smith sometimes does. Skitz told her how fortunate she was to have a door that opened via skeleton key. Honor stared in reply. It wasn't a detail that interested her.

Before the night was out, Honor accused him from the corner of her bed. "You're just a ghost, a negative of HIM," she cried, although in reality Skitz was sheet-white. As he headed for the door, she tried to call him back, to explain that she had meant it as a compliment.

Honor writes up her date in a letter to Robert Smith. "He had some of your beauty," she notes, "but none of your terror. He played in a band called Visionary Flowers. You would never call anything by such a dumb name, I know."

She addresses the envelope by heart and doesn't expect a reply. Honor has been sending Robert at least one letter a day for six months now and nothing has changed. He won't write, she knows.

He'll show up at her door.

There are days when she panics. Days when, all morning long, things keep evaporating. Her heart pounds as she uses her fist to hold down stamps that threaten to curl in flight like the uncancelled ones she's peeled off letters from home.

Times, too, when her handwriting fluffs and puffs and runs together, turning into indecipherable fat clouds of words.

Nights when she talks to herself so much she thinks she should get a pet, to have an excuse.

But today she has completed her letter. She dresses to go out to mail it, but when she discovers it's not morning, she returns to get her nightmarish big black coat.

After she drops the letter into the box, Honor heads for the Palindrome to get something to eat. The Pal is a burger restaurant with a fifties motif spoiled by hippie wood panelling. It hurts to look at it too closely. Honor sits in a booth and removes her notebook from her oversized black purse. She writes poetry while she eats.

Honor goes to the bathroom and distractedly reads the graffiti on the metal stall. In thick black pen someone has written, "I SLEPT WITH ROBERT SMITH." It's okay. Honor has read this before. What's new is the response, in timid thin pink: "At least," it reads, "at least you remembered HIS name."

Safely back at home, Honor continues working on a poem called "Without a Trance." But her concentration is poor and before too long she starts scribbling "Robert, Robert, Robert in a Big Black Coat," until it becomes a piece of its own:

Corpse flowers
feed on loveblood
have ghosts for eyes
when reaching
their roots entwine skulls

and I stare at the ground
when we kiss
drowning in dust
drowning at night
a generation of two
making love over stones
of another

The next morning there is a pummelling at Honor's front door. She gets up from the matted and torn black futon where she had fallen and goes to see if it is the postman. It isn't—it's her landlord, a balding young man whom Honor thinks stupid. When she doesn't open the door, he slides an envelope through the crack at the bottom. Honor picks up the note after an interval, once she's sure he's gone. She sails the paper out the window and it falls like ticker tape.

The telephone rings and it's her landlord again. "Listen," he tells her, "I know you're there. You've got two choices. One, pay your rent. Two, find another place to roost. Me, I prefer the latter."

"What ladder?" Honor thinks as she gently replaces the receiver. He sounds like he's getting suicidal. She goes into her square kitchen to make a cup of tea.

The ladder, portable stair, dark at the top of the stars. Suicide case caught hanging stars by their tinsel tails. Hunting accident.

She hears someone at her door again. It's a girl she knows called Ecs, formerly Stacy, i.e. ex-Stacy, then the drug, and now Ecs. Ecs comes in and sits on the lumpen futon.

"You look like you just got up," she tells Honor.

"I was in the kitchen."

"Don't you ever clean your place?"

Honor thinks, I'm glad she's come by.

"The reason I stopped by," Ecs says, "is that I need a roommate."

"Where do you live now?"

"In the Fontenoy, on Whitley. It's really cool. It's a twenties skyscraper, all crumbling now. But my roommate just left." She rolls her eyes. "Acting."

"I like living alone."

"Don't we all. I just can't afford it. Can you?"

"Sometimes," says Honor. "But why would you want me?"

"I want to help you," says Ecs. "I heard you were having some hard spells and I thought I could help, I don't know, cast out your demons or something."

"No, thanks," Honor says. "And besides, exorcised demons have to go somewhere, you know. They aren't thin air. They land places."

"Well, if they can pay rent, they can move in with me. I don't mind."

"I'll think about it."

"As long as you'd promise to be tidier," Ecs says. "All the Robert Smith junk can stay, is fine, but if you could put it in some kind of order . . . Call me tonight and let me know."

"Oh, I wouldn't know by tonight," Honor replies, realizing she'd have to write to Robert first, see what he thinks. Plus, give him her change of address, give it time to set in. "I can let you know in a couple weeks."

"A couple weeks? I'll keep looking, then. See you." Ecs lets herself out.

Honor makes herself another cup of tea and sits down at the kitchen's card table.

Dear Robert,

I read somewhere that the Goths did not build ruined castles, still that's what we think of, when we think of them. The reason I bring this up is that I'm moving to this twenties skyscraper kind of thing. It's all decaying now, which is what people like about it. I don't really care. It's boring to me but I wanted you to know, so you'll know where to find me. For where but in puzzles do uneven edges meet?

Yours,
Honor

Ecs assesses the vacant space in her two-bedroom apartment. She finds solace and companionship in the emptiness, and order in the absence of things. The rest of her apartment, the part she lives in, is so perfect it looks like a model home. The only aberration is her bedroom, where the bookcases are stacked with nearly one hundred copies of the same paperback: *Edie*, by Jean Stein. They give the effect of a black and silver-white, unending ellipsis.

It isn't that Ecs is obsessed with the sixties' most psychotic superstar, it's just that she thinks she ought to have the book about Edie's life. All her copies come from secondhand stores, where they look the most vulnerable.

When Honor moves in, Ecs hopes, she won't bring too much clutter.

Honor disconnects one of her speakers, a huge archaic thing, and then she remembers something. She was at a club and when a song by the Cure (Robert Smith's band) came on, this guy walked over to one of the gigantic speakers (he was dwarfed by it) and leaned his head in. Honor squints to recall his face, and when it comes clearer she thinks it was Skitz.

She wraps the cords around each unwieldy speaker and carries them down to her car. Then she comes back up the stairs and when she puts her key in the lock, it strikes her that she won't be doing this again. Suddenly she knows why people collect keys and doorknobs—it's about hands and the past, touching things that are gone.

"I get so lost," she writes in her mental letter, "all I can do is look straight ahead."

Honor drives the few miles to the sub-Hollywood Hills, where she'll be living on the eleventh floor with Ecs. She parks and unloads a box marked FRAGILE that's filled with Cure posters, records, buttons, articles, stickers, and so on. Also in the box are her journals.

At the front door, she calls Ecs on the intercom and Ecs buzzes her in. Ecs makes way for Honor, who steers the huge box, and then together they unload the car. A limp stack of clothes is, Ecs observes, as weighty as a dead body.

What furniture Honor has folds, collapses, or unscrews. Nothing is stable. When it's all in Honor's new room, Ecs says, "Your furniture looks like you stole it from a motel."

Honor doesn't reply but remembers she's forgotten her bathroom towels. It's okay, she decides. Maybe her landlord can use them wet for a noose, string them together as a means of escape.

She arranges her things in her new room and it takes until nightfall. From the box of memorabilia, she removes her latest journal but when she tries, she is unable to write. She feels frightened, nauseated, like grief. So she lays down on her futon, pulls a sheet over herself.

"I'd never sleep uncovered," she'd once written to Robert. "It'd be like lying in an unmarked grave."

Honor thrashes from side to side in her makeshift bed until she sits up and looks out the barred window. Bars on the eleventh floor? She must be dreaming it. Or maybe it's shadows. She closes her eyes tightly, sees the same ornate latticework grille. Squinting harder, she wills the image into reverse: a white trivet on the inside of her eyelids.

It doesn't work.

She pretends Robert's here with her, that they make love until their bodies are numb from too much feeling.

When she awakens the next morning, Honor gets a sheer and pale blue air letter from her shelf. She wants to write Robert and, finding herself able, she is relieved. She writes about a dream she just had.

Isn't it weird how in horror movies women run toward terror? Their negligees part like sheer curtains over an open window. Then, when they get what they want, the damsels scream and despair like sexual ghosts.

I don't know. I know people say you're obsessed with suffocating and they say you're obsessed with drowning since there are 74 references to it in your songs but I think it's kissing you're obsessed with. Kissing which is, when you think about it, equal parts of both.

Love.
Honor

Honor opens her room door quietly, sheepishly, and peers out. She is stunned to find Ecs sitting on the living room floor, surrounded by boxes of envelopes.

"What are you doing?" Honor accuses, certain that Ecs is up to what she herself has been up to, only Ecs is much more organized, more businesslike about it.

"Pardon?"

"That. What are you sending?"

"Coupons, Honor. It's my job. It's what I do. I stuff envelopes and get paid for it. You should try it."

"No, thanks." Honor looks away and over at the t.v., which isn't on.

"Don't you have to do something? I mean, how are you going to pay the rent?" Ecs asks. "This isn't that bad, you know. At least I don't have to go out anywhere."

"It's okay," says Honor, still staring at the t.v. "My parents send me a little bit of money every month. Could I watch a Cure video?"

"Sure," says Ecs. "Put 'em on. I can watch while I'm working."

Honor retrieves a videocassette from her room and sits on the sofa to watch it while trying to ignore the deliberately sharp and rustling paper sounds coming from over her shoulder. After a time she turns halfway and asks Ecs where the nearest mailbox is.

"It's about two blocks. I'll be going there in a little while if you have something you want me to take."

"It's okay," says Honor flatly, rewinding the videotape.

On a blurry gray day in slightly North London, Robert Smith drives to his management group's offices. He parks partially on the curb and rushes inside to collect his mail and messages.

A blonde woman smiles her greeting and then embraces him. "You've got more letters from your American friend," she says good-naturedly as she hands him a plastic crate full of mail.

"Which one," Robert says, not as a question.

"You know—the one you like. Horror or what's-it."

"Oh, Horror. I'm actually thinking of writing her back."

"Your choice, Robert," the woman says as she directs his attention to another piece of paper, a shiny fax.

The pattern is always the same and Ecs is sick of it the way you get sick of looking at a rug. Boxes will come, full of coupons for her to put in the business-size envelopes. Bulk rate. Sometimes Honor might answer the door and bring two or three boxes into the living room. Ecs will then transport them to the dining room table where she has to work now since Honor's always watching videos.

It's happening right now: Ecs can see the back of Honor's head, where her black hair is shaved short, nodding slowly and lullaby-like to Robert Smith being interviewed. He's talking about how he hates people who try to claim and keep the Cure as their pet group. He says the word "hate" with such staccato Ecs nearly jumps.

From behind her barricade of boxes, Ecs keeps looking at Honor, who's curled and comfortable as a stuffed toy cat, and she hates her. Hates her so much her saliva goes down like venom into her veins, her fingertips, her hands, any part of her that goes into her job.

"Does your tongue ever get sore?" Honor asks, out of the blue.

"I don't use it," Ecs replies. "I have this little plastic bottle. See?" She holds up what looks like a doll's baby bottle, without the nipple.

Honor gets up and goes into her room as Ecs imagines stabbing her hard with a letter opener. When Ecs goes down to get the mail she finds a creamy bonded envelope inside the box addressed in a slanting, reassuring hand. It is for Honor with a return address of North Nog, on Long Island. Ecs holds up the envelope to the listless, hazy sun and although she can't see through it, she knows there's a check from Honor's parents inside. A check that Ecs will keep, even if she can't cash it.

In her room Honor feels edgy and agitated, like she's not appreciated. Even Ecs hates her. She gets a copy of the Cure's latest press kit from her file and thumbs through it. Two glossy black-and-white photos—one of Robert alone and one of him with his band—temporarily stick together and Honor panics. But the pictures come apart, unscathed as two romanticized lovers. Honor reads the press release.

" 'The band is a magnet for unstable types,' Smith acknowledges," and for Honor today this goes down like precisely the wrong thing.

On a piece of paper she scribbles blue felt circles around an idealized image of her face: her black hair perfectly refracts bluish light and the rings become a kind of halo leading into a bull's-eye.

I'm sure you lump me into your unstable faction, but there are things you need to know, if you haven't intuited them. I do *have talent. But I don't know what to do with it. It bothers me like a headache, a sickness. I didn't ask for it, didn't cultivate it. So I look to you and you salve it a little bit, or tear it open, which has the same effect.*

It's exactly like Matthew Arnold said about something or other: It's like I'm trapped between two worlds, one dead, the other powerless to be born. Talent with no direction, like offering up dead air.

Oh, I have been in therapy but it's just that it seemed so pointless, like charm school. So rude just giving answers without asking courteous boring questions in return. How does that *prepare you for the real world?*

I also don't believe in quiet support from other people. I knew this guy, Skitz, who probably could have given me it and it might have been okay for a while but in the end it has to be a lie. I'm sure they secretly, sullenly want what they're supporting for themselves. And I don't want to live my life like Everyman backwards.

A poem I did by that same name:

At the Palindrome
we move
on quicksand
in our tattered cathedral skirts
we wake opaque nightmares
He who I have loved
with such commotion
now makes my skin crawl
in both directions
Still we might as well dance
til the end of the world
when the sky will soften
and the dead will hide from the living

I do still love you Robert, with all my being inside and out.

Love—Honor

Honor seals the letter, her tongue lingering long and kiss-like. Then she runs out into the living room.

"I've done it!" she announces to Ecs. She is dizzy with adrenalin.

"What?"

"I've written the letter that will make Robert love me."

Honor grabs her black velvet coat (even though it's hot outside) and rushes out the door toward the mailbox. When she gets to the blue metal receptacle, a letter carrier is kneeling in front of it, scooping letters of different shapes and colors into a white carton marked "U.S. Mail."

"Can I take that for you?" she asks Honor, who slowly extends her arm.

"Thanks," Honor says and turns to go back, walking this time.

"Excuse me," the carrier calls after her. "I can't accept this."

"What?"

"We can't take mail for Great Britain. They're having a postal strike. Nothing's being delivered."

"What?"

"It won't go. I'm sorry." The woman's eyes are dark and lush, the color of sympathy. "You might try again in a few days."

Honor feels like crying but it's not a release known to her. Instead she just takes the letter and goes back up the hill.

Back at her apartment she walks past Ecs without looking at her. In her room Honor listens to *Kiss Me Kiss Me Kiss Me* straight through without flinching once or even dancing.

In a telegram office near the West End, Robert Smith stands in the queue. His ratted hair renders him taller than the others in line. Robert hasn't decided what he's going to say in the telegram—he'll wait until he gets the form and then wing it.

Ecs observes Honor as stranger and stranger. She never watches videos anymore, just stays in her room doing god knows what. One day Honor asks Ecs if she's seen any letters for her from her parents and Ecs says no—maybe there's a partial U.S. mail strike too, or something.

"Yes, a sympathy strike," Honor agrees quietly before going back in her room.

A little while later there is a knock at the front door and because Ecs is out, Honor has to answer it. A skinny, pimple-pocked boy in an oversized cap looks up from his clipboard and says,

"Telegram for Horror."

"Who?"

"Horror. It's from England, you know, that's in London."

Honor signs for it shakily, taking care to break apart her script in the appropriate place to match the intended name. The boy leaves muttering, without a tip or a clue.

Honor reads the words which jump and jolt like their own kind of Morse code:

Dear Horror
Enjoy your letters
I'd like to meet you and would if it weren't for Mary
As if all love demands a witness
Yours faithfully
Robert Smith

Honor goes to her room and places the telegram precariously atop a stack of Cure cassettes. It looks like a pair of giant wings crowning a building.

Horror? she thinks. Ho*rr*or? How can she claim this telegram when it's not really addressed to her? How can she keep it? She hears the sound of Ecs at the door, Ecs with people, ugh, company, but the company turns out to be Honor's parents who've just come from the airport. They're full of concern and mock-sincerity, worried about Honor, who hasn't cashed their checks. When they didn't receive this most basic communication—her endorsement—Honor's mother had phoned and spoken with Ecs, who told her yes, her daughter was in trouble and yes, they should probably come as soon as they could.

The parents are mild-looking, dull, and unassumingly deadly. Honor's father is completely bald. Her mother wears glasses and gloves.

When Honor sees the two of them she screams.

"Honor, Honor," her mother says, trying to smooth her daughter's back-combed hair with a gloved hand. "We thought maybe we should all take a trip together. Would you like that? We thought we could go to London, the three of us."

"I . . . don't . . . want . . . to . . . go to . . . London," Honor says between breaths and sobs. Ecs stares from the doorway, amazed. She's never seen Honor cry.

"We thought you'd like that," her mother continues. "Let me help you pack some things."

"No!" says Honor. "I won't go."

"You will go," says her father, who stands near Ecs, and Honor gets up, wobbly, and starts putting her memorabilia into the box.

"I have to take this," she says. "I have to take my things."

"Okay," her mother says. "Where are your clothes?"

Honor points at a shopping cart bedecked with studded belts, large earrings, scarves. Clothes are in the basket, shoes on the rack beneath.

"Oh dear," says her mother. "Everything is black."

"This is ridiculous," her father intones. "Let's hurry it up."

By the time Honor is trapped between her parents on a plane, Ecs is using part of Honor's back rent "plus a little something extra to hold you until you find another girl to take Honor's room" to buy a videocassette of Edie Sedgwick in *Ciao! Manhattan*. Ecs will be able to watch the movie undistracted by her envelope-stuffing job which she won't need, at least for quite a while.

If Honor weren't so sedated, she would know the flight to be too long for one to London. She'd also be more surprised to disembark and find herself in ice-beautiful Switzerland.

The countryside is so ordered, Honor thinks, as she's placed on a train, it's so SAME it's just like Ecs's room.

In the clinic just outside of Vevey, Honor's room is quiet. She thinks of Robert Smith for the first time in a month. And, for the first time, her head is clear and doesn't hurt. She remembers looking at a picture of him when she first arrived here and how the sight of his hair made her itch, made her scratch all over.

She begins to identify all the things she has to tell him: how one doctor told her her behavior at times was "ecstatic" (how saintly!), about the woman, Perla, who's always sneaking smokes and who told Honor one has to enter madness to escape death.

Honor thinks, too, of a boy who tried to commit suicide at a Cure stadium show in Los Angeles.

I'm sure you remember him, too. How stupid he was, how tasteless. How doubly embarrassing to have lived. *It's bad enough he was stuck on some girl and can't you just see her, some So. Cal. stupid mindless girl who knows nothing except this boyfriend-thing, having a relationship. How functioning of them, how adjusted. People like that shouldn't even be allowed to go to your shows.*

But I wonder too sometimes about you and Mary, that you didn't just settle for the first person you could talk to. It seems too pat or easy at times—a girl from your school, from your hometown. I tend to think that one's true love is in the remotest world-corner from where you are at any, at every given moment, like polarized figurines.

I saw graffiti once from someone who'd slept with you and while it didn't really bother me then, it does now. I once knew this girl who had the back of a t-shirt she was wearing signed by Andy Warhol. She always said she knew then how the art felt, the pen to the well and I'm sure that's how your sex is.

I know you use your dreams a lot in writing and I'm not sure how I feel about that now that I'm forced to dwell in mine and recount them for my doctors. Maybe dreams' beauty is their privacy. So I never tell the truth but I will tell you one last one that I keep having about you in that you're in this room and it's a harsh-white cocoon, restrictive belts wrap like tight veins and there's all this fog inside. I keep calling for you to speak French to me—I think we're in the Côte d'Azur—

but you can't see me; the spark of recognizant love that's tangible as lightning (me) can't be seen.

I told you about this dream but I'd never tell my doctor. Instead I tell him I dream of cats and streams. I know now it's pointless pinning hopes on people, they'll only pop like helium balloons. And I know too that goodbye notes are never signed "Love."

Honor
(not Horror)

That afternoon when Honor is supposed to be in dance class, she rushes out in her pale pink leotard and trumpet-like tutu, in her hushing ballet slippers, toward the edge of the hospital. No one stops her—people are freer here. Honor walks toward the gate where she waits for someone who'll be going to Vevey, someone who can mail her letter.

She looks like an upended tree, her hair like roots and skirt fanned and funnelled. Finally a man driving a horse and wagon comes along and stops at her beckoning. Honor speaks her best French to him and he takes the letter from her and then kisses the hand that wrote it.

Honor skips slowly, half dances back to the building, which was once a convent. When she's close enough, she sees that everyone is outside on the front lawn, milling and flitting like butterflies.

There's been a fire in one of the wings, she's told. Someone was smoking. No one was hurt, fortunately, but some of the rooms were harmed. Honor's memorabilia has been damaged beyond repair: records like pools of flat sticky tar; tapes, melted worms; Robert in pictures with even blacker hair now, and curled at the edges.

Honor's parents arrive two days later and ask her for her version of how the fire started. She shrugs and replies she's sure she'd be the last to know.

In Deep Shape

I'm not an American," Honor says defensively in a London pub.
What, then?
"I'm a Mystic."
She means it. She's a girl who, having been through much (next to nothing, really—not even a boyfriend), simply directs all her human feelings toward ghosts.

Honor comes to be in London fresh from a clinic in Switzerland. She likes the city for its broken high clouds that make the days so night-heavy. She likes the scented silence of the parks.

And she likes her flat, as much as she can like anything.

Honor is doing differently from her past now, having realized that she can't understand anything that doesn't have a deep, drawing undercurrent, an emotional subtext. She drinks, despite her doctor's advice, in a Portobello Road pub of a late Sunday afternoon, having spent the morning listening to reggae in her flat. Reggae music, a boy outside the ICA once told her, is the true soundtrack of punk.

In the iced and opaque-ribboned glass behind the bar, Honor recognizes the reflection of Gaudy, with whom she once lunched (drank, really) one afternoon in a garden pub by the canals of Little Venice, near Regent's Park. Gaudy is a minor pop star who hasn't had a hit record yet, not for want of trying. He is thin as a grate and has the most alarming blue eyes.

The afternoon he'd shared with Honor, they left the garden and went to his flat. Together they washed and dyed each other's hair the deadliest shade of black widow black; only Gaudy—far more drunken than Honor—misjudged his application to her hair. Honor's scalp repelled the potion as best it could, but her hair still fell out in clumps balled at the middle. Her locks dotted the sink like spiders.

Honor held back her tears and Gaudy turned up the stereo. "If you want quiet, move to the country," he shouted when a neighbor bleated for him to lower the volume.

Next daylight found Honor in deep shape, on the floor of Gaudy's sitting room. Gaudy was asleep in the bathtub, the water gone sheer black with dye all around him. Incredibly, once he got out and dressed, his hair looked perfect and the dye only gave his pale skin a more lucid, Lucite cast.

Honor left Gaudy and ran quickly to the Underground, where she was assured a modicum of darkness. She has always disliked daylight for, while there's a trace of bluish, pure light in darkness, there's no hint of darkness in light.

When Gaudy caught a look at his spider-spattered basin, he cursed Honor and decided then and there she was a harpy.

And so now, with his singular wit, he approaches Honor at the bar and asks if he can buy her a pint. "Harp, is it?" he says, smiling just enough to keep the skin around his eyes from crinkling.

"She's a Mystic, this one," the bartender tells Gaudy.

"Oh, I know," he replies. "Weaving her psychic web."

It's not that Honor wants to be with Gaudy that much but rather that she doesn't wish to say no to a drink.

"Right, then," says Gaudy as he passes a fat glass to her. "To blackout!"

Their glasses clink together like tap shoe heels and Honor takes a lengthy sip as Gaudy proceeds to tell her about his latest rock star adventure.

"I was in America last week, you know. My management company thinks my sound is somehow more . . . American, I guess. So this mini-tour showcase thingy was set up for the Americans to have a look. Just three dates: New York, Los Angeles, and some other place. It was in L.A. where after my show I got some coke although I wanted Ecstasy. Wouldn't you know the old nose started bleeding. THIS nose. What could I do? All these record company parasites in the next room—we were back at my hotel—and what could I do? It didn't look good, y'know. The Next Big Thing with a Nosebleed sort of thing."

"What did you do?"

"Waited 'til it stopped, didn't I."

Honor sighs, can't conceive of telling such a long story that doesn't have a point. "I have to go," she says, and Gaudy looks back at her with no reaction.

"Are you off, then?" he says.

"Yeah."

"I may come 'round later."

"Okay," she says, certain he doesn't know where she lives.

She lives on the tail of Portobello Market—she could throw rocks at the Westway. Her flat is small and damp, too damp to put up posters. The walls are a uniform cream and the carpet has a water-marked deco pattern. One way or another, all the furniture came from the Market: purchased or gleaned from discards abandoned after the vendors have packed up.

Monday afternoon Honor has an appointment with her psychiatrist, although she is loath to go. She feels she's the kind of girl hysteria becomes, and steadfastly vows to resist the pathological world of happiness that the doctor tries to impose.

Monday night she's out at a club, High Hell, and it's no different. Honor looks at the people around her and feels so physically apart it's as if there's a trough, a melancholy ditch, between herself and the rest of the world.

In a compassionate moment her doctor had called her condition Romantic Despair, but Honor knows it better as loneliness. And tonight she feels so alone she thinks she'll turn to stone, become a pillar, a prop, a maypole for others to gaily pivot around.

When she leaves the club she heads for home, to just sit. And the next morning she wakes up looking rough, for of all the emotions, longing is the most visible.

Honor dresses like a somnambulist (lots of lace and floral print) and tops her outfit off with a pea-green velvet coat that has an ample hood. She appears in the street, a druid on acid, and walks toward Kensington Church Street for Kensington Market. In the chimeric set of stores, she wanders only to pause at a stall where she sifts through a tree rack of silky scarves that hang weightless, like candyfloss wings.

She pulls at one in particular and angles her plush elbow into a passing boy's stomach. She looks at his face, which is predominantly curtained by filmic black hair. It's a face she has seen a hundred times before but could never place just where—and while she knows it's clumsy to believe in love at first sight, she feels a kindred weakness and silence. She's certain he's the one person who can make her life worth living or ending.

Honor runs her hands between and down the scarves as she watches him make his purchase, a velvet-trimmed waistcoat.

"He's sweating flowers, he is," says the cashier to a girl on a stepstool, who's intently shoving t-shirts into a wooden cubicle.

"Who, Simon?" the girl replies.

So he's called Simon, Honor thinks over a cup of tea in one of the market's cafés. It really sounds more like a name for a cat.

The remainder of the week passes but Honor can't make herself go out. She would do so, she decides, if it could be guaranteed that every face she saw would be Simon's. Everyone: street cleaners, shop assistants, tea ladies, restroom attendants, news agents, ticket sellers, the entire Underground, thousands of Simons, everyone. She feels dizzy with the thought of it, a perfect world.

But when she parts the velvet, muslin-lined curtains to peer through the lace panel at the street below, she sees the crown of a woman's head. The woman has champagne-rinsed gray hair—definitely not Simon.

So Honor contents herself with his name, which she repeats over and over. It slides off her tongue with such sibilance it's like a spell. Simon, Simon. It becomes her favorite thing to say, replacing a long ago phrase: "People like that, I really hate. I really hate them."

Honor lies back on her patched and weather-parched divan and a memory invades. She is in Hollywood walking down a steep street in a particularly nasty neighborhood. She's looking down and in a frame of the sidewalk someone has written "Mary-13" in fresh chalk. Instantly Honor starts scuffing out the words with the sole of her boot, much the way some horses are trained to paw their hoofs, 1-2-3 for yes, 1-2 for no.

Then a boy who's nearly blindfolded by a bandanna comes out of nowhere, rushing toward Honor as he screams and swings a bicycle chain.

Honor runs and jumps out into the street, causing an oncoming car to swerve into the curb. Its driver, a huge man, leaps out and grabs Honor by the shoulders, yells at her and pulls her up onto the sidewalk. A crowd collects and the avenging youth watches until he gets bored. Then he leaves.

Why this now, Honor wonders, safe in London. And why she hated the name Mary, she's no idea. She should probably mention this to her doctor, instead of diverting him by saying things like she's been entertaining thoughts of suicide. Entertaining? Did she have to throw a party?

Honor yawns and decides to watch Open University, instructional t.v. Eventually the phone rings but it's only Gaudy calling to see if Honor wants to meet him at a wine bar in the Kings Road. She declines. You're not Simon, she wants to tell him, but he'd never understand.

Gaudy is baffled that she would say no to him, unaware that he was merely the object of a crush of convenience. Such an infatuation, while not to be underestimated, is only potent and partially debilitating until the next thing, the real thing, comes along.

On Saturday morning Honor makes her ritual trek to Camden Town, where she goes to the open-air clothes and antiques market. She feels like a spirit walking, as once again she slowly shuffles through racks of skirts and babydoll dresses, leggings and decorative bras.

Inside what is usually the Electric Ballroom, Honor picks up a heavy-soled shoe and sees Simon's profile reflected in the steel-plated toe. His nose is so sharp it obscures the other side of his face.

Honor says hello and he looks at her, past her, and then back at her eyes. Were there ever eyes this gray? she wonders, thinking they are the color of the moon.

Simon introduces himself and she shakes his hand, which is weighty and cold with antique rings. He wears one of the scarves Honor had clung to when she watched him that day in Kensington Market.

"Did you get this in Kensington Market?" she asks, looking at his neck.

"Portobello," Simon replies, still holding her slim hand. Honor puts the shoe she has been evaluating back on the table and she and Simon walk up the stairs and outside, where it is beginning to rain. They go up Camden High Street to the cobbled part of the market where Things outnumber Clothes.

Because it's raining heavily now, they take shelter beneath the arches by the canal, Camden Lock. There they embrace, hook together tightly.

"You're trembling," Simon tells her. He talks so softly it's like he speaks in parentheses.

"I'm just feeling my love for you," she says as the rain seeps through the cracks in the bricks to drip on Simon and then Honor. It is late summer rain that melts Honor's ice-insulated skin.

When they do small talk, Simon says he used to go to a club called the Batcave and Honor thinks that's it, he's the Beauty of the Batcave.

Simon lives in Battersea, in a tiny rehearsal space, though he has no ambitions toward artistic ends. Rather he just likes to spend his time reading and propping up his faith, a kind of arch-Anglicanism that twists at will like a Gothic stairwell.

He takes Honor by both wrists, focuses on the water that's delicately beaded her ragged-hem hair. "Come over Monday night," he tells her. "I'll cook dinner for you."

Honor nods her assent, wonders how she will wait that long, and, deeper, how he could.

When she arrives back in her flat, she assembles a lump of laundry, realizing she has nothing to wear for Monday night. In the launderette she is drifting, distracted—a phantom washing clothes. While she's out, Gaudy calls and leaves a message that he has been asked to do a BBC radio session. It is a big break for him.

Honor thinks about returning the call, thinks of Simon's hands like heavy silver baubles around her slight wrists. Frenzied, she calls Gaudy and directs his way by.

In his flat, Simon is scattering papers and books on the floor until they encircle him like a collapsed, makeshift clothesline. He should write a letter, he knows, write one to his wife who's in New York working for a while. He should tell her what has happened, about the girl in Camden Lock. But instead he listens to the Cocteau Twins.

Gaudy comes by Honor's very late but he looks radiant, the way good news can alter someone, make them taller even. He must be over six feet now, able to look down his straightened nose at anyone, every critic who's condemned him. Honor can only stare before she thinks to wave him in: he just doesn't look real, eyes tinted too blue, hair perfect and spiky-soft. He comes in; his low-slung leather trousers hang right, so right they beg for Honor to pull them off as he lounges on her settee: He reclines his perfect head further back into the fringe-trimmed pillows as Honor, a virgin, takes his sex in her mouth, her lolly-tongue soon sweet with the taste of him.

She rises to display what she's wearing, a Victorian lace-white dress, gauzy as scrim, which she unbuttons and unhooks without drawing the drapes. Gaudy doesn't get up; he motions for her to come to him and she does, determinedly but awkwardly offering him her veiled chastity until it cuts in her. Gaudy thinks she must have her period but when she keeps wincing, he reconsiders, sure that she's had that operation some groupies undergo. Honor would tell him otherwise, only the occasion doesn't seem that momentous, doesn't really call for anything. She stays on him, toying with his uncoiled snakeskin belt, one foot nestled in the puddle of her cheesecloth dress as the cars on the Westway whiz by like pearls on a snapped and rotted strand.

"Harpy," Gaudy whispers in, and then bites, her ear. "Enchantress."

Gaudy stays with Honor all the next day, then takes a taxi home when he realizes he's missed the last train.

On Monday morning Honor finds herself looking forward for the first time to her appointment with the psychiatrist. She'll tell him what she's done, what she plans to do, and how she thinks that all this time she's been mistakenly calling her sexual drive loneliness, and now that she knows this, her feelings of abandonment might subside, might melt like balm into her skin.

She declares all this strongly, courageously, to her doctor and hates him for the way he stares her back, saying nothing. She knows his pause is a way of condemning her, of making her feel insecure by willing her to keep talking so she'll contradict herself. But she doesn't do it, just sits down and twists her elephant's hair bracelet.

"Are there other things you'd like to accomplish now?" her doctor asks finally, solemnly. She takes him to mean artistic pursuits.

"I know what you're going to say," Honor replies. "This is about the little engine that could, now, isn't it? Well what about the little engine that couldn't? Or how about, better still, the little engine that could, but just didn't feel like it?" She lifts her suede purse from the floor and leaves.

She feels uneasy – she's never walked out in the middle of a session. But then she smiles, remembering she's never told the truth in one before, either.

That evening Honor takes a bus to Simon's in Battersea. She sits on the top deck because it's more momentous. After she gets off, she has to walk a distance and it feels like it might sleet so she puts on the hood of her velvet coat and draws her arm around herself.

In her coat pocket is a loaded camera; she's not really sure what prompted her to bring it.

Simon opens the door and Honor notices he's cut his hair around his ears – it's dead even with his cheekbones like they were a finish line. The top is still long and tall except for where it falls arbitrarily.

The first thing Simon notices about Honor is the camera, which she now holds in her hand.

"I hope you don't mind," Honor says shyly about it. She pauses inside the square room, a kind of corral with a roof. "You're not one of those people who think cameras steal your soul, are you?"

"I'm not a Pagan," Simon replies. "I've no objection to the camera in and of itself. What I object to is how I look different in each photograph."

"Maybe it's the camera, and not you," Honor says, trying to help. Then she adds, "In some ways the whole idea of pictures is insulting. I'm sorry—I shouldn't have brought it." She puts the camera back in her coat pocket.

"Don't be like that," Simon cautions, helping her out of her coat. "Your skirt is amazing, like it's tiered with flocks of bats."

Honor's smile wavers at the corners as Simon steers her toward a dark wood table with carved and matching chairs. He returns from the cooking corner brandishing a bottle of red wine as if it were a trophy. He fills Honor's glass.

"To blackout," she says.

"To us," Simon corrects, and Honor feels an eerie closeness to him. They are intimate already, a kind of wordless intimacy usually reserved for children, who have both the time and the ability for it.

"Are you a writer?" Honor asks. "Because you have a lot of books."

"Oh, no. I just like to read. I'm sure I haven't got a postcard in me."

"Then again," he continues, replenishing her now empty glass, "sometimes when I'm really pissed I think about it."

"Hmmm," Honor replies. "I remember F. Scott Fitzgerald said, 'There's no use to make mysteries simply because one has drunk a few bottles of wine.' I've never forgotten that."

"Seems so despairing somehow," says Simon. "I think despair is very empty."

"Empty! I think it's empathy!"

"So you have no faith?"

"None. Well, in a way. I believe in eternity in that I think it's unsolved. Just one unsolved, unending ordeal."

"Oh, I disagree," says Simon, putting down his glass to emphasize his statement. "I don't think that living is the actualized part. We're preparing for what's next." He gets up, remembering the food that's cooking. "Excuse me," he says, even though he's only going a few feet away. "I hope you like salmon."

"I do," she says, knowing that while she loathes it, she loves him. Everything he says pulls at her, echoes through her, even if she doesn't agree.

"Where in the States did you grow up?" he asks. Honor is slow to answer, hating to talk about her past.

"Long Island, but I lived in Hollywood for a while. How about you?"

"Salisbury. Have you been?"

"No."

"We should go then, sometime. Not so much for the city itself, for there's nothing much to see apart from the cathedral, but there's Stonehenge. I think that should appeal to a Pagan such as yourself."

"I'm not a Pagan," Honor laughs.

"Well, then, you'd like the countryside, at least."

"I'm not sure. I've never cared that much for scenery. I always kind of thought of it as being a backdrop for drugs, mainly."

"We can take 'E,' " Simon proposes, "if it would make it easier for you. As for me, I just want to go somewhere cold, where I can wear my punk-rock jumper. Here, I'll show you."

From the lower drawer of a wardrobe, Simon withdraws a pink matted sweater, dreadlock-like tendrils dangling from it like mohair udders.

"I love it!" Honor says, toying with the furballs of yarn. Simon responds by putting the sweater on her. She raises her arms like surrender and he smooths the matting down around her body, lingering and languishing over her breasts. By his day bed they kiss and he lifts up the first tulle layer of her skirt, followed by the satinet one. He pushes down his leggings, slides off her silk and velveteen-bowed panties. His sex in her is unlike Gaudy's—less confident, softer yet more supple.

He smiles after he's come, mentions something about having forgotten the dessert, petit fours. Honor's pout is like the frosting indications on each of the little cakes and between bites she and Simon kiss.

"Do you want to watch videos?" he asks her later, after he's cleared the table. "We can look at the Cure." When Honor doesn't reply, he asks her if she likes them.

"I guess," Honor shrugs, uncertain. Together they watch a video compilation until Honor can't put up with it anymore. "This is so stupid!" Honor shouts as she watches a nubile schoolgirl running through an empty sanitarium, oblivious to the presence of the Cure but aware of the spectre of herself in a past life. "How can she not see the band members when they're right there in plain sight?"

"Maybe she's trying to ignore them," Simon laughs. "Seriously, I think you're missing the point. The thing is that the girl is time-slipping."

"In that case I wouldn't be afraid," Honor says. "I'd be fucking relieved."

Simon turns off the video. "Why don't we take no notice of all that," he says, "and plan our trip to Salisbury instead?"

"Call me about it," she answers. "I really think I should be going now."

A few days later Simon phones and Honor is unnerved by his reliability. They make plans to go to Salisbury that weekend. "It might be nice," she agrees, "to see a sky petalled with stars."

At the weekend they drive in Simon's car to Salisbury, where they check into an inn. The blaring pop music from the lounge belies the hotel's high-beamed antiquity.

After they've seen their room, Simon takes Honor for a walk through Salisbury's not particularly enchanting streets.

"I like the night," Honor says into the crescent lapel of Simon's jacket. "I wish there'd never be another day."

Simon nods. "I think it was the druids who measured time by nights, which is where we got 'fortnight' from."

"I like that," she says, rubbing cat-like against him.

"They wanted to touch the stars, you see," he continues. "Do you notice how many more stars there are here than in London?"

"I'm trying not to," she says. "They're not what I expected, and when I look up there for comfort, all I see is a chain of teeth."

Simon hugs her tightly, places her face inside his jacket. He heads her toward a corner pub, where it's warm and aglow inside.

"Tomorrow, before we set out for Stonehenge," he tells her over pints of Guinness, "we'll go to Salisbury Cathedral. I think you'll like the churchyard there."

They toast and their glasses clink the notation of hours.

Back in their room, it takes Honor and Simon forever to fall asleep, partly because of the lounge band but also due to things inside each of them.

In the first daylight, when it's finally quiet, Honor wakes just before Simon. She's unaware that he watches her get dressed, watches her unfurl her skating skirt, display her jewelry on the bureau, and use her palms to iron her musty flowered shirt. At once Simon feels uneasy, the pain of observing someone who really isn't comfortable being on earth. He stirs and turns so she'll know he's awake.

Honor goes to his side of the bed, wearing her 1950s black slip—the definitive kind one can only find in the States. She stands even with his profile on the pillow and he addresses his face to the slip's beige lace hem.

Later, they take a continental breakfast in the lounge, the room that was a source of their torment the night previous. Honor looks gloomily at the stage that is still set and dreams of dismantling the p.a. and donating the equipment to a struggling band who'll doubtless be rehearsing later in a basement somewhere near.

Everyone around Gaudy in the BBC1 Green Room slouches—band members, the sound engineer, a secretary—but Gaudy sits up straight, taut as a suspended marionette.

He's told the deejay he plans to be the ultimate fashion accessory, as timely as a magazine and every bit as disposable. And earlier that morning, over egg and chips in a café just off Portobello Road, he'd explained to a journalist that he believes all art to be prostitution, in the way that he will stand out in any crowd, especially the pitiful one he's in the midst of at the moment, by his ostentatiousness, his striking carriage and demeanor. He will be selected.

Honor and Simon meander through the churchyard, dwarfed and darkened by the behemothic Salisbury Cathedral. Honor listens to reggae on headphones and it adds a lilting rhythm to her step as she negotiates the statuary and crypts.

"It bothers me," she says too loudly to Simon, "all these people buried like footnotes."

"But they're not lost," Simon replies, "not lost at all. That's what the markers are for, partially."

"Oh no! Those are what I hate the most! They just sit there like accusations. And I think the more ornate ones are the most offensive—

like big hypodermic needles draining the blood from the buried beneath."

"It could be even worse, I guess," she continues, skipping away. "At least we're not plundering their crypts in the name of history or whatever." When Simon starts to reply, he sees her headed toward a grove of oak trees where leaves hang damp and limp like drooping bats.

"Let's get on toward Stonehenge," Simon calls. When she comes near, he grabs her elbow.

"Oh," she says, pirouetting out of his grasp. "I forgot. I brought my camera." She snaps a picture of Simon, who looks wary.

Together they walk (most of the way in silence) along the narrow and uneven road toward Stonehenge—a road made for cars and not the homaging curious on foot.

Simon tells Honor what he knows about Stonehenge, that there are fifty-nine stones, each one full of witchcraft, that its builders probably venerated the rocks, trees, and wells also. He remembers he's forgotten to bring Ecstasy but produces a beaker of vodka which he pours into bell-shaped cups he's carried in his Peruvian backpack.

"This is my favorite way to drink," Honor giggles, off balance. "Hidden and forbidden." Simon is afraid she'll fall but she seems to steady with each swallow.

When the stones first come into view, in the late afternoon's fading light, Honor gasps. For Simon they always produce a kind of genetic memory, the kind that can't be articulated or disturbed by words of explanation. But to Honor they're frightening, a huge gaping mouth with doorlike slabs of teeth hanging at odd angles.

At first she refuses to walk inside the circle, but Simon persuades her, envelops her with his shoulders. "To me, it's like a crown," he tells her, but that doesn't make it any better. Simon is so pure and sincere, she knows things will always make way for him.

Honor walks apart and then sees, carved in mossy green in one of the rocks, the words "Mary-13" or "Mary-B" or "Mary-P"—she doesn't bother to ascertain precisely which. Instead she turns back to Simon, falling on her knees. She places one hand on her head and the other on the sole of her boot. "I give thee all that is between my hands," she whispers to him. "Everything."

Simon sinks beside her, terrified. There they sleep curled, knee to chin until a guard wakes them up.

"It's nearing sundown," he explains.

Honor is shaking; she has dreamt of being up and away and

nowhere until the Cure's Robert Smith comes down from a just-higher cloud, his black angel-hair blowing sharp and inviting as atmospheric heroin.

Now, in her half-sleep, she mumbles to Simon about needing to go back to Switzerland. Instead they begin the long trek back to Salisbury.

Simon is able to hitch a ride for them and he and Honor sit huddled in the back of a truck, Honor's hair woven into Simon's punk-rock sweater as she raises her face only to stare into his pale, uncomprehending eyes.

"Positive punk," he whispers to her, having nothing else to say. "Around 1983 or so. A nice flip to Gothic and the Batcave scene."

The next morning they're readying to leave their room. Honor changes from black clothes to gray, just as night color yields to dawn.

Simon asks, "What were you saying about Switzerland?"

"When?"

"Yesterday. At the monument, you were saying something about going to Switzerland, do you remember?"

"I don't know," she replies, stressing the *I*. "I've only been there once and all I could think was it's not the rich, but the Swiss who are different from you and I."

"Same difference, isn't it," Simon replies, securing the buckle on his backpack, while Honor thinks that the Englishperson's best trait is the ability to say a question as if it were a final, absolute statement.

On Monday Honor disregards her psychiatrist's appointment and generally ignores the days until Saturday. After taking a perfunctory turn around Portobello Market she returns to her flat to smoke opium, alone. She gets the idea to go to a Saturday evening Mass (anticipating Sunday). To cover the thick and clinging smell of the drug, she dabs her skin and douses her clothes with lavender scent.

She's not a Catholic – if anything, she was raised Unitarian – so she has to observe the gathered to know when to stand, to kneel, touch her forehead, her bow-shaped lips, her slow-pounding chest. The priest says something about "a near occasion of sin" but then fails to give any examples.

Communion is given and instead of joining the parade to the altar, Honor reaches into her satchel for the parcel of opium, wrapped in aluminum foil. She scrapes the substance with the nail of her tiniest finger, puts it under her tongue.

She leaves before the final blessing and heads up Kensington

Church Street for Notting Hill and then Portobello. In her flat she picks up the ringing telephone.

"It's Gaudy," a voice says. "From your past."

When Honor doesn't say anything he continues: "I suppose you missed my BBC appearance. Never mind. I did want to invite you, anyway, to my release bash-up promo-thingy at the Electric Ballroom. You know, the press pitted against the usual suspects, a near occasion of sinners . . . "

"Okay," says Honor, laughing now, stunned that priests can actually foreshadow things. "When is it?"

Gaudy rings off, picks up *Sounds* to re-read his latest confrontation/consultation with the press. He has perfected a technique of repeating journalists' questions to trivialize their content. Too, he specializes in labyrinth-like, serpentine responses that confound at best. As a result he's most often quoted when he's angry and answers in clips. "Go fall in love," he'll say as a curse. "Then come back and tell me about the flowers of romance." Still, he talks and talks, knows he needs the press as much as they (whether they admit it or not) needle him.

Simon is late meeting Honor at Gaudy's party because he has been writing a letter to his wife, Lisa, in New York. "I don't know what it is," he prints, about Honor. "I can't explain it. She's so frail and sweet I would give up my happiness to be with her."

He adds in script, as a postcript: "Lisa, can you ever understand? Does our physical distance correlate?" He seals the envelope and takes the Underground to Camden Town, for the Electric Ballroom. He joins the waiting throng at the door and is in trouble because he doesn't know the band's name (Visigoth). He also doesn't remember Gaudy's, which he had scrawled on the envelope he'd hastily posted to his wife.

"Oh, God," he says, just audibly, but near enough for a doorgirl to interpret as "Gaudy" and Simon's in.

He finds Honor, who wears her camera like a sixties shoulder bag. She totters on stiletto, suicide heels that curve and point downward like existential punctuation marks.

Honor hugs Simon, but out of deference to Gaudy doesn't kiss him. However, Gaudy is across the packed room, explaining to someone about his arch hairstyle and the title of his record, *ODE*, which stands for "Off the Deep End."

"I should have dedicated it to you," Gaudy says to Honor when he's finally made his way to her. Simon gives him a disgusted look and walks away.

Gaudy pretends he doesn't notice. "I thought you'd be dancing," he says to Honor and motions toward the floor.

"Don't confuse me with that mire," Honor insists. "I pulled hard to get out of that quicksand."

"I'm going to America again this week," he says. "Wish I didn't have to fly, though. Wish that I could go over on the QE2, like the Cure. What was it Smithy said? 'Five days and fifteen bars'? I could do with that. Yes, I could definitely do with that."

Honor looks away, spies Simon by the side of the stage talking to Richard, Gaudy's bass player. Richard's bass has drawings of violin spiders on its neck. The frets and strings suspend them in a crostic web.

Richard tells Simon he studied at the Royal Academy of Music after coming down from Glasgow. "I used to think I hated being in a pop band," he admits, "but then I realized I just hate Gaudy."

Gaudy is on the stage now and with his glare he pulls the rest of his band up from the audience to join him for a song.

Honor snaps a photo of the band and then asks Simon to take a picture of her watching them. Simon agitates, says he hates the music, so Honor indulges him by agreeing to leave.

They pass a journalist who sets down her lager long enough to write in her notebook: "Gaudy writhes, and when the band leaves the stage," (they are still performing) "strong riffs and a trace remain, like the patterns snakes swirl in sand."

At home alone in her flat that night, Honor feels strange and desired, caught between Gaudy and Simon. It is a feeling that almost makes her happy, and an emotion that makes her sick.

A few days later Gaudy stands, incongruous, in a gift shop at JFK Airport. He wears a knee-length black dress over leggings and boots. Rubbing the temples of his high forehead, he scans the racks for a book to read on his flight to Los Angeles. A perfect picture of Honor comes to mind as he selects and purchases a self-help title called *How to Win Back Someone Who Never Loved You*. He sees Honor's face superimposed on the pages as he reads and waits in the departure lounge, his feet atop a trash can. Gaudy knows Honor thinks she's solved her problems, most likely with Simon. But nonetheless he's confident: as a lifelong soap opera addict Gaudy knows there's no problem that has a solution which can't be thwarted.

Several mornings following the release party, Honor calls her psychiatrist to make an appointment for that same day. As if the lapse in their professional relationship had only been to the good, she tells him a truth about Gaudy's party, how it had frightened her.

What in particular, asks her doctor.

"The squeamish attention Gaudy received," she replies. "I mean, the only thing I think fame could be good for is to afford one privacy. Like being able to have bodyguards to keep people from getting near you."

Fame isn't for privacy, says the doctor.

Right-o, thinks Honor. One has madness for that.

But what about you? Are you feeling as strong as before? he questions.

"I guess," says Honor, "but almost like a precursor to misery, like I'm saving my strength just for IT. And it does bother me to go on, like the opposite of what my mother always said, that brave people are never scared. I think they're the only ones who are, the ones who are brave enough to feel terrified."

Have you heard from your mother?

"Oh, yes," Honor laughs. "God, yes. She sent me a notice about my high school reunion, as if I'd be interested."

So you're not.

"No, no one would remember me." She rats strands of her hair with her thumb and index finger.

Why do you think that?

"Don't know. Guess I was just too ethereal to be noticed."

Honor leaves her doctor's and walks the way back from Maida Vale, all the while imagining Simon is by her side. She stops at a pharmacy in Portobello Road to drop off two rolls of film and he doesn't protest.

Simon is making a cup of tea when his telephone rings. It is his wife, Lisa, calling from JFK Airport en route to Los Angeles, where the chic deli she works for is opening a West Coast version. If Simon has any hopes or cares for the two of them, he will fly to Los Angeles and meet her, come join her where she'll be staying at the Hollywood Roosevelt Hotel.

He has to, he knows. Simon rings off and arranges a flight for late that night He packs his backpack, remembers Honor at Stonehenge when he sees it, and decides to drive to her flat.

Battersea Bridge looks like a suspension bridge, like it's made of rope and wooden slats and wings, as Simon drives across it for Ladbroke Grove. Before he knocks on Honor's door, he listens and hears the sounds of the soap opera, "Brookside," from within. On it, a character is explaining her heartfelt Catholicism and Honor punctuates the dialogue with laughs and yelps.

When there are three raps at the door, Honor throws off the black shawl she's wearing and lowers the volume on the t.v.

Simon's face is the color of stone and about as turgid. He tells Honor his story, his truth.

Honor picks her shawl up off the settee and wraps it around her. She paces the small sitting room and turns to face him. He looks not at her face but at the profile on a ribbon-strung cameo she's wearing.

"Married, Simon," Honor says. "Why?"

He hasn't an answer. "I'm not sure what will happen," he tries to tell her. "Maybe things won't work out. Maybe she won't have me—or I, her. Honor, I have loved you. I'm not sure that I loved Lisa. It was more like a vision of her I fell in love with, and not her. She's rather shallow by comparison."

"Please go," Honor tells him, pushing off his arms. Still he hangs on with the tenacity of a loose tooth.

"I'll call you," he says, while Honor stares at the television screen. "Honor, at least look at me. Be fair to me."

She doesn't turn as he leaves and she hears him go down the stairs, their love reduced to a concerto of retreat, a grammar of descent.

Honor keeps the t.v. set on without sound the remainder of the night. When she finally leaves her flat days later, it's to pick up the film she'd turned in. She doesn't remove the photos from the packet until she's having cafeteria tea in the British Home Store on Kensington High Street. There she spreads the pictures in rows on her tray, surveys her face and Simon's framed in white border like cement around a pool, four walls, or a page.

She picks up the pictures blithely, as if she were winning at cards, and puts them in her coat pocket. Honor fastens every clasp as it is bitter cold outside but she has to turn back at the escalator, for she's left her scarf at the side of the table. When she returns, it has slipped snake-like to the floor, and that's where she retrieves it from, balling it up around her fist and then shoving it in her other pocket.

It's colder than death, Honor thinks as she steps into the street. That was like the title of a book she'd seen in Waterstone's, *Love is Colder than Death*. Not love, she'd argued to herself, but life. Love was the pretend thing, like a muffler around life, a muffler that was really just rotted with crocheted lace holes.

It starts to sleet as Honor passes the church where she'd gone to Mass. She ducks inside and sees a priest or priest's helper, she's not sure which. With one mittened hand to her mouth, she approaches him, saying, "I've lost my soul and I can't afford to buy another," but due to her affect and her accent the man can't understand her and he hurries away.

Honor keeps on walking home, one covered hand feeling the photos in her pocket. She tries to recall what was on them, but it's the untaken pictures that come to mind, like Simon smiling beneath the arches at Camden Lock, waiting for her at Fulham Broadway station wearing all shiny black like a taxi, or holding her, afraid of her, at Stonehenge.

Gaudy wakes by alarm in his hotel room at the base of the Hollywood Hills. The room is plain, done in motel gold and avocado plaid. He moans and rolls over, falling out of bed as he does, jolting his bony hip.

He curses and stumbles to the bathroom, where he showers and then fixes his attention on his hair. The current cut sort of sways inward and then curves out, like the shell of the Hollywood Bowl he'd seen yesterday. Gaudy considers calling his band members, who are sharing a room down the hall, but decides against it.

The maid comes in while he's watching "Highway to Heaven" on t.v., so she works around him. At eleven A.M. there's a knock at his door and it's a woman from his record company, dressed all in white like a nurse. She's accompanied by a numb-looking man of indiscernible age.

"Hi," says the woman. "Gaudy, I'd like you to meet so-and-so from the *L.A. Music Review*." Gaudy is speechless, can't believe he's heard right, but then he finds out the man really is called So-and-So.

They sit on the sofa and So-and-So places his tape recorder on the low table Gaudy usually likes to put his feet on.

"Shall I call room service?" asks the woman, Cathy, as she picks up the phone and asks for coffee.

After a cup, Gaudy is sitting erect and leaning forward at the tape recorder, although So-and-So assures him it would pick him up half a room away.

Gaudy starts to explain how in London the center always shifts. "We don't need earthquakes like you lot," he says. "Our own creativity keeps things moving. Like now, the center of the universe is right in my flat, and just outside, stretching as far as, say, Camden Town, you're still in the proper orbit."

He has another cup of coffee while So-and-So laments the tardiness of his photographer, who doesn't show.

Gaudy is so wound after the interview that he leaves his hotel and walks east toward Hollywood Boulevard and the heart of Hollywood. In a bar he asks a long-haired boy wearing a photo-badge with "MIT" written on it if he's from the FBI.

"No way, man," says the youth. "Why? You wanna score?"

He puts Gaudy on to a guy in a flannel shirt, who sells him some Ecstasy. Along with the drug, he hands Gaudy a business card. "Call me if you need anything else," he offers hospitably.

Back in his room Gaudy takes the "E," hoping to slow things d-o-w-n, but instead he becomes afraid of the macramé owl that's hanging just above the sofa. He sees its brown bead eyes as spiders in a thick rope trap, so he runs out by the sinister and tiny pool. Longing for a larger one, he phones Cathy, who says she can oblige. L.A.'s full of swimming pools, she laughs.

At her dining room table, Honor has decided to write a letter. "Dear Dr.," she writes, "dear dr dream, down and dreaming," as she slumps over headfirst into a thirty-six hour sleep.

There's a mare in Honor's dream, a Hollywood silent movie horse being led down her street by a man who's dressed as a sheik. He speaks to the side of the animal's face.

"IN DREAMS!" Honor calls to the man, knowing this isn't real. But he keeps walking, doesn't hear her, as Honor lifts her head from the table, aware that only her body is sleeping.

She feels a dim trance, observes heroin-thick clouds, cracked and struggling in the noonday Los Angeles sky.

Honor sees herself back in an apartment she'd once lived in. Simon is asleep, an invader in what was her bed. She pulls the top sheet off him but he's still covered head to toe in a pitchfork-printed muslin shroud.

Honor covers him back up and goes outside to look again at the clouds that are dirge-like now that it's turned night. She sees a black London taxi: it must be Robert Smith coming to collect her.

At his parents' home in Sussex, Robert Smith is on retreat, trying to fall asleep in his childhood room. Various toys surround him like they once did Oscar Wilde, when he, too, was being hidden. But Robert can't sleep right, feels like he's dreaming a fraction of someone else's dream.

It's night, he sees in sleep. "BEGIN RESPONSIBILITIES," he writes on a notepad. But he feels tedious and hellish when he sees he's stuck in Los Angeles. He drives a Range Rover on the English side of the road, on a foothill street, and turns the steering wheel erratically, anything to end this dream.

Honor waves at Robert, but instead of stopping for her he swerves defiantly (as one would a toy car, knowing it's on a track) and hits Simon, who falls instantly, his head in a pothole filling up with blood.

"Dream!" Honor screams, accusing.

Robert drives his Range Rover to the edge of Lake Hollywood, as far as a car can go, and gets out to walk. A shadow is following him, impossible at night, so he turns to grab the thing and throws it in the water. It pulls him in, too, and they struggle and splash until Robert stabs the shape with a hat pin. It deflates and sinks like a popped pool toy.

Robert Smith awakens, wet with sweat, with the idea for another song.

Simon, languid in the chaise-longue beside Lisa, stretches his long white legs in the winter sun. His skin is waxy, like trick-or-treat fangs. He looks at the bottom of the Hollywood Roosevelt's pool, which was painted by David Hockney. The adorning swirls and curves are affectionately known as "swimming parentheses," but lifeguards protested that the dark marks posed a safety hazard, and the hotel had been forced to seek historic status for the pool, to protect it. Simon turns on his side and closes his eyes as two blonde expatriates do breaststrokes beneath the water's smooth surface.

"You really should be in the shade," Lisa cautions him. She looks American now, with her hair a woven brown color, close to natural. But Simon just puts on his dark glasses.

Cathy's wearing a different white outfit as she escorts Gaudy poolside, a length away from Simon and Lisa. Gaudy doesn't listen as Cathy runs down, for the thousandth time, the remainder of the week's schedule. He barely catches her saying that a photographer may be joining them at the pool but when she keeps on talking, he tries to wave her quiet. It's then that he sees Simon.

Gaudy gets up and goes over to him. "Well, well," he says, eyeing Lisa. "The other side of the coin, is this. Well, we'll see who wins the toss, shall we? One thing, though. Do you consider Honor heads or tails?" Simon stands up wobbly, speaks softly to Gaudy but Gaudy keeps shouting until he shoves Simon into the pool. Simon bobs up amidst the design, tall, a floating accent mark.

Meanwhile, the photographer has arrived and is busily snapping pictures. "Gaudy's a publicist's dream!" squeals Cathy. "He even pushed this guy off the deep end."

That evening, Gaudy's arrival at a dance club is expected, and in the dark, in his room, he prepares for his appearance. One last look in the mirror validates and verifies his beauty, so he's off.

He starts to cross the narrow street for a waiting cab, but is cut dead by a speeding car. During his last, he sees (in place of stars, tornadoes, and asterisks) bats, spiders, owls, and snakes all hunting each other. The final thing he sees is Honor's pretty, pale face.

Two daylights later, Honor awakens and her neck is stiff to her shoulders from slumping at the table. She turns on Breakfast T.V. and an announcer says, "Coming next: Was rock's latest fashion accessory murdered?"

After advertisements for cereals and British Telecom, after little clouds and suns that symbolize the country's weather, Honor sees Gaudy's face with words in the far reaches of his hair, looking like a chintzy crown, "DEATH ROCK?"

She hears of the hit-and-run, and how a possible clue in the form of a Scottish plaid scarf had been found near the body. "Perhaps it had blown free of the car," speculates the announcer.

"Perhaps it would have throttled the driver, then," replies Honor sarcastically, out loud. "Perhaps it would have gotten tangled in the tire spokes and wrung his neck right off."

She sees Simon being interviewed, following questioning by police, because of an earlier poolside fracas. She sees him ghost-like, walking static on the screen.

She hears a description of the "phantom rock star" suspect, who drove a British car and had high, spiky hair. An alleged eyewitness insists he saw a man get out of the car after the impact. "He did," says the young boy, who secretly flashes his gang sign to the camera. "He had on Air Jordans and flood pants, man; they were too short, and trimmed in plaid, man. I couldn't make that, man."

Honor sits in her doctor's office, talking about someone she knew who died. "They keep making a big deal about whether he was murdered," she says, "and I mean, I can't believe they don't know."

That afternoon she stops by the photo area at the pharmacy to pick up some prints. She has ordered two enlargements of the picture that shows her watching Gaudy's band. Honor plans to send one copy to Simon, since he took the photo. He should have it.

She addresses the envelope at her dining table, and removes the snaps from their packet. Honor looks long at the picture: Gaudy is wrapped in a kind of fog that yields to his features, which are crystal-sharp. He appears like an image in a fortune teller's orb. In this bigger print, however, Honor has faded; overexposed, she looks dead, without even a ghost's hope of mobility.

Instead of keeping the second copy, she puts it in an envelope to mail to her high school reunion committee. If she's already dead, she thinks, she may as well go home.

Sex Off Balance

Honor is flying home to America from London. She is listening to Glenn Miller on the flimsy, filmy headset, when all of a sudden it hits her: in the afterlife, everyone has high cheekbones. She raises the plastic window blind and sees a rococo angel perched on the plane's wing. It's her old friend Gaudy, gnawing at the bolts.

Her plane is stuck in a wiry tree, skewed like a kite hopeless on a branch. For Honor, the dying is the frightening part; a wind-full, self-deprecating entrance followed by the indifferent closing of a door.

In time she can barely see her grave site through the haze. When she thinks she does, she is horrified to discover she's been planted in London's Brompton Cemetery, a little rich for her (now-drained) blood.

At least she likes her headstone. "Honor Lake," it says, "Better, then Nothing." How she got what she wanted is puzzling to her. She never specified it and there's no one who could have known.

She quickly finds out the grave is no private place. People of all sorts stop by to peep, and most of them are people she never wanted there, like her parents and her ex-love, Simon. She starts to worry she has no chance of ever being alone.

Honor reads her epitaph one last time. "Better, then Nothing."

But that's what she thinks.

Call it H, not heaven," she hears someone say but she can't make them out in the gray monoscape, which is even grayer here on the other side. Honor unleashes her black spider boots to walk barefoot on the clouds, but she quickly learns she can't—they're made of a substance like angel hair fiberglass. She nurses a sharp cut in the crease of her third toe and then puts her boots back on.

Her hair, however, is sticking up perfectly, the way she always imagined it.

Honor keeps walking until she stumbles upon a headless stone seraph and, leaning up against it, Sid Vicious. Sid looks downcast and it would stand to reason: people who are ahead of their time must suffer even more in heaven, in H, where virtually everyone's earlier than they are.

In a Victorian chapel, Honor slides into a pew that's cold with the necrophiliac likeness-kiss of an enamel tub. She observes people worshipping what she gathers is the past, the one thing they probably can't have. Honor becomes aware she's on a pilgrimage, and if she's careful it's one that might afford her a version of heaven, and a vision of hell.

Honor leaves the church and keeps walking in a straight line, through a path of trees. In a clearing, she sees a carousel of horses, griffins, and marble beds that have cherubs dangling by their necks from the head posts. The hand brake is operated by a bored-looking Ian Curtis from Joy Division. Honor calls out to him to stop the merry-go-round so she can ride it, but he ignores her. It dawns on her then that people can't see or hear her; she's like the perfect eavesdropper.

The carousel finally reels to a stop and two Jazz Age women get on. One wears an ostrich plume headdress that matches the carved horse she selects. Honor sits on a bed behind them, keeping her head down to avoid the swinging stone infants.

One of the women sighs and then says, "It's always early when you've got nothing to do."

"Where shall we go after this?" asks the other, a redhead.

"Oh, Hide Park or Covert Garden; it doesn't really matter."

So this is heaven, thinks Honor. HHHH, a gust of wind reminds. H, a sort of toppled London all askew, seen askance.

Honor hums to the carousel's music but when she enunciates the words to "Love Will Tear Us Apart," the ride slows to a halt. Ian Curtis points his index finger until it settles on Honor. He swiftly tells her to dismount, to go away. She stares back her disbelief, wants to ask why he suddenly sees her, but his alienation and vehemence send her scurrying.

She heads for an aviary where no birds are singing. Instead, a gray woman prunes a silver rosebush. "Grandma!" Honor calls out, oddly nostalgic for a member of her family.

The woman sees Honor and screams. She gathers a friend by the arm and says she's seen a monster, a spectral zombie. The friend sits the woman down on a kind of throne and calms her. "You just have to ignore them if they're going to start coming 'round here," the friend counsels. "It's a shame, you know. T'was a regular Valhalla 'til THEY came along."

Honor goes on but when she comes across Victoria Station, she enters the skeletal edifice. She climbs up onto a white tightrope rafters-high above the train tracks. From this vantage, the central platform looks like a dance floor, a waiting room. Honor keeps looking at the wooden boards and regrets not dancing with her friend Gaudy the last time he'd asked her. She misses him until he appears clearly, smiling and waving from the opposite platform.

"Can you see me?" Honor calls to him. "Gaudy, can you hear me?"

"I hear you," he says, "and I see you."

"How come you're not screaming and running away, then? That's what everyone else does!"

"That's because you're on the wrong side," he says. "It's better over here; you'll see. Come down that stairway beneath the sign that says 'Dominion' and I'll help you from there."

After Gaudy grasps her gloved hand, he motions to a place between the railway ties, a sheer hell where things appear as if through screens instead of glass.

"I'm glad you came down," Gaudy says, "but I must admit I enjoyed looking up your kilt when you were there."

Honor surveys his still-perfect face, his porcelain pallor. His eyeliner mimics sleeplessness.

They go through a smoked-glass door, through a shabby room, and down a few more precarious stairs. In an entryway, cordoned and curtained off, Gaudy turns to Honor. "I'll make you forget you were ever alive," he says as he pushes her sideways. Honor's kilt falls away like shredded silk and Gaudy's soon inside her, deep, at an impossible angle.

"This is the best thing about hell," he explains while he's coming, "you get to have sex off balance."